FLIGHT OF THE BUMBLEBEE

Balestier Press
Centurion House, London TW18 4AX
www.balestier.com

Flight of the Bumblebee
Original title: 野蜂飞舞
Copyright © Huang Beijia, 2018
English translation copyright © Nicky Harman, 2022

First Published in Chinese by Phoenix Juvenile and
Children's Publishing Ltd in 2018
English edition first published by Balestier Press in 2022
Published by arrangement with Phoenix Juvenile and
Children's Publishing Ltd

This book is published with financial support from the
Jiangsu Literature Translation Programme

A CIP catalogue record for this book
is available from the British Library.

ISBN 978 1 913891 34 3

Cover illustration by Zhang Huaicun

All rights reserved. No part of this publication may be
reproduced, stored in a retrieval system or transmitted in
any form or by any means, electronic, mechanical, without
the prior written permission of the publisher of this book.

This book is a work of fiction. The literary perceptions and
insights are based on experience, all names, characters, places,
and incidents either are products of the author's imagination
or are used fictitiously.

Huang Beijia

FLIGHT OF THE BUMBLEBEE

A Novel

Translated from the Chinese by

Nicky Harman

*Best wishes from Nicky
1/4/2023*

Balestier Press
London · Singapore

Translator's Foreword

This story stands on its own feet. It explains itself, so you don't need me to tell you very much about it. But here are just a few things you might like to know.

In Chinese, surnames come first and given names afterwards. In this story, I've used their given names for all the children. So Shen (surname) Tianlu (given name) is referred to as Tianlu.

Orange is the only name I actually translated, because the author, Huang Beijia, explained to me that she called her that because she is such a bright, sparky character. What a great name for a girl! It suits her.

'Uncle' and 'Auntie'. These are terms of respect that a younger person will use for an older one. So when Orange talks about Professor Tao as 'Uncle Tao', it doesn't mean he's her real uncle.

Ms Huang tells us in her Afterword that she found a very

useful history book about what life was like in Chengdu in the war years when the universities moved there from East China. She was able to make her story historically accurate and, yes, the football match between the British pilots of the RAF and the Chinese students really did happen. You can find out anything else you want to know about the Second World War in China (where it's called the War of Resistance against Japan) by looking online.

And finally, the songs. As Orange tells us, 'In those days, everyone used to sing, it was a favourite pastime, no matter whether you were happy or sad.' The families in our story were very cosmopolitan. Many of China's professors were educated in America or Britain, and knew their Italian opera just as well as their Peking Opera. They also knew gospel songs, revolutionary songs (Soviet Russian as well as Chinese) and the British singer Vera Lynn's wartime ballads. All the adults, men and women, would have known Chinese folk songs, and so did the children (who also had one favourite which they sang to the tune of the French song Frère Jacques.) All the songs that Orange talks about are real songs and are available online. Chinese Books for Young Readers, an independent blog run by three translators, have been kind enough to host a special page with links to a selection of them on Spotify and Youtube. We hope you enjoy listening. Just go to https://chinesebooksforyoungreaders.wordpress.com/2021/06/25/flight-of-the-bumblebee-the-playlist/ or scan the QR code here:

I'd like to take this opportunity to thank Ms Huang and the publishers for letting me translate *Flight of the Bumblebee*. It was a great privilege. I hope you enjoy reading it as much as I enjoyed translating it!

Nicky Harman
October 2022

Contents

Translator's Foreword

Prologue 1

Chapter 1 Mulberry Tree Mishap 12

Chapter 2 The Pencil Case 30

Chapter 3 The Cockerel Loses Some Feathers 52

Chapter 4 Our Night-time Walk 62

Chapter 5 The Christmas Party 78

Chapter 6 The Youth Militia 91

Chapter 7 The Profs 103

Chapter 8 Air Raid! Air Raid! 118

Chapter 9 Flight of the Bumblebee 136

Chapter 10 The Flying Tigers 152

Chapter 11 Shuya Leaves Home 166

Chapter 12 A Girl in Love 187

Chapter 13 Rice, Wheat, Cotton, Corn 202

Chapter 14 The Book That Flew Across the Hump 218

Chapter 15 The Translators 226

Chapter 16 The Bookshop 243

Chapter 17 Sports Gala 260

Chapter 18 Sad Times 272

Chapter 19 Catching a Spy 286

Chapter 20 Mum's Fur Waistcoat 300

Chapter 21 Joining Up 315

Chapter 22 Letters Wing Their Way 325

Chapter 23 Happy Times 343

Epilogue 357

Afterword, by Huang Beijia

Splendid Land, Endless Days 364

Prologue

Go on, have a guess, how old do you think I am? Ninety, you say? Huh! How could I be that old?! I'm eighty-eight. At least seven hundred days off ninety, and that's a long time! Seven hundred sunrises, seven hundred sunsets, and make no mistake, girl, I'm gonna live them all!

There's nothing wrong with my eyes. My younger daughter's only sixty and she's not in as good shape as me; she carries two sets of glasses around in her bag, one set for reading, the other for driving. What a bother. I don't need any at all. That mobile you're holding, you just click and bring up any news item, and I'll read it out for you without making a single mistake.

My hearing? That's not bad either. The right side is pretty good, the left side not quite so good. That's why I asked you to sit on my right. Back when the war began, that was in August 1937, I think – I remember there were still melons for sale, the cicadas were still making a din in the trees, and the evenings were so hot, you had to splash water all over the yard before you went indoors to sleep – well, that was when the Japanese planes came. You lot have never been through anything like that. When the bombs dropped, the air got so hot you could see sparks. The classroom windows shivered and shook like they had malaria. The porters, the store owners, the school children, and the workmen, they all swarmed into the street, desperate to get into any air raid shelter they could find. It was a mad scramble. There wasn't room for everyone. Some of them got their heads through the door but their bums were stuck outside. One day, we were in class when the alarm sounded. Just as the teacher was herding us out of the classroom to a shelter, a bomb landed right in front of us. There was a huge blast, and the school gateway was gone. I fainted from shock, and when I came to, I couldn't understand why the world had turned into a silent movie! The blast had perforated my left eardrum and there was blood coming out. That ear hasn't been right since then.

Our home was on the campus of University of Nanking in Nanjing. My dad, Huang Yuhua, had been employed there since he returned from Cornell University in the United States with a doctorate in agronomy. He started as a lecturer and then got promoted to deputy dean of the Agricultural College, then dean. The Chinese lived from farming back then. There's something miraculous about sowing in spring and harvesting in autumn, and the kind of people who became agronomists did it because they were patriots and wanted the best for their country and people. Before the Anti-Japanese War, there was an improved wheat variety called Jinling 26. I don't know if you've heard of it. Ah, silly me! Of course you wouldn't have! You're much too young. You should have heard of Yuan Longping though. 'The father of hybrid rice', they called him. Anyway, Jinling 26 was originally discovered by an American professor in a wheatfield near Nanjing, just one seedling. They dug it up with great care, and carried it back to the college where they cultivated it for eight years. That was the first time a plant had been selectively bred in China, so it was quite something.

My dad came back from America, and took up where the professor had left off. He came up with a brand-new variety called Jinling 2905, which had larger grains and a higher starch content, and produced bumper harvests. The papers were full of what they called 'China's Green Revolution'!

I'd better stop going on about wheat. I only brought it up to show you what a wonderful man my dad was. He made a huge contribution to his country and his people.

Let's go back to the Anti-Japanese War. As soon as war broke out, the government mobilized the people. The slogans went, 'Your country needs you – all of you, men, women, old and young! Sacrifices will be required of you! We have to fight the Japanese!' As soon as the order was given, people from all walks of life responded, workers, farmers, shop-keepers, and students. They said goodbye to their loved ones, and left for the frontlines, or worked behind the lines, and threw themselves into the war effort, the 'National Salvation Movement', as it was called. Those were heroic times.

I was eight years old when war broke out. My brother Kejun was fourteen, my sister Shuya was thirteen, my sister Su was four, and my little brother was still in my mum's belly. University of Nanking moved to West China, away from the war. They hired three steamers and we all boarded at the Xiaguan Docks, and set off upriver. First, we arrived in Hankou, and had to change to small steamboats to go through the Three Gorges to Chongqing, and finally to Chengdu. It was a terrible journey, as you can imagine. My father, as the dean of the Agricultural College, was responsible for getting a huge quantity of books, improved plant varieties, and lab equipment and materials safely to Chengdu. He was also responsible for the dozens of teachers and students who came with us. So he had no time to take care of his family. My poor mother was seven or eight months pregnant, and had to struggle on and off boats, and in and out of carts, with her huge belly sticking out in front of her, dragging me along with one hand, and my younger sister with the other. And when there was no transport, we had to walk. Mum had had her feet bound as a girl, and although she'd unbound them, she still didn't find walking easy. She had terrible blood blisters, and her legs were so swollen that when you pressed down, it left a dent as big as a broad bean. The rest of her got so thin, her face was no bigger than a spinach leaf. But she never gave up and finally we arrived in Chengdu, and found a small house in the Huaxi Fields district, where the universities were.

Pomegranate Gardens, that was what it was called, and there really was a pomegranate tree in the garden. Our house was built of red brick, and there was an upstairs and a downstairs, and a carved doorway at the entrance. Inside, there was a dark, creaking wooden staircase. The paint was peeling off and the banisters were rough so if you weren't careful, you could get splinters in your hand. Upstairs, a walkway ran around the outside of the building, and through the thick wooden railings, you could see the courtyard down below. It was full of flowers and trees, and a pair of Rhode Island Reds belonging to Professor Mei from the Department of Animal Husbandry and Veterinary Medicine lived there too. The cockerel and the hen had fantastic red combs, and they strutted around in the mud, threatening small girls and fluffing up their feathers menacingly. They were brutes. We were in no doubt about who ruled the roost – they did!

Our family lived in two rooms in the southeast corner upstairs. The rooms were shabby but a good size and very light. They had unusual wooden parquet floors, although the wood was pitted and cracked and you could easily lose a pencil down the cracks and never get it back again. My dad's colleagues helped him build a partition in the back room, with a bookcase. We girls slept on one side, and our brother on the other. The outer room was my parents' bedroom, and was also our living room, dining room, and Dad's study. His desk was their bed base on top of four wooden chests. It made a good-sized table top and my dad was very happy with it. But the chests held our clothes too, so if my mother wanted to get stuff out for us, she had to clear the 'desk' of all the books, pens, test tubes, and glass bottles and she'd tell us to lift the bed board out of the way, so she could open the chest underneath. Then the bed base had to go back, and everything on the table had to be returned to its original position, all neat and tidy. My dad was very easy-going, but he didn't like anyone messing with the things on his desk. He'd go into a sulk, refuse his dinner and bury his head in a book. If you talked to him, he ignored you. He was just like a child.

What I remember most clearly was the plane tree in front of the house, which was taller than the first floor windowsills. One summer, I climbed onto the small table by the window, and reached out and grabbed a shiny black cicada chirping loudly on the branch outside. I got some twine my mum used when she made shoe soles, tied a bit around the cicada's middle, and put it back in the tree. As soon as it took off, I gave a yank, and the poor cicada fell on its back on the windowsill, all four legs in the air. It didn't know what had happened to it and started screeching. Shuya came over to the window and gave me a terrible scolding: why couldn't I learn to behave myself like a proper little girl, instead of spending all day annoying the bugs and the birds?!

You get the picture? I was a skinny little tomboy, built like a beanpole, with cropped hair and a scrawny neck, always dashing around, into everything, no wonder my sister was always criticizing me.

Shuya was very pretty, she really was. In fact, she was one of the prettiest girls in her school. I remember once she stole my dad's bike and wobbled on it all around the school playground, followed by a group of yelling boys, all with arms outstretched to grab her in case she fell off. All the other girls were jealous.

Kejun and Shuya were both full of enthusiasm for

everything. Once he taught me and little Su to sing a song called 'Save China', and I can still remember it now, 'Save, save, save China. Let's all move forward together. Work, work, work so hard. To save China, we must fight!' We used to sing that song so passionately!

And then there was Shen Tianlu, my lovely big brother Tianlu...No, I'm all right, don't you worry. Old people get teary like this sometimes. So let me tell you about Shen Tianlu. You can see a photo of him in the Anti-Japanese Aviation Martyrs Memorial Hall in Nanjing. He's tall and thin, with a narrow face and clear, bright eyes, and he's wearing an American-style bomber jacket, khaki breeches, leather boots, and holding a pair of leather gloves in one hand. Behind him is his American Curtiss Hawk III fighter plane. He looks so handsome!

Tianlu was not actually related to us. A long time ago, before I was born, his father and mine were at Cornell University together, and shared lodgings. My dad was doing agronomy, and he was studying horticulture. Farming and gardens are close, and they became close too. In fact, by the time they'd finished their studies, they'd become best friends. My dad used to say that even the tuxedo they wore at their graduation ceremonies was shared: they bought one between them and split the cost.

Back in China, though, they went their different ways. My dad went to University of Nanking to teach, breed plants, and educate people. Tianlu's father was recruited to the Communist Party by a cousin, and went to Moscow to study for a year, and then worked in the Jiangxi Soviet area, apparently in a very responsible position. In October 1934, the Long March began. Tianlu's parents set off with the rest of the Soviet. Their group managed to get across the Xiangjiang River, but then the Kuomintang army machine-gunned them and they were killed. Tianlu was lucky – he'd been sent to his grandparents' home in Sichuan as a tiny baby, so he was safe. But not long after his parents' death, the old folks fell ill and died too. Tianlu was still a little boy. He used to roam around the village, and one relative or another would give him a bite to eat, but he hardly ever stayed in one place for more than a day or two. He'd become almost feral by the time my dad arrived in Chengdu with his university, and set out to search for his old friend's son. When Tianlu arrived at our house from the village in West Sichuan, he was fourteen years old, the same age as my brother.

It's been eighty years, but I've never forgotten the first time I set eyes on him. Even today, if I shut my eyes, I can see it all...

Chapter 1
Mulberry Tree Mishap

By the end of May in 1938, the wheat in Huaxi Fields was golden, the mulberry trees were laden with dark purple berries, and the pomegranate trees were covered in red flowers.

My little brother had been born and was four months old by then.

My mother was badly malnourished during her pregnancy, and had had a terrible journey to Chengdu, so it wasn't surprising that my brother only weighed a pitiful two pounds and eight ounces at birth, no more than a kitten. He didn't even cry like a normal baby – he sounded wheezy. When Doctor Fan, who lived downstairs in Pomegranate Gardens, saw him for the first time in the maternity ward of the Union Hospital of West China, he gasped in horror.

Luckily, the Fans had some American milk formula, which they gave my mother. Two tins of that and he began to grow in leaps and bounds. Within three months, he had turned into a beautiful chubby baby with little dimpled hands and arms, who gurgled with delight when anyone teased him.

As I said, Doctor Fan was our downstairs neighbour. He was American, a Christian, and a professor of surgery at the West China Union University. He was a wonderful doctor. Top government officials and their families came all the way from Chongqing to consult him. His wife, Mary, taught piano at the Conservatory of Music of West China Union University. Every evening, we'd hear piano music flooding out from the Fans' living room, wave after wave of it. Then all of us, upstairs or downstairs, crept around on tiptoe, so as not to disturb the dreamlike beauty of the melodies.

But most of the time, the 'music' was more of a crashing and banging. That was when Mrs Fan's piano students were having their lessons. For a while, I was one of them. My mother used to frogmarch me to piano lessons, the reason being that I was such a restless, energetic kid, and my dad hoped that learning piano would smooth off some rough edges.

The Fans had just one daughter, Sheona. She was blonde, with cherry-red lips and eyes like a Persian cat, with pupils that gleamed when she was out in the dark. We were the same age, in the same class at primary school, and we were best friends. When I went to catch fish in the stream, climbed trees to raid birds' nests, or slipped into the experimental fields at the Agricultural College to pick melons and steal peaches, she was always there to cheer me on. Too bad she was a chubby girl, and that slowed her down, so most of the time she watched me. Every time I climbed a tree or paddled in the stream, she would pat her chest and exclaim, 'Oh, my goodness gracious me!'

I reckoned that the other reason why she was happy just to watch, was because she always wore a skirt. Skirts were no good for climbing trees because your knickers showed and that was embarrassing. Why did foreign girls always wear skirts? I never understood.

But I never held it against her. She had her role. I had mine. Every performer needs an audience to cheer her on, after all.

Back to my baby brother. At four months old, he

still had no name because my dad was too busy to choose one. Once the institute arrived in Huaxi Fields, he was busy taking his students out on field trips. They co-organized the Crop Promotion Pilot Zone with the local government, set up farmers' associations and cooperatives, distributed the improved wheat and cotton varieties to the farmers, and taught them how to plant them, all free of charge. My dad always said that the economy needed to be developed behind the lines, so that the soldiers at the front could be fed properly and fight effectively. His words, as always, made sense. Anyway, my mother did not feel it was her place to choose a name for my baby brother in Dad's absence, so everyone just called him 'Kid'. Every time he heard his name, his mouth widened in a gummy smile, and his big eyes twinkled, as he looked around to see who was calling him with dribble running down his chin.

Kid was a delight by day but a nuisance at night. He would start to cry as soon as dusk fell, and wail inconsolably. My mother was always afraid he would disturb the neighbours, so she used to carry him round and round the room for night after night to keep him quiet. As Kid got chubbier, my mother got more haggard. She grew so sallow and thin that it seemed like a puff of wind might blow her away.

The Fans' housekeeper, Mrs Xing, was upset. 'Mrs Huang, you can't go on like this. It's not doing you any good,' she remonstrated with my mother.

Mrs Xing was from Shanghai and although she had come to Chengdu with the family years before, she never gave up speaking Shanghainese. She probably didn't want to. Shanghai folk are famously proud of their dialect.

Mum sighed, 'But what am I to do? I can't put him back inside me.'

Mrs Xing thought a moment, then said, 'Write some prayers on strips of paper and stick them up. See if that works.'

Mum was worried that my dad would think this was superstitious. 'Will it work?' she asked hesitantly. Mrs Xing took charge. 'We'll never know till we try,' she said.

My mother, in some trepidation, asked my sister Shuya to write the strips for her. Shuya shook her head adamantly, her face full of scorn, and declared, 'It's just superstitious nonsense!'

Whenever there was a family drama, I threw myself into the fray. 'Mum, I can write! I'll write them for you!' I offered eagerly. My sister glared at me. 'You're so dumb!'

I ignored her. All I wanted was to be involved.

Relieved to have found a helper, Mum quickly gathered the writing materials – brush, ink, and a big piece of yellow paper which she cut into foot-long strips – and soon had everything ready for me. I followed her instructions and wrote in my wonky handwriting the same rhyme on each strip:

'Heaven up there

Earth down here

We've got a cry-baby at home.

Read this thrice, ye passers-by,

And Kid will sleep soundly till dawn.'

My older sister watched me scrawl and snorted in disgust, 'You never work for your tests in school and now look at you beavering away! And look how wonky your writing is. You should be ashamed of yourself!'

I was happily engrossed in my calligraphy, and ignored her. She was competitive, I knew that. And she was dead jealous that our mother was paying me all this attention. But my mother was always indulgent to any one of us who did what she said.

I wrote out ten strips. 'That should be enough,'

my mother said. I thought it was enough too. Ten times I'd written it! Now we had to stick them around outside in the hopes that some kind person would see one of them and stop long enough to read it aloud three times, so that Kid would sleep right through the next night and our mother would be saved.

Mum made a bowl of flour paste so my little sister, Su, and I could go out and stick up the strips. Su could carry the bowl of glue and I found an old worn-out brush of my father's to paste it on with.

Su and I sneaked along the deserted street, with the bowl of flour paste and the brush, half anxious, half guilty. We took a quick look to make sure no one was watching, and pasted a strip on the wall outside Pomegranate Gardens, then another on the corner of Lantern Alley. We pasted one at the back of Tingbi Teahouse. That was enough for the moment. I pulled Su out of sight, and we found some shade and watched to see if anyone passing by would stop for a read.

We hung onto the tree trunk like geckos, our hearts in our mouths, not daring to take our eyes off the strips of paper, even to blink. After a while, a man in a long gown came bustling out of the teahouse, one hand clutching the hem of his jacket, the other clasping his belly. He looked like he was looking for a place to do a poo. He got to the corner of the street, looked up and saw our strip, still wet from the glue. He stepped forward, ripped it firmly off the wall, scrunched it up, then turned and disappeared.

Su was frantic. 'Sis, Sis!' she cried. 'He's torn it off and gone away with it! Go after him!'

But there was no way I was going to catch him. He was scurrying faster than a rabbit. Besides, he was a big man. Even if I did catch him up, I wouldn't dare challenge him.

I pretended not be concerned. I rapped Su over the head with the remaining strips and said, 'Let's go and find somewhere far away to paste them up.'

'Far away, will there be someone who can read it three times?' she asked.

'Of course,' I snapped back.

Su was my little tail. She always stuck right behind me, no matter what craziness I was up to. We walked along Shaanxi Street, over the cobbles, past a store selling brooms and dustpans, straw mats and hats, then a dilapidated clan hall guarded by a stone lion with half its head missing, and an inn with brilliant red canna flowers around the door. There were a few houses with tiny yards here and there alongside the street too. It was only May, but already hot. The sun was glaring down and there was no one around. Weeds poked through the gaps between the cobbles, their prickly leaves scratching my ankles. My legs felt itchy, as if bugs were crawling up them. The broken bricks and tiles that lay against the walls had been in the sunshine for hours and stank of cat poo and dog pee. Su pulled a disgusted face, and held her nose.

As we went past the inn with the canna flowers, it occurred to me that there must be guests coming and going, so I stopped, looked around, and then motioned to Su to hold the bowl up. I hurriedly dipped my brush in and slopped some paste on the gate, then pulled out a strip, unfolded it, and pressed it down onto the paste. 'Run!' I hissed, and pulled Su with me.

But Su was quite little and besides, she had the bowl of paste in her hands. When I jerked her, she went flying, and so did the bowl. It broke into pieces on the cobbles and the grey-white paste slithered out all over the stones and in the gaps. It looked yucky, like snot.

I was terrified that the inn-keeper would come out and catch us, so I yelled at her, 'Why are you so clumsy?!' Her little mouth turned down and I knew she was about to cry. I flung her off and marched away. She was so scared at being left behind, she scurried after me, snivelling, 'Far away there's no one…far away there's no one…'

Poor little thing, she was only four, and had only just started kindergarten. I relented. 'Don't be such a pain! Just keep quiet, will you? If you keep quiet, I'll pick you some mulberries.'

That hushed her up in no time, and she stopped snivelling. Her eyes were still teary but she stared around her eagerly. 'Where? Where are the mulberry trees?'

I remembered my mother saying, 'You mustn't lie to a child. If you do, she won't believe any adult next time around.'

So I let her into my secret: the mulberries were in the woods by the river. The tree was full of them, so many you couldn't count, ripe, purple berries, sweet enough to die for. Su listened to me entranced, lips parted, her baby teeth gleaming in the sun, big eyes staring, blinking as if she hardly dared believe me.

It was true there were mulberries in the woods by the river, but we'd picked all the ones on the branches that were low enough for our short arms to reach.

Every day when Sheona and I got out of school, we'd been going there and eating till our lips were purple. It got so that when we burped, we got a winey taste in our mouths. So there weren't any left for Su, that was for sure.

But I'd said it now, so I couldn't take it back, could I? I told her there were mulberries, so there must be some.

I took her by the hand and we went to the river. I put her on a knobbly old tree stump and told her to wait for me, not to move. Then I squinted upwards, my hand shielding my eyes, before I bent double and crashed into the undergrowth. I was praying fervently, *Mulberry tree, bring them to me! Please God, let me find a few mulberries!* It didn't matter if they were green and so unripe they made her mouth pucker, I had to find some to keep Su happy.

It was cosy and warm among the trees. Mottled sunlight filtered through the canopy, it was hot underfoot, and there was the dry smell of the earth, the whiff of rotting leaves, and the sharp scent of countless flowers and grasses. A black centipede boldly crawled onto my shoe, and there was a wasp as big as my thumb buzzing around the back of my neck. It didn't sting me, but it wouldn't go away either.

What was it trying to do? The leaves of the mulberry trees were beginning to go yellow and even the green ones were rough-looking, no shine on them anymore, unappetizing if you were a little white silkworm. I stood under the mulberry tree and looked up. The highest branches were laden with clusters of berries but there was nothing within reach. We'd had them all. If only we'd left a few behind!

I could hear Su whimpering, 'Sis! Sis!'

'Coming!' I called. There was nothing for it. I'd have to climb the tree. I was good at climbing. There was no tree anywhere around our house that had beaten me yet. Besides, the mulberry tree had lots of leafy branches and a short trunk and rough bark. I'd be up at the top in no time at all. What I had to look out for was the ripe berries at the top. If I didn't take care, I'd bruise them and get covered in sticky purple juice. And I wouldn't be able to hide the tell-tale stains on my clothes, so I'd be in for a beating from my mother when I got home.

I made my way up the trunk, carefully reached out, and picked seven or eight berries from the nearest branch, cradling them gently in the palm of my hand. I couldn't help myself. I began to drool with anticipation. My mouth opened and in one gulp, they were gone. *They're Su's...Su's...*I told myself firmly, and tried my utmost to keep my fist closed over the few I had left.

Suddenly I heard a shriek from the edge of the wood, 'Daddy! Daddy!'

My heart in my mouth, I propped myself against the trunk, and stood on tiptoe so I could peer through the branches.

My dad hadn't been home for two or three weeks, and my mother was still waiting for his salary, so she could buy material to make us summer clothes. I saw two people coming along the road. The tall one was my dad. His clothes were covered in dust and he was wearing a pair of cloth shoes with holes in the toes. His hair was long and tangled, and looked like a bird's nest from where we were. If it weren't for the tortoiseshell-framed glasses he wore, no one would think he was a university prof. Even our primary school headteacher dressed better than he did, with his long gown and leather shoes.

But who was the boy walking beside him? Why had I never seen him before? I guessed he was about my age, judging by his size. He only came up to my father's armpit. He was more ragged even than my dad, with half of one sleeve missing from his jacket and his trouser legs hanging over his ankles. He was barefoot, his feet black with filth, and he scuffed along kicking up dust with every step. He kept turning his head as he walked along, though I couldn't see what he was looking at. In any case, he looked pinched and miserable, and very unwilling.

Was he a beggar? My dad had once brought a beggar boy home, for my mother to feed him up. The trouble was, with five children in our family, there was no knowing where the next meal was coming from. We really didn't have anything to spare.

I stood in the tree fork, making myself as tall as I could, and waved frantically towards the road. 'Dad! Dad!'

My father stopped. He shielded his eyes and looked suspiciously towards the wood. The boy stopped too. He was looking down at the ground, completely uninterested, as if all this had nothing to do with him.

Su was already running towards her daddy, her little arms outstretched, laughing and calling to him. Su adored our dad, because he was strong enough to swing her high in the air, something my mother couldn't do. I started to climb down as quickly as I could. I was keen to grab hold of my dad's bag, sling it over my shoulder, and carry it home for him.

But I still had a bunch of ripe mulberries in one hand, and didn't want to throw them away. So I had to come down with only one arm around the trunk, the other arm held high in the air, and I slid faster than I meant to. I felt a stabbing pain in my knee, as if I'd been stung by a wasp. I ignored it. My mother always said I was tougher than other little girls, though I never knew if that was praise or blame.

I hurtled towards the road, still clutching the berries. Su was already having a cuddle, her arms around Dad's neck as she giggled happily. Dad's bedroll had spewed dirty clothes onto the road. The boy stood behind the bags, shoulders drooping, looking dully at the sky, the ground, and the woods, anywhere but at us.

I was a big girl, I'd had my eighth birthday, I was almost nine. I couldn't expect as many cuddles as Su, but I was just as happy as she was to see Dad come home. I acted very grownup and went over to pick up my dad's bags and bedroll. The boy still didn't turn his head. It was obviously deliberate. He must have been jealous that we three were so happy to see each other.

'Orange!' my father suddenly yelped. 'Look at your leg!'

I looked down. My knee was a mess. I must have cut myself coming down the tree, and the wound looked deep. The blood was trickling down in a thin stream. It was bright red, like leeches had been sucking my blood. No wonder it didn't feel right when I was running. My knee felt stiff.

Su was terrified at the sight of the blood and buried her head in the crook of Dad's neck. He tried to put her down so he could attend to me, but she wouldn't let go of him. She locked her legs around his waist and her arms around his neck, and stuck like a limpet.

To be honest, even I was scared when I saw the blood pouring down my leg. I was afraid I'd get tetanus. Sheona had told me that if you got tetanus, you died. If I died, I wouldn't get any more mulberries next year.

My father crouched down and tried to coax and scold Su into letting go. I stood there dumbly, just wishing I knew how to make the bleeding stop. In the middle of all this, the boy suddenly hurtled away. We saw him in a bit of scrubland back from the road, scrabbling around in the bushes until he found a plant, which he pulled up. He ran back to us, crouched down in front of me, and stuffed the herb into his mouth. Then he chomped away at it, his cheeks bulging, until he'd made a sticky mass of bright green paste. This he spat into his palm and, to my astonishment, slapped onto my leg.

I was dumbstruck. I had no idea he was going to put spit on my leg. What a disgusting idea!

But strangely enough, as soon as the stuff was stuck to my knee, the wound cooled down, and felt nice and slightly ticklish. The bleeding stopped, and I could flex my knee a little bit too. That was better.

'Look, Dad, look!' I exclaimed.

My father grinned at the boy and gave him the thumbs up. 'You're a good boy, Shen Tianlu!' he said.

Ah-hah, so he had a name. He wasn't just a beggar boy who'd been tagging along after my dad.

I was even more astonished by what happened next. Tianlu stood up, thought for a moment, then bent down in front of me, put his hands behind his back and grabbed me, and hoisted me firmly onto his back!

'Let's go, Uncle,' was all he said.

'Can you carry her?'

'Sure.'

'Let's go then.' And my father set off briskly, with his roll slung over his shoulder, and Su in his arms.

Good heavens, Dad was letting this stranger carry me! How did he know I wasn't going to be kidnapped? This boy was strong too, even though he was only a tiny bit taller than me. He wasn't even puffing as he piggybacked me along.

I was terrified as I lay on his back, the thoughts flashing through my mind. But I dared not move, let alone protest. On his back, I smelled the sweetish smell of his sweat in his neck. It really was sweet, to my surprise. In our textbooks, 'sweat' was always described as 'sour', but his neck smelled like sweet rice wine. There was something else strange: a child's hair is usually too slippery to get hold of. But his hair was all short, stiff bristles, so I had to keep my chin well up so that I didn't get spiked in the face.

I had completely forgotten that I was still holding the mulberries. By the time we got home and I opened my fist, they were thoroughly squished, and the sticky juice had run all over my palm, outlining the creases in bright scarlet. It was quite a grisly sight.

Chapter 2
The Pencil Case

Shen Tianlu was the odd one out in our family for quite a long time. He was totally unlike the rest of us – Kejun, Shuya, me, and Su. He was remote and strange and he just didn't fit in.

He was short and rather scrawny, with fine features but a big head and unusually big hands and feet too. The different bits of his body looked weirdly mismatched. When we arrived home that first day, my father told us who he was and introduced him properly. When he said Tianlu was fourteen, the same age as Kejun, Shuya's mouth fell open and she gaped in astonishment. She made a show of inspecting him front and back, before drawling, 'Mum, he's a dwarf. I thought he must be a year younger than Orange.'

And to get me on her side, Shuya dug her elbow into my ribs and said sarcastically, 'Orange, if he's fourteen, we better be polite and call him "big brother". What do you feel about that?'

Tianlu had just carried me all the way home, so what could I say? I pulled a face instead.

Tianlu had gone red to the ears, and was scuffing the ground with one big foot. There was an odd expression in his eyes. I couldn't decide if it was embarrassment or annoyance.

Anyway, Shuya got a big telling-off from our dad for being rude to a guest. 'So what if he isn't tall?' he told us. 'Some people grow their bodies first, others grow their heads first, and that's much better, don't you think, Kejun? Orange?'

Kejun smiled and went over and gave Tianlu a matey pat on the shoulder. Under the combined onslaught of our father and brother, Shuya looked crestfallen, though still rebellious.

To be honest, my sister always ruled the roost at home, because she was the smartest and best at everything. She always got top marks in her homework, and she was good at things like music, chess, calligraphy and art. At school, she could always be relied on if there was a song or dance to be performed, so the principal and teachers all loved her. She had a very good opinion of herself and didn't like being roundly told off by Dad one bit, especially in front of Shen Tianlu. I couldn't help gloating.

Shuya scowled furiously at me. She could always see right through me.

Compared with Shuya, Kejun was everything you'd expect in a big brother, although he was only one year older than her. He was tall, with broad shoulders, and a handsome, open face. He was also gentle and reasonable, never argued, and was always kind to Su and me. It was typical of the two of them that when Tianlu arrived, Shuya poked fun at him, but Kejun threw himself into cleaning the bedroom they would share. Then he cleared a space by the window, brought in benches and some boards, and in no time at all had cobbled together a bed for Tianlu. He also found a face cloth and other basics he'd need, and made a bookcase for him with bricks and more boards. My mother exclaimed gratefully, 'How kind you are, Kejun!'

I could see where she was coming from, but half of me felt she should have praised me too. After all, I'd just given up my writing table for Tianlu. Without it, I had to do my homework on the bed, and my writing came out all wonky. Why didn't Mum see that?

Shen Tianlu was a leftie. I was the first to spot this. You see, I was interested in people. My schoolwork wasn't up to Kejun's and Shuya's, and my mother complained that I was a wild child, couldn't sew, and didn't even look like a girl, but actually I was, and am, very observant. Not much slips past me, and I have a good memory too. Otherwise, I wouldn't remember things that happened seventy or eighty years ago so clearly. I realized that Tianlu always used his left hand whether he was using chopsticks, washing his face and wringing out a towel, or helping with the housework – sweeping the floor, wiping the table, and bringing water. And the left side of his body was stronger too. For a while, I amused myself by imitating his left-handed movements, and started clowning around and making my left shoulder higher than my right. My mum got cross and whacked me on the shoulder with the fire stick to make me stop.

'What kind of a person only imitates someone's bad points and not their good ones?' she scolded me.

She defended Tianlu as well. 'Don't make fun of

lefties. Lefties are very bright, you'll see.'

And so it turned out. When Tianlu started in high school, he made rapid progress. Soon, he was almost level-pegging with Shuya. But she was determined to keep her position at the top of the class, come what may. She put every ounce of effort into her school work, I could see that.

We found Tianlu's dialect difficult when he first arrived. It took a long time for us to get used to it. We hadn't been in Chongqing very long and didn't know Sichuan dialect, and he had a very thick accent. Sometimes, my mother talked to him in Nanjing dialect but it was a dialogue of the deaf – I had to translate for them. Tianlu was very self-conscious about his accent and used to play dumb. When my mother served him more food, or told him to take a shower, or gave him clothes or shoes to try on, he either shook his head, or forced out his attempt at mandarin, 'Awesome', which came out as 'Ow-sum'. At first, every time we heard another 'Ow-sum!', we three girls collapsed laughing. Of course we got a thorough telling-off from my father, so eventually we stopped mimicking him out loud. Instead, we used to mouth 'Ow-sum!' behind his back whenever he said it, and pull horrible faces.

Tianlu knew exactly what we were up to, but he couldn't stop us. He had no one to defend him, not classmates, nor friends, nor family. He was an awkward kid, and we didn't help. When I think about it now, I wonder how we never realized just how alone and lonely he must have been. We had it so easy in our nice, warm family, and my parents gave us so much freedom to grow up.

After the summer holidays, school started again. I was in primary school, my big brother and sister were both in junior high school, with Kejun in the third year, and Shuya in the second. My dad took Tianlu to register and tried to get him into Kejun's class. The teacher tested him, but then said no, because he didn't know a word of English, and couldn't do algebra either, and so would not be able to keep up with the work. So he was put in the same class as my sister.

Dad didn't want us to look down on Tianlu because he'd been put in a year below his age. He explained that Tianlu was an orphan and had never had his parents to look after him. He'd been lucky to get a full belly, let alone an education. He'd only been to school on and off, so he'd fallen behind and needed time to catch up. 'I'm willing to bet it won't take him long,' said Dad. 'His father and mother were highly educated, truly exceptional, and Tianlu will outstrip them, for sure. Isn't that right, Tianlu?' He looked at him earnestly, but Tianlu went pale. He bit his lip, and for once he didn't say any 'Ow-sums'.

Under her breath, Shuya said scornfully to me,

'What's Dad thinking? Why should I call him "big brother" when he's in the same year as me? It's ridiculous. He's so short that he gets to sit in the front row!'

I shrugged. I couldn't see why it was ridiculous to be put in the front row. After all, with my long arms and long legs, I'd always been put right at the back, from year one onwards. I was probably being laughed at too!

Shuya couldn't get over me siding with Tianlu. 'Do you like this short-ass, or something?' she asked.

'No! I like Kejun, he's so good-looking.'

'Idiot!' she said.

'I'm not an idiot!'

'Shut up! If I say you're an idiot, you're an idiot! You don't understand anything.'

Obviously I didn't agree but I couldn't get the better of her. 'You wait and see. It'll end in tears,' she went on.

'What?'

'You wait and see.'

What was she talking about? Shuya was getting more mysterious by the day. I'd never be as clever as her.

But Shuya must have had second sight or something, because something happened that really did end in tears. It started with my dad buying Tianlu a very smart pencil case. I was madly jealous.

But a bit of history first. After University of Nanking was evacuated from Nanjing to Huaxi Fields in Chengdu in 1938, it found a new home on the campus of West China Union University, along with Beijing's Yenching University, Cheeloo University, and Nanjing's Ginling College. All the administration, teaching, catering, and accommodation were amalgamated. With five universities squeezed onto one campus, space was at a premium. There were three thousand students and fifty or sixty departments, all crammed in together. At the same time, prices for everyday things were going through the roof, teachers had all taken pay cuts, students had to borrow money to eat, and teaching conditions were horrendous. Students today couldn't even begin to imagine it.

On the way from our home in Pomegranate

Gardens to the primary school, there was a big stationery store. The district had thousands of students, and they all needed paper, ink, and inkstones. The stationery store did a roaring trade. Before the term began, there were some colourful metal pencil boxes on display, probably imported from Britain. I remember there were two different designs. One had a white boat bobbing in the sunshine on the sea, its sail billowing in the breeze. The other had bright green grass, and red and yellow flowers, and a red house with a pointy roof. And in the middle of the picture was a cute little white rabbit.

I went home and started to work on Mum. 'Can you buy me a pencil case?'

'Money's tight this month. By the time we've paid your school fees, there won't be enough for food.'

'Sheona has one, it's so pretty!' I whined. 'And she's got a new pencil and a rubber.'

'That's different. She's an only child. You're one of six.'

How did she make it six? Kejun, Shuya, Su, Kid, and me. Then I realized she'd counted Tianlu. I was annoyed. Why had Dad brought him home? My parents were paying for his food and clothes and school fees. No wonder my lovely pencil box had vanished in a puff of smoke.

All the same, that pencil box drew me as if it were a magnet. Every day on the way home from school, I sneaked into the stationery store and looked at it. The ocean scene ones quickly sold out, but there was a rabbit one left. I was stubbornly convinced this rabbit was mine, and I'd just let the store have it to look after. I needed to check every day whether it was happy in its position in the display cabinet. I squatted down to talk to it, and pretended I was stroking its furry ears through the glass. One day I brought a stalk of bristle grass in and waved it in front of my rabbit's nose, imagining it sniffing, jumping off the lid, and out of the case into my hand.

Sheona was very sympathetic. She was a kind-hearted girl. The whole family used to attend church, where God was, and God loved everyone, so she told me. She got out her brand-new red-and-white rubber, cut it in half, and gave me the red half.

'For you,' she said. 'I know you like red.'

I held the half-rubber in my hand but my mind was still on the rabbit pencil box.

'Hey, if you really love that pencil box, say your

prayers every day and God will give it to you,' Sheona advised me.

I wasn't really convinced because Professor Mei and his wife (our downstairs neighbours, the ones with the Rhode Island Red chickens) used to go to church every week and pray and sing hymns, but when they had a baby girl, she only survived a few days and then died of pneumonia. Mrs Mei cried her eyes out over that. Obviously the Lord didn't give everyone what they wanted.

One day after school, I paid my usual visit to the stationery store, but at the counter, I got the shock of my life. The rabbit had gone. There was just an empty space, a pale rectangle in the dust, where the pencil box used to sit.

'Where...where's it gone?' I stammered and pointed. I could hardly speak for shock.

The shop assistant had acne scars on his nose. 'Where do you think?' he smirked. 'It grew legs and upped and ran away.'

'Where to?'

'I dunno. Maybe someone caught it and took it home to put it in the pot,' said the assistant, bored.

'Rubbish.'

'It's true! Rabbit meat is delish! With Sichuan pepper!' His pockmarked nose twitched as if he could smell it.

Su might have believed him but I wasn't four years old any more. Besides, I didn't like him joking about my rabbit.

I glared at him furiously, then turned and barged out of the shop. As I ran down the cobbled road, I looked at the evening sun shining over the field in front of me. At that moment it didn't look like a red ball of fire to me; it looked black, pitch-black, and it was sinking and dragging me down with it, into an abyss of despair.

That evening at dinner, I messed with my bowl of rice porridge and hardly ate anything. My mother was worried. She kept feeling my forehead and asking if I was ill. I didn't dare tell her what was upsetting me. She'd tell me not to be such a baby. Mum took my uneaten food and scraped half of it into Kejun's bowl. Food was too precious to waste.

It never rains but it pours. That evening, my dad turned up at home with a long thin thing wrapped in paper which he pulled out of his gown pocket and, right in front of the rest of us, gave to Tianlu. 'It's for you, Tianlu,' he said kindly. 'For school.'

Our heads swivelled towards Tianlu and we all watched him open the package. If my dad had picked me out and given me a present, I would have been all over him, at least three kisses and three pinches on his shoulder to show how happy I was. But Tianlu didn't seem very excited. He looked wooden-faced, dull, and listless.

He was all fingers and thumbs too. The way he tore the paper off, it was like he'd never had a present before. First, the triangle of folded wrapping paper at one end, then the one at the other end. Finally, he turned the thing upside down and pulled the paper apart. I could hardly believe my eyes. It was a brand-new pencil box! The lid was painted with green grass, a red house, and a sweet little rabbit! The sides and the bottom of the case were painted gold. In the dim light from the weak electric bulb, this beautiful, gleaming gift dazzled me!

So it was Dad who had bought the last remaining pencil box. And given it to Tianlu.

At that moment, I was nearly spitting with rage.

Didn't Dad know what I felt about the rabbit pencil box? I'd been going on about it every day at the dinner table: pencil box, pencil box...Hadn't he heard? Obviously he wasn't my real dad, he was Tianlu's? I didn't know what to think!

Dad must have sensed our outrage because he added, looking us each in the eye, 'Your mother's made bags for your school things. That'll do you fine. It's war-time. We all have to scrimp and save.' Then he went on, 'Tianlu's just started school and your mum's busy with Kid. She hasn't had time to make a bag for him. That's why I bought him a pencil box.'

That was his explanation. Well, at least he took the trouble to explain. That was his democratic side coming out.

Shuya muttered, 'Yesterday we had our monthly test. Someone flunked it.'

Dad rapped his pipe on the table-top. 'Speak up! I won't have you muttering about people behind their backs!'

Shuya plucked up her courage. 'Yesterday we had tests – '

'And what does one test mean?' Dad interrupted. 'Tianlu has only just started. It'll take him time to catch up. Even if he's behind now, it doesn't mean anything. You don't know how well he's going to do in the end.

Besides, Tianlu's one of the family now. It wouldn't matter if he got zero. We'd still look after him the way parents should.'

Shuya bit back her words. She didn't dare say anything more.

Dad seemed annoyed, and waved us all away from the table to read or do our homework. All except Tianlu. Speaking so softly that we couldn't hear, he talked to him for a long time. I caught a few words: 'Your dad used to…', 'National disaster'… 'You can't do anything without learning…'

I strained my ears, but I never heard a word from Tianlu.

In the lamplight, he was sitting there looking at the floor. I had no idea what was going through his head. *He's so stupid!* I thought furiously. *My dad's been so good to him and he can't even say thank-you.*

The next morning, Kejun went out into the yard to draw water, as he always did. Then he tramped up the stairs carrying the bucket and tipped it into the water jar. Shuya got the fire going and made breakfast. I swept the floor, and Su took the rubbish out. We each had our jobs in the morning. Tianlu didn't have any particular task yet, so when our mother went out shopping with Kid in her arms, he carried the basket for her.

My sweeping took me to the part of the bedroom where the boys slept. Tianlu's school bag was on his bed, open and I could see the brand-new shiny pencil box inside. Suddenly, some devilry took hold of me, egging me on to do something very, very bad. I found myself by his bed, picking up the pencil box, and hiding it inside my jacket. What was worse, I closed the bag up, then sneaked downstairs, out into the yard, and round the back to where there was a tumbledown wall. I hid the pencil box in a crevice between the stones, stuffed some dry twigs in to cover it, then scuttled back indoors, and carried on sweeping, wiping the table, making the beds.

I could hear my heart thudding in my chest. It was so loud that I was amazed that Kejun and Shuya didn't hear it too.

But no one noticed anything strange in me. They were too busy. The early morning was always the busiest time at home. Even my father, who always let things go on around him without apparently noticing, had to do his bit, passing out the bowls and chopsticks.

Tianlu had a double maths class that day. In the

second hour, the teacher handed out everyone's tests and went through the answers. It was when she asked them to correct their work that he realized his pencil box was gone, and his pen, his ruler, his rubber, everything that had been in it. He scrabbled around in his schoolbag but it wasn't there. Frantically, he tipped the contents of the bag out onto the desk: the books were all there, but the pencil box had completely vanished.

According to my sister, the teacher was very annoyed. Not only had Tianlu failed the test and pulled the class average down but, to make matters worse, he didn't have his writing things with him either. In her eyes, he was sloppy, careless, and generally a useless student. She flew into a rage, grabbed Tianlu's maths book and test paper, and threw them out of the window. Then she hauled him outside and yelled at him that he had to stand on the walkway and watch the class through the window as a punishment.

Class went on, and it was so quiet in the corridor that the teacher completely forgot that there was a student being punished out there. When the bell rang, she remembered Tianlu. Maybe he had come to his senses and repented, maybe he deserved a few kind words. She went to find him. But Tianlu wasn't there.

That was the kind of wild child he was.

She didn't bother to go looking for him. It was a big school with more than two hundred children of all ages. Some were hard-working, some were mischievous, and more than a few sometimes skipped classes.

But no one skipped lunch in our family. When Tianlu didn't come home, my mother thought it was a bit odd. She sent Kejun to the school to look for him. He searched but there was no sign of Tianlu. My mother got really anxious. What if something had happened to him? Shuya had to tell her that Tianlu had got into trouble in class. Mum was frantic, and sent me to Dad's laboratory to tell him. My dad was just as worried as my mother. He got two of the lab students to help him, plus us three eldest, and we searched all over Huaxi Fields. It took us until the middle of the night to find him. He was in a melon shed on the banks of the Jinxiu River.

The thing was, Tianlu was a bright boy. When his pencil box had disappeared into thin air, he immediately guessed who was responsible. Being humiliated in front of the whole class by the teacher was the last straw. He was so upset that he decided to run away from Chengdu and our family, and go back to his home in West Sichuan. But then he realized he didn't know how to get there. He walked round and round by the Jinxiu River till night fell. Then, exhausted and hungry, he went and stole two young corn cobs from someone's field and fell asleep in the shed.

My mother shook him by the shoulder. 'You're so stubborn! Didn't you think about how worried your family would be?'

He stared at her. 'I don't have a family.'

That wounded Mum, and she wiped tears from her eyes with the front of her jacket.

My father was hurt too, but he was a man, he couldn't start crying like my mother.

He was silent for a long while, then pulled himself together and said kindly, 'Fine, Tianlu, if you really don't want a family, as soon as you're grown up and you can make a living, you can leave Huaxi Fields. But I was your father's best friend, so until you've grown up and finished your schooling, I have a responsibility to look after you. You agree?'

Tianlu acted awkward like he usually did, only this time he scowled rebelliously too, and refused to say another word.

My dad sighed, ruffled Tianlu's hair, and set off slowly down the road to the institute. He was always the optimist, and it was rare for us to see him so gloomy.

Tianlu certainly set the cat among the pigeons that day. But I had to admit that it was me who had started all the trouble, or rather, the little devil inside me.

I went and pulled the beautiful pencil box out of the crevice in the wall where I had hidden it and, in floods of tears, I took it to Dad. I steeled myself for a beating, or even expulsion from the family. But my father looked down and thought for a long time. Then he waved me away.

I couldn't understand it. I'd done something terribly dishonest, hadn't I? My father had always brought us up to behave honourably.

'He obviously thinks you're a hopeless case. There's no point beating you,' said my sister.

I panicked. Did Dad really think I was so bad that nothing could be done with me? Would he give up on me? Forget I even existed? For a whole week after that, I was on my best behaviour. I ate up the pickles that I normally hated and didn't touch any of the other dishes; I swept all the way down to the ground floor; I conscientiously copied out new words into my homework book – the other children copied each new character ten times, I copied them twenty times. When it came to washing the dishes, carrying Kid around, helping Dad with his bag and passing him his shoes, I made sure to get in there first.

I slaved away at home as my way of punishing myself for my bad behaviour.

Kejun didn't miss a trick. He knew exactly what was going on. He made sure to lavish praise on me, 'She's a clever kid, Orange. She's admitted she did wrong and now she's making up for it.' Then he whispered to me, 'If Dad's not shouting at you, it's because he knows how much you wanted that pencil case. It's just that money's tight. He only had enough to buy one, so he couldn't get it for you.'

Really? Did Dad really know how much I wanted it? Would he forgive me? The tears came to my eyes.

As for the pencil box, Tianlu refused to take it. He said it was too pretty and girly. He said he'd swap with me. I could have the rabbit box and he'd use the bag Mum had made for my pencils.

But if Tianlu didn't want it, then I certainly didn't, either. I had my pride.

Shuya was only too happy to have the pencil case. With a syrupy smile, she assured our mother that she would pass it on to Su when she started school.

That was the kind of girl Shuya was. She could put on a goody-goody act to get what she wanted. I was getting big myself but I'd never get to be as crafty as she was.

Chapter 3

The Cockerel Loses Some Feathers

Up to the age of ten, I was always getting into scrapes.

My mother worried about me. 'Between seven and eight is supposed to be a difficult age, but you're nine, and you're still naughty. No man's going to want you!' She was tormented by the idea that I'd never get married and would stay a spinster for the rest of my life.

Some were big scrapes. For instance, I was never allowed to go swimming in the river, because I could only do doggy-paddle. When the river was high or if there were hidden currents, I might get dragged under and drown. But I loved the feeling of immersing myself in the water on hot days, so I used to jump in whenever I got the chance. Once, Mum made me a new pair of cloth shoes. I took them off and left them on the river bank before getting in. When I'd had enough of floundering around in the water, I climbed out. No shoes! Some pesky kid must have run off with them. A brand new pair of shoes! And I'd just casually left them lying by the river! My mother gave me such a beating that she raised three bright red welts on my bottom. She wept as she hit me, 'I've never known a girl to be as naughty as you! There's never a minute's peace with you around! Why aren't you more like your big brother and sister?'

I was furious at the thief who'd got me this beating. I swore I'd find them wherever they were hiding. For days after that, whenever I went out, I kept my eyes glued to other kids' feet, hoping against hope that I'd catch someone wearing my shoes. I'd pounce on them, grab hold of them, spit in their face. Of course, I never did get my revenge. The thief was no fool.

Then there were the small scrapes. Like breaking a glass test-tube belonging to my dad, picking up my little brother to cuddle him but tripping over so he banged his head and got a big bruise, having a new outfit to wear to school for once and fooling around and getting ink all over it…I got so many things wrong that I used to wonder whether my mum had got it wrong even giving birth to me.

Early one Sunday morning, Professor Mei came to see my dad. He was holding his majestic Rhode Island Red cockerel, and looking distraught.

Of all the people who lived in Pomegranate Gardens, Professor Mei was the closest to my dad. Dad taught agronomy and Mei, animal husbandry and veterinary science. They shared a common language. Professor Mei had studied biology at the University of Wisconsin, and came back to China after he completed his doctorate. He switched to the department of animal husbandry, where his work had something to do with genetics. The couple had no children, so he had time on his hands and loved to have long chats with my dad. He used to bring a chair outside and sit in front of his door downstairs, smoking a pipe and waiting impatiently. No sooner had my dad put his foot through the gate than he'd be on his feet. Then he'd stomp up the stairs after him and they'd brew a pot of tea and sit and chat about how the war was going, what the Chongqing government was up to, and what the Americans were thinking. They tended to slip into English, especially when it came to talking about the United States, and the pair of them would get very angry, and shout at each other.

I asked my father once, 'Why do you talk English when you shout at each other?'

'Because it doesn't sound as vulgar in English.'

'But why do you shout at each other?'

'We're expressing our feelings.'

What a strange explanation.

But most of the time, they talked quite calmly, about things to do with teaching. One of my dad's students was going to write a dissertation on 'Genetic and Cellular Studies of Wheat-Rye Hybrids'. My dad had no special knowledge of biogenetics, so he asked Mei to be his co-supervisor. Professor Mei said yes, immediately. Another time, my dad and his students planted some rows of a particular kind of American cotton in the far test fields one spring. By autumn, they'd produced a bumper harvest. The plants were nearly three feet high, and covered with cotton bolls, each one as big as a child's fist. The local farmers gazed at them greedily, then sneaked back at night and everyone picked a few. By morning, more than half the crop had gone. My dad was so upset that his lips came out in cold sores. Professor Mei stood calmly smoking his pipe as he put my father straight, 'Stealing happens. If people steal off you, it means you've got something worth stealing and that's good. If what you've got is no good, no one's going to steal it. They won't even accept it as a present.'

That made sense to my dad. He went and told his students not to bother investigating. Sure enough, next spring, the local farmers used the new cotton seed, and promoting the improved strain was no trouble at all.

That morning when Professor Mei banged on our door, holding his cockerel under his arm, my father guessed something was wrong. He brought a stool for him and poured him some tea.

'It's outrageous! Absolutely outrageous!' the professor spluttered, out of breath from having run up the stairs.

'Please, sit down, old boy. What's up?'

Mei ignored the offer. 'Every parent has a duty to educate their child, you know what that means, Huang?'

'Of course I do, yes, indeed.' My father reassured him.

Professor Mei had obviously come to demand justice. My father and mother always felt guilty when we did wrong. Other people had only one or two children, you could keep an eye on them. But we were six, including Tianlu, and it was hard to stop us getting into trouble.

Professor Mei lifted up the cockerel and turned it around so its bum was sticking under my dad's nose, so he couldn't miss it. 'Its tail! Look at its tail! Three tail feathers are gone! Three!'

He stuffed the bird back under his arm again, freed a hand, and ruffled the cock's remaining bright red tail feathers. 'Do you have any idea how precious this rooster is? It's come thousands of miles. We brought eighteen head of cattle, seven pigs, six sheep, and a pair of Rhode Island Reds, all of them priceless, all so we could use them for hybridizing, to improve the local strains! You have no idea how hard the trip was, Huang. We were shelled all the way. We were lucky to get here alive! I've been rearing them for breeding. No one touches them but me, I – I – '

'Stop right there, Mei.' My father was looking doubtful. 'This compound is full of families with children, all of them up to no good. How can you be so sure it was mine?'

'Because none of them are brave enough to go near the cock and hen, except for your Orange!'

He was spot on. Whenever I had nothing better to do, I'd mess with his birds. Once, I got hold of a stray cat and tried to give it a ride on the rooster's back but the bird wasn't having any of that. It glared furiously and its hackles stood on end. Then it stretched its neck and charged me. The watching children all scattered in terror. And what happened then? I actually caught it, and held it down. Meantime, however, the cat had taken its chance to wriggle out of my arms, and fled with an ear-splitting screech.

Now, I had no one but myself to blame for being careless. I must have been seen when I stole the rooster's feathers yesterday, and whoever it was must have been mean enough to tell on me to Professor Mei. Probably it was Shuya. She was always scheming to get me into trouble, while she played Miss Goody-Goody.

No one knows a girl like her own parents, and besides, I had always been the troublemaker in our family. At the mention of my name, my dad had it figured out. He looked around for me but I had hidden in the back room, and locked myself in. A clear admission of guilt. My dad sighed and apologized to his old friend with complete sincerity, 'She's a naughty girl. She's done a very bad thing. I'm so sorry.'

Professor Mei was still raging. 'Three feathers! Your daughter owes my cockerel a very big apology!'

My father turned to the bird and addressed it, 'Right, right, I'm so sorry, cockerel! It must have hurt!'

'This must never happen again!' thundered the irate prof.

'Don't worry, old man. It won't. Believe me. I'm giving you my personal guarantee!'

My dad, quite shamelessly, kept offering his condolences to the man and his bird. In the end, he made my mother scoop out half a bowl of rice from the big jar, and gave it to the precious bird, so its tail feathers would grow back quickly.

Even after Professor Mei had hurried away, I sat tight, refusing to open the door, no matter how hard my father knocked. I heard my sister outside, telling Dad I'd pulled the tail feathers out so I could make a shuttlecock. She must have found my shuttlecock and shown it to him because I heard his angry voice, 'Throw it away! Throw it down the toilet!'

At that, I flung open the door, hurtled out, and grabbed the shuttlecock off my sister.

I sunk my teeth into her too, and she screamed. My dad was really mad by now. With one big stride, he was in front of me, his hand raised above his head, ready to give me a slap. But my dad had never beaten one of his children before. His hand shook, and he wavered, maybe trying to work out how much force he should use.

Suddenly Tianlu appeared and squeezed in between me and my dad. He looked up at my father's hand.

'Uncle, don't be angry with Orange. She wants to be first.'

My dad looked mystified. 'First in what?'

'Kicking the shuttlecock. It's a competition, all her classmates have good shuttlecocks.'

'And what does that have to do with pulling the cock's tail feathers out?'

'Everything! Maybe you've never played shuttlecock. If the feathers are long enough, the shuttlecock goes up and stays steady. It doesn't go sideways, you can do it with one kick, it's brilliant, and you win!'

My dad thought a moment, then lowered his hand. 'Well, that's interesting, this little monkey's certainly competitive!'

He decided to forgive me. He turned away, clasped his hands behind his back while he considered the matter, then turned back to ask me, 'Do you get a certificate if you win?'

'Yes, the teacher's alrcady got it, locked away in her drawer.'

'That's good,' my dad said decisively. 'After the competition, go and show your certificate to Uncle Mei and confess. See if he'll forgive you.'

I grinned and then burst into tears. I had no idea why I was crying. It was very strange.

There were other things I couldn't work out, like why Tianlu stood up for me at the critical moment, when I was the one who stole his new pencil box, and I was always making fun of his accent and the way he did things left-handed.

And another thing, Tianlu was not even in the same school as me. He kept himself to himself and hardly ever opened his mouth to anyone. How had he found out there was going to be a shuttlecock competition in our class, and that I desperately wanted to win? Very weird.

How difficult it is to really understand someone.

Chapter 4
Our Night-time Walk

In November, the weather in Huaxi Fields began to cool down. I'd been keeping a green grasshopper over the summer and one day, I found it lying on its back in its little bamboo cage. It wasn't moving. I prodded it with a blade of grass and realized that it must have died during the night. Its body had gone stiff. Su wanted to feed it to Professor Mei's cockerel but I refused to let her, and buried it in a flower pot on the walkway. Su was fascinated and kept asking if the grasshopper would come back to life next year, just like the plants in the flower pots put out shoots every spring. I couldn't be bothered to answer her funny questions. I told her to go and ask Kejun. He knew everything. He had the *Young People's Encyclopedia* in

English, which was supposed to have all the scientific knowledge in the world in it, but sadly my English wasn't good enough to read it.

That winter, Mum made cotton padded coats for the four of us children who were at school. Shuya and I had dark blue ones, but there wasn't quite enough cloth, so she made collars from an old patterned silk cheongsam she cut up. Shuya loved the collar, which magically gave her ordinary padded coat an instant touch of luxury. She was so happy that every time she crossed a bridge, she wanted to stop and look at her reflection in the water. My brother and Tianlu got black, school uniform cotton-padded jackets without any decorations. Su had no new clothes. She got my big sister's old jacket, cut down to fit. Mum told her we were wearing school uniforms, and reassured her that when she started school, she'd have one too. Su believed her. She began to tick off on her fingers the days until she could go to primary school.

So we all had winter outfits, but what about the soldiers at the front fighting the Japanese? There was a photo in the Ta Kung Pao newspaper which showed a group of soldiers in a tunnel wearing unlined jackets and trousers, and shivering from cold. We Huaxi

Fields young people, from college down to primary school, had to do something, and we threw ourselves into organizing Winter Uniform Relief Concerts to raise funds for the soldiers at the front line.

The performance my school was due to put on was scheduled for the end of the month, in the auditorium of West China Union University. Our principal had personally arranged to borrow the auditorium. He was on the Chengdu Anti-Japanese Fundraising Committee, and was Huaxi Fields' most famous resident.

We were going to do a concert, so we had to have solo singers and choral singers, and soloist instrumentalists and an orchestra too. Sheona was the best piano player in our school, so she got the piano solo. She discussed with her mother when she got home, and came back to school to report that she was going to play a piece called 'Homesickness', by the Prussian-born composer Albert Jungmann. The music teacher gave her approval. There were a number of people living in our area who had fled from enemy-occupied Northeast China, and they must have been homesick all day every day.

The fifth grade were rehearsing the Salvation

March: the whole class dressed up in Scout uniforms, each carrying a small drum, and beat them as they marched in military formation. Then they sang the rousing chorus, 'Guns at the ready! Advance! Don't hurt the people. Don't hurt your own. Defend the Chinese nation. Forever be free!' They rehearsed on the sports ground, and we could hear the skirring of the drum beats and their loud clear voices. All of us from the other classes were green with envy.

We were in the fourth grade and our teachers were determined that we should not be outshone by the class above. How were we going to outdo them? Voice and instrumental solos were not exactly rousing, no matter how good the soloists were. Our teacher proposed that we should form a choir and sing the children's war song, 'Dig, Dig, Dig for Victory', which went, 'Down with the Japanese soldiers! Dig, dig, dig for victory! Pick up your gun and aim it true. I am a little volunteer, not afraid of dying. Advance, hold hands, advance together!'

Suddenly I heard my name. 'Orange, I want you to play the piano accompaniment.'

Oh my God! I couldn't do that! My hand shot up, and I blurted out, 'Miss, I can't! I'm scared!'

The teacher looked at me. 'Oh, so there is something you're scared of, is there, Orange?'

There certainly was, and unfortunately it just happened to be the piano. Sheona's mother, Mary Fan, had been teaching me off and on for nearly a year but I still couldn't plonk out the Czerny Exercises for Beginners. Mrs Fan was quite disappointed with me. I'm guessing that every time we started a new lesson she regretted having remarked on my long fingers, that first time.

'Sheona plays really well! She's going to go to a conservatoire in America,' I said, with exaggerated enthusiasm for my friend's playing.

'I don't need you to tell me how well Sheona plays,' the teacher snapped back. 'She's a soloist, she can't be distracted by playing accompaniments.'

I nearly cried. After all that, even if I bravely managed to play as she wanted, the teacher would regard it as 'just an accompaniment', child's play.

But I was pig-headed too, and I wasn't going to admit defeat. No matter what the teacher thought, I'd give it my best shot.

But how? There was nothing for it. I'd have to knuckle down and practice, even though I didn't believe that a week's practice was enough for me to be able to play along to 'Dig, Dig, Dig for Victory'.

Mrs Fan had a rule that those of us who took classes with her had to come to her house for lessons, but they couldn't drop in and practice on their own on her piano. She suffered from migraines and noise set them off. To practice the piano, we had to rent the piano room in the music department at Ginling College, and it had to be a time when their music students weren't using it, so it wasn't often available, even just once or twice a week. This particular month, several local schools were organizing concerts, and the piano room was even more in demand. I only got two nights to practice, and that was after 9 o'clock.

From Pomegranate Gardens to the Ginling College music department was quite some way, at least half an hour on foot. The distance didn't matter but the nights were dark, and you had to go through thick woodland, past an eerily silent cemetery, and down a narrow alley flanked by courtyard walls painted black, and a Catholic church where candles flickered in the windows. Just thinking about doing the journey alone made the hairs stand up on the back of my neck.

I begged Shuya to come with me. 'I'll give you my

pencil,' I offered.

She pulled a face. 'I don't want it. You've only got half of it left.'

'We've got to rehearse at night too,' she went on. 'We're doing the play "Put Down Your Whip", and I've got the lead female role. I can't refuse to rehearse and see you to and from your piano practice, can I?' She was sitting on the edge of the bed dipping red paper in water to colour her nails. She had dyed the pads of her fingers red too, and when she spread her fingers, they looked like vampire claws.

'That's ugly,' I said.

She raised her eyebrows. 'None of your business!'

I tried Kejun instead. He was a gentleman, and he hardly ever turned a girl down. Sure enough, he agreed straightaway. But when I told him what night it was, he looked embarrassed. 'Oh that's too bad. It's the same day we have our school reading club. Qian Mu's been invited to come and talk about Chinese culture and China's youth. Qian Mu!' He repeated the name with great respect.

I had no idea who Mr Qian Mu was, but I did know that I'd have to walk that road at night alone, and I was really upset.

My mother took pity on me. She was sitting in the walkway winding some wool into balls, and saw me running around like an ant in a hot wok, and poked her head into the house. 'Tianlu can go with you,' she said firmly. And she shouted, 'Tianlu!'

Tianlu always obeyed my mother. As soon as she spoke, he put down his copybook and got up. 'Owsum', he blurted out.

He had to go with me because my mother had told him to. All the same, it was a comfort to know that he would be on that hair-raising road with me.

All these years later, I still remember the stars that night. There were myriads of them, and they were spectacular. They were so dense I felt like I could bring them crashing down from the sky if I opened my mouth and gave a yell. Along the path as we set out from home, there was a light dusting of frost that glittered in the starlight. The air was fresh and clean, so cold that it stabbed me in the nostrils as I breathed, filling my airways, catching in my throat, so I almost choked. I had to open my mouth wide and expand my chest, and after a few gulps, I could breathe properly.

Tianlu walked in front of me, holding a short shoulder pole he used to carry the bags of rice and vegetables when he went with Mum to help her with the shopping. He was swiping it side to side, as if he was Monkey in *Journey to the West*. I ran and caught up with him. 'Why did you bring that stick?'

'To fight ghosts,' he said.

'Rubbish!' I told him. 'Ghosts don't exist.'

He leered at me. 'Then why are you scared?'

'I'm scared of the dark.'

'That's where ghosts hide out, in the dark.'

I couldn't think what to say to that.

The trees around us grew thicker. By day, this wood was paradise for Sheona and me. We came here to watch how the ants transported the bodies of butterflies several times bigger than they were, and to collect the pale yellow cicada sloughs that we could sell to Chinese herbalists. I used to try every kind of bright red berry I could find – they looked so inviting but numbed my tongue and made my throat swell. Once, I caught a shiny black cricket in some tree roots. Sheona told me that it was called a gladiator cricket. She'd seen them for sale at the market and they fetched a high price. People used to make them fight and lay bets. I got all excited at the thought that the bug I was holding might make us a lot of money.

Holding it in cupped hands, we hurried to the market, but the stall-holders laughed at us. They told us that it wasn't a fighting cricket but just an ordinary bug, and advised us to take it home and feed it to the hens. Sheona was mortified. We'd already been planning what to do with the money. We were going to buy *baba* rice cakes.

'Did you ever catch gladiator crickets in the countryside?' I asked Tianlu as we walked.

'What are they?' he asked, sounding interested.

'Crickets that can fight.'

'Oh, why didn't you say so? What's this gladiator stuff? There are tons of crickets in the country – coffin heads, gourd crickets, gunshot greys, vine purples!' He explained them all so vividly and clearly, the different kinds of head shapes, their mouths, how hard they bit, how to feed them, and so on. I was astonished at this outpouring. Tianlu had found something he enjoyed talking about! I also realized that a story told in Sichuan dialect sounded much more gripping than it did in our Nanjing mandarin.

'You won any fights?' I asked him, trying to imitate his accent. But he kind of shrivelled up and refused to answer.

'Ah-hah! You were having me on!'

He was furious. 'Having you on! There are all sorts of clever people in the countryside!'

I laughed so hard that I had to stop walking. It was so easy to wind Tianlu up. When he got angry, you could see all the muscles in his neck, and he was so earnest that his voice shook. He was funny.

But Tianlu was not stupid. He immediately realized that I was making fun of him, and he was not happy. He turned and strode away, leaving me behind, just like that! He was almost running. I ran after him, begging him to slow down and wait for me. He ignored me, kept walking, and in the blink of an eye had disappeared into the darkness. I really panicked. The night was completely different from daytime. I decided to run but really I was stumbling. I was in such a panic that I didn't know where I was going anymore, and I got my hair tangled in some thorns. I pulled and pulled, but I couldn't pull free. In my terror, I yelled at the top of my voice. He must have heard my fear because he turned around and came back for me. Then he was at my side, peering to see what it was that had caught my hair, and clumsily trying to get me out. He managed to pull out a good few of my hairs, but finally I was free.

'I expect that was a ghost, coming to take revenge,' he taunted me.

I didn't dare answer back.

I thought of the cemetery where owls hooted mournfully and the church where the candles flickered like will o'the wisps, and decided to stop being an ass. I asked him sweetly, 'Brother Tianlu, can you hold my hand?'

It was the first time I'd called him 'brother'. He acted surprised, and looked at me silently for a long time. In the darkness, I couldn't see the expression in his eyes, but I could hear breathing heavier than usual, and he seemed flustered.

'Brother Tianlu.' I repeated it again, playing a bit cute.

He struggled to make up his mind, but finally allowed me to hang onto him.

Maybe he was embarrassed because he didn't know whether it was all right to touch a girl. He was silent for a while, then thought of a compromise: he offered me the short shoulder pole and held one end, so I could hold the other end. He walked in front and I walked behind. I complained that I felt like a blind beggar boy. In a low voice, he gave me an ultimatum.'You want me to come with you or not?'

'Yes, yes,' I said hurriedly.

Luckily it was nighttime, and there was no moon, so we were walking by starlight. Even so, I walked along behind him, holding the stick, looking anxiously around me, terrified that one of my schoolmates might pop up and see me, and carry the tale of this ignominy to school the next day.

By the time we got to the door of the piano practice room, my nose had started to stream from the wintry cold.

I quickly sat down on the piano stool, opened the piano lid, and began to practice. The tune was simple but powerful. I didn't need to read the music. I knew it off by heart. We'd sung it so many times in school. I just needed to find the right white piano keys and bang away, making it sound as rousing as I could.

The piano room was tiny. There was only room for the piano and one person. Tianlu had to sit on the doorstep. He looked bored to death as he gazed up at the sky, or at the patch of grass plunged into darkness opposite him, or the Dutch cows brought by Professor Mei from Nanjing, lying down to rest. Occasionally, I stopped and turned to follow his gaze; the grass outside had turned purple and indigo in the starlight, and the blades seemed to glow faintly, as if they were covered in fireflies. But it wasn't fireflies, it was dewdrops. The sturdy black and white cows did not behave like a herd. They just plonked themselves down anywhere, like so many large lumps. They had grazed their fill and now they chewed the cud, occasionally raising their heads when something stirred their interest, and giving a low moo. It sounded like they were greeting each other. They were big eaters, and did a lot of peeing and pooing, and sometimes the ripe smell wafted into the piano room, making it difficult for me to breathe. But Tianlu seemed to find it intoxicating. I heard him sniffing loudly, and then he stood up and whistled through his fingers. Obviously he liked these silent cows. Maybe he'd been a cowherd in the countryside?

The hour passed very quickly, and someone else had booked the next hour. We gave the key back and left. All the way, I was going over the note and finger positions in my head, and didn't say anything. Nor did Tianlu. I think he liked me better when I was quiet and didn't tease him.

But just as we passed the church buried in the

shadows, something moved him to say, out of the blue, 'You play really badly.'

I was taken aback. 'What?'

'I said, you play really badly,' he repeated. 'You hit the keys like you're hammering a chopping board. You've given me a headache.'

I let go of the carrying stick and stamped my feet in annoyance. If it hadn't been for a flock of bats suddenly flying up from the churchyard and frightening me, I would have given him a push and then run home by myself.

I brooded over his comment for days after that and refused to talk to him. He was so annoying, he'd never even touched a piano, he had no idea how many black keys and white keys there were. What gave him the right to criticize me? Huh, I'd give him hammer on a chopping board! Could a hammer play 'Dig, Dig, for Victory', or make a whole class sing to the tune it was playing?

Perversely, Tianlu's comment made me want to play the piano better, and get as good as Sheona, and surprise him one day.

I was hugely excited by this idea, and I started to take my piano classes seriously and practice hard. I would even hum Beyer or Czerny as I walked along. No one was more surprised than Sheona. Had I been touched by the hand of God, she asked me?

I told her, 'God's a ghost because he doesn't exist.' Sheona went pale with fright and patted her chest. 'Lord Jesus, forgive her!' she implored.

What's interesting is that I actually set myself my first goal in life because of something Tianlu said.

Maybe one day Tianlu would have to take back what he said, and how would he look then? I couldn't wait to see.

Chapter 5

The Christmas Party

It was December and although we were in the south of China, the weather was bitterly cold.

The trees carpeted the ground with brilliant golden leaves, then almost overnight, turned into naked skeletons. Only a few withered leaves shivered feebly on the branches. The shrubs looked like whisk brooms standing on end, scrawny and ugly. The crickets and the 'golden bell' bugs had stopped singing. I wondered if they had found a nice warm cave to hibernate in. When I set off for school in the morning, the sky was a pale grey, and so was the ground underfoot. I could see my breath in little clouds that rose into the air. It felt warm to the touch if I reached out quick enough.

The fighting at the front was not going well. The

Japanese had landed troops and captured Guangzhou. We heard the whole city had gone up in flames, and there were many dead and wounded. In Changsha, it was our own army that had set fire to the city, a 'scorched earth' tactic. In an attempt to reassure the army and the populace, Generalissimo Chiang Kai-shek issued his 'Wuhan Retreat: Report to the National Army and Civilians'. In it, he vowed that the whole country would remain united against the invaders, and would never surrender.

I remember my big sister, Shuya, wrote an essay called 'Winter in Paradise' and got it published in her high school journal. She brought it back and showed it to us. The first sentence was, 'Huaxi Fields has winter too...Human beings living on earth and in hell, imagine paradise as somewhere happy, comfortable, serenely peaceful, ringing with songs of freedom, without fear or poverty or storms, the home of God's beloved sons and daughters...If that's what people really imagine, then they must be very happy. They have created in their minds a paradise more heavenly than heaven is. Those with imagination are indeed blessed...'

My dad puffed on his pipe as he read her essay. He thought for a while and said, 'It's good, it's reflective and you make clear arguments. You've made progress.' Then he added, 'The problem is, you sound too pessimistic. China is not defeated yet. We're still resisting. At the beginning of the war, the Japanese military told the emperor that it would take three months to occupy China. How long ago was that? One year and three months! Have they occupied China? Look at us in Huaxi Fields. Aren't we teaching, and performing, and giving lectures, just like normal?' He waved his pipe, pointing it at each of us in turn, 'China's hopes lie with you. There's no such place as paradise. We're going to build one. Your job is to read, study, enjoy your childhood, and learn as much knowledge as you can. And remember, once we've won the war against Japan, rebuilding China depends on you.'

Kejun did not totally agree with Dad. 'Sure, studying's important, but right now, the war's even more important. Huaxi Fields is full of hot-blooded young men, and they're burning to join the army and fight!'

'And what about you?' Shuya mocked him. 'Are you joining the army? The Youth Militia maybe?'

'We'll be grown up soon,' said Kejun.

'By the time you're grown up, the war will be over and done with!'

'And what does "over and done with" mean?' retorted my brother. 'Defeat or victory?'

My father grinned as they argued. In his view, the way to establish the truth was to argue it out.

But when would we grow up? The day seemed so far away that I couldn't see it even if I stood on tiptoes. I couldn't imagine what defeat would look like, or victory for that matter. I was a lanky ten-year-old with big hands and feet, and my skin was stretched so thin over my muscles and bones that it was almost transparent. I hadn't an ounce of fat to spare. I was always hungry, always craving more food and more snacks. If I couldn't find anything, I'd drink a bowl of brown sugar water. That soothed my hunger pangs for a while. When I compared myself with Kejun and Shuya, I knew I'd never be as clever as them. More than that, I was afraid of not living up to my father's expectations. When the day came for rebuilding China, I'd still be a stupid girl who couldn't do her maths.

Tianlu never joined in these discussions about the current situation or the future. He just buried his head in his homework, mumbling his English to himself, plodding through one test after another, no matter what was going on around him. The only one of the family who could drag him away from his studies was my mother. She made sure to praise him for wanting to do better, and sticking at it – little by little he'd get there. And he was part of the family, a brick in its wall. 'You just see if I'm right!' she declared. We all know that she was trying to encourage him. He had had a difficult start in life and it wasn't a simple matter to catch up with Kejun and Shuya.

Very soon, it was Christmas. The Huaxi Fields schools were all run by the churches, and Christmas was the most important holiday in the year. The Winter Uniform Relief Concerts organized by the schools had been very successful, and everyone was brimming with enthusiasm and eager to do more to raise money. All the schools were planning their Christmas performances. The competition was fierce.

West China Union University's repertoire was naturally Handel's 'Messiah'. They had started rehearsing almost six months before. Mrs Fan would play the piano accompaniment herself, and the conductor was to be Miss Greve of the Music Department. I don't know why we called her Miss because she was actually a silver-haired old lady, petite, with a kindly expression but keen eyes. She always wore her hair in an elegant bun on the back of her head, and her erect figure, in an indigo cheongsam, was often seen around the campus. The lead soprano was the wife of Professor Mei downstairs. She had permed hair, and wore Western-style clothes. She was tall and strong and cut an imposing figure as she strode along, looking exactly like the professor's Rhode Island Reds. Once we heard her singing the famous song of the exiles of northeast China: 'My home is on the Songhua River...' Her beautiful voice wove through the intricate melody, and our neighbours all fell silent. It was like the whole world had filled with sorrow.

Cheeloo University's National Theatre Company were rehearsing arias from two Peking operas, 'Famen Temple' and 'Yang Silang Visits His Mother in the Palace'. The actors sang and played and rehearsed every detail, accompanied by a tremendous crashing and banging from the gongs and drums. So many people came to watch the rehearsals that they were more crowded than the actual performance. I went with Shuya once, and we arrived just in time to see part of 'Su Wu Tends His Sheep'. The actor sang, 'White-haired mother / Watches for her son's return / At the third watch, both fall asleep in separate places / Who dreams of whom?' Below the stage, my classmates hummed along, their voices choked with tears.

Ginling College had chosen Cao Yu's play, 'Sunrise'. Apparently the playwright himself had come from Chongqing to direct it, and the costumes and scenery were splendid. The students were a stuck-up bunch, and hid themselves away while they prepared. No one was allowed in to watch rehearsals in case it spoilt the surprise on the night. So we were all on tenterhooks, waiting for the posters to go up advertising the performance.

Kejun and Shuya, although only high school students, were determined not to be outdone. They decided to be ambitious, and chose Shakespeare's *A Midsummer Night's Dream*. It was just right for teenagers – the plot was weird, the language was gorgeous, and it was full of elves and fairies. Kejun took it upon himself to delete some of the longer, duller speeches, and what he called the 'soppy' bits – some of the love scenes and the kissing. His new, improved version was fantastic and colourful, and lots of fun.

My brother even offered me a part. 'This is your chance, Orange. You can be a fairy,' he said.

I was taken aback. 'But I'm only at primary school!'

'That's what we want for fairies. It's called fitting

the person to the part.'

My sister overheard and sniggered. She was going to play Titania, and was happily deciding whether to wear her hair loose, or in a more elaborate, aristocratic style.

'That's no fun,' I objected. 'I can't act.'

'Can you learn lines?'

'Yes.'

Kejun clapped his hands. 'Then what's the problem? All you've got to do is go on stage dressed as a fairy, stand in the middle and recite your lines, and walk off again.'

'And that's all?' I said doubtfully.

'That's all.'

'Simple as that?'

'Absolutely simple as that.'

'Will there be *baba* cakes at rehearsal?'

'When we've done the performance, I'll buy you *baba* cakes. Two – no, three!'

I gave it some thought, but I still wasn't convinced. It was going to clash with the Peking opera, so I wouldn't be able to go and listen to Su Wu sing the aria, 'White-haired mother.'

'You really don't want to?' Kejun looked at me with a slight smile. 'All right, I'm going downstairs to ask Sheona. She'd be better than you anyway. She can go on stage without any makeup.'

He headed for the door. I yelled after him, 'Don't go! Don't go! I'll do it.'

Of course, this was exactly what he was banking on. He shrugged and gave me my lines. 'Learn them in three days.'

I felt a bit dazed. What had I let myself in for?

Tianlu was going in and out helping my mother prepare the dinner, fanning the flames in the stove, fetching water to wash the vegetables, and then rubbing the dishcloths in the used rice-rinsing water. I was still standing looking dazed, with the paper in my hand when he muttered, 'You're so easy to con!' I was furious. I yelled at him, 'If I want to do it, it's none of your business!'

His lips curled in what looked like a smile. He was obviously winding me up, and I got even more furious.

After that, when I finished classes each day, I sat at the dining table, learning my part. The sentences were so long-winded that I could hardly get my tongue around the words.

'Over hill, over dale,

Through brush, through brier,

Over park, over pale,

Through flood, through fire…'

Tianlu was hard at work on his calligraphy. Without even looking up, he corrected me. 'It's "bush" not "brush".'

'You're such a pain!' I yelled at him. 'Mind your own business!' He raised his eyebrows and carried on writing.

I carried on to my second speech:

You spotted snakes with double tongue,

Thorny hedgehogs, be not seen.

Newts and blindworms, do no wrong.

Come not near our fairy queen.

Philomel, with melody

Sing in our sweet lullaby.

Lulla, lulla, lullaby, lulla, lulla, lullaby…

I sneaked a look at Tianlu. He was still looking down at his copybook but his pen was poised in mid-air and he hadn't written a word. I figured he must be listening to my lines. *That's good*, I thought, and raised my voice. That woke my little brother, who'd just been put down for a nap, and he wailed.

My mother had to stop her sewing, and told me off. 'Are you crazy?'

Tianlu finally burst out laughing. He threw down his brush and looked up at me. 'What kind of a lullaby is that?

You're shouting so loud, you'd scare the Thunder God!'

Who cared if I was shouting? I'd taken on the role of the fairy, and dammit, I was going to do it well, and make Tianlu jealous of me.

We began rehearsals. It was only then that my sister discovered that she was not the heroine. There were two other female leads, Hermia and Helena. She pouted and looked annoyed. But then she found out that Titania was a good part, because she had a lot of power. She had a bunch of little fairies that she could order around, and had some fine speeches, which was brilliant.

I was disappointed. Kejun had lied to me. I wasn't the only fairy. There were lots of us, and we were all on stage together. My brother hadn't recruited Sheona, because her blonde hair and blue eyes looked too different from the rest of us, but lots of other children from Pomegranate Gardens were there. When we weren't on stage, my fellow fairies chattered like sparrows, only noisier. But I was the First Fairy. I had a big speaking part, while the other children just had to stand behind me providing the backdrop. My brother had chosen me.

As for our fairy costumes, the school's art teacher who was the stage director was racking her brains about what to do. First of all, no one was sure what fairies were supposed to wear, and then there were too many of us and no money for so many costumes. Finally, Kejun came up with an idea. He covered some large sheets of newspaper in yellow paint. When they were dry, we cut holes in the middle, and put our heads through the hole. The bottom of the newspaper had strips stuck on to represent wings. When we danced and waved our arms around on stage, the 'wings' flapped, and the yellow paint shone in the stage lights. Somehow or another, it worked.

'You fairies look like a swarm of wasps!' Shuya jeered.

But I didn't care. I wasn't like her. She was so desperate for Titania to have something to wear on her head that she'd begged two silver hairpins off our mother.

But luck was against me. When everything was ready, the day before the performance, I suddenly came down with a high fever. I was delirious and my mother went downstairs at night to ask Sheona's father to come and look at me. Professor Fan got his stethoscope and listened front and back. Then he said I had acute pneumonia and would have to go to hospital.

This was too bad. I had my performance the next day! I had two big speeches! Kejun and Shuya were frantic. How were they to find someone to stand in for me at such short notice? My lines were really difficult!

You'll never guess what happened. It was Tianlu who went on instead of me. He actually volunteered. My brother and sister were amazed, and so was I. All those days I'd been learning my lines at home, they'd gone into his head as well as mine and he knew them off by heart. Besides, he was quite short, and if you didn't look too closely, he didn't stick out in a group of primary school kids.

Afterwards, Shuya told me that Tianlu had recited his lines in quite decent mandarin. She had no idea where he'd learnt that from. She said we shouldn't have looked down on him the way we did. He was very intelligent.

There weren't many people in this world who my sister admired.

Meanwhile I was lying in my hospital room, drinking the pig's lung soup that my mother sent over, and feeling depressed. What was the point of spending all that time and effort learning my lines, and having Tianlu laugh at me? I would have had more fun spending my days listening to 'Su Wu Tends his Sheep'!

Chapter 6
The Youth Militia

That year, four members of our family joined the Youth Militia: Kejun, Shuya, Tianlu and me. The three of them were in high school and I was in primary school, but our uniforms were the same.

Tianlu was short so he had to roll his trousers up twice over. The hem of the jacket hung down to his bottom. Altogether, his outfit looked like someone else's cast-offs. Mine too, for the opposite reason, I was too tall and too thin. It was baggy and my arms and legs stuck out of the cuffs. I looked like a scarecrow, especially when I went to school on a winter's morning. An icy wind tunneled down the front of my jacket, and my chest and back froze. It was horrible. My mother couldn't bear it either. She took the jacket in around the waist, and made the waistline of the trousers a few inches smaller, so it fitted a bit better. Even so, we had one inspection from a visiting city official and had to line up in front of the school in our uniforms, and with our scout sticks. My sister was passing by and saw me. She went home and told my mother, 'Orange looks so skinny that you could snap her waist in two with her stick, and they've got her doing sentry duty!'

I hated these sneering comments from Shuya. So what if I was skinny? I could drill and sing military songs just as well as my fellow soldiers.

The Youth Militia had us doing 'A Good Deed A Day'. For a while, we spent our whole day looking around us wherever we went, in the hopes that we would come across someone who was blind or lame, and could take their arm, or offer them a glass of water. But we primary school kids couldn't compete with the high school students as far as good deeds went. For example, Shuya and her school friends made small things for the frontline soldiers. They sewed tobacco pouches, knitted gloves, and plaited hemp string into sandals. They were always coming up with new ideas, but no one wanted to teach us how to do anything. Once, we heard that a group of wounded soldiers had been admitted to the Union Hospital of West China, and all the Huaxi Fields kids turned out in force and mobbed the hospital, offering to help. But we got no further than the gates before we were chased away by the matron. She didn't want any girls from the high schools either – they might scream at the sight of blood. In the end, only a dozen male students were allowed in, including Kejun. They emptied slop buckets and potties, washed bandages, and helped the patients to the toilet. For a few days, Kejun had a glimpse of hell. When he came home in the evening, he couldn't eat his dinner. He shut himself in the room and cried. Then he swore he'd join up as soon as he reached eighteen, and wouldn't set foot through our door again until he'd destroyed the Japs.

It was not easy to find a good deed to do, but that made me all the more determined. There was a well near our house, and I discovered that old women with bound feet went to draw water there every day. The cobbles were slippery and a full bucket was heavy. It worried me to see the women staggering home with their buckets. One day I got up early in the morning and waited by the well. Every time I saw an old woman, I rushed over and offered to help. But strangely enough, they all turned me down. It was as if they'd made a collective decision. When I tried to grab the bucket, they dodged away and the water splashed out. We all ended up with wet socks and shoes. Eventually one said, 'It's very kind of you, but it's hard work carrying water. And look at you, you've got sticks for arms. You'd never manage it. If anything happened to you, your mother'd be really upset.'

I really didn't think my mother would be upset. After all, she'd had five children, and if something happened to me, there'd still be the other four. Anyway, I just couldn't find a good deed to do. I kept coming up against a brick wall. At every Youth Militia meeting, when we had to report what we had done that week, I was so embarrassed, I wanted to go through the floor.

Sheona understood what I was going through. She reminded me, 'You could help your mother. That's a good deed.'

'That doesn't count!' I objected. 'When you help someone in the family, that's not a good deed, it's your duty.'

'We're all God's children, and all God's children should get help,' she said.

Well, if you put it like that, it made sense. I started

diligently helping my mother with the housework: washing the dishes, sweeping the floor, lighting the stove, boiling Kid's nappies, and going with Mum to the market so that I could carry the bags of rice home for her. Sometimes I cleaned the walkways and stairwells of our building. That meant getting a bucket of water and a rag, and wiping up and down the stairs, so the brickwork and bannisters were spotless.

'How you've grown up, Orange!' said my mother approvingly. Then she added, 'If you work as hard as this, you need never worry about finding a good husband.'

I wanted to yell at her, 'Why don't you listen?! I'm doing a Good Deed a Day, not looking for a husband!'

But I said nothing. My mother would never understand. After all, she was just a housewife.

When spring-time came, the Youth Militia did a training march. We put on our uniforms, got our sticks, and slung a bag of grain across our chests, the kind that a field army carries. We started from the school sports ground and marched to Zhaojue Temple on the northern outskirts of Chengdu, camped overnight, and marched back again. It was going to be well over twenty kilometres, quite an achievement for primary school kids.

On the morning of the departure, we formed up in impressively long lines. Accompanied by drums and gongs, we all sang at the tops of our voices, 'We are the Chinese people's youth soldiers. We may be small but we have big ambitions!'

We marched, and rested, marched and rested. At around midday, a third-year boy had an accident. He was overcome by a bout of diarrhea, couldn't see a toilet and was too embarassed to ask to drop out. Right where he was, he messed his trousers. He was so upset, he began to cry. The school head got one of the teachers to take him home. Then there was a girl whose father was someone important in the Chongqing government. She looked as fragile as a china doll, and actually fainted before she'd walked five kilometres. The PE teacher pressed the acupuncture point under her nose and brought her round, but she clearly could not walk any further. There was no one to spare to get her back home, so they bought a large wicker basket from a villager, and put her in that. The men teachers took turns to carry her. She was so embarrassed that she ducked her head down into the basket. That way, no one could see her and she couldn't see anyone. Just like an ostrich.

My food bag had fried soybeans, a few *shaobing* sesame cakes, two salted duck eggs, and a small packet of toasted rice cakes. Sheona had shortcake biscuits baked by her mother, and cooked semolina mixed with dried fruit and sugar. It was only because we were camping that the two of us had so many delicious things to eat all in one go. We were as happy as could be. As soon as we'd left Huaxi Fields behind us, we dug a little hole in our bags and began to winkle bits of this and that out of it. We hid the crumbs in the palms of our hands and had a good look around. (We couldn't let the teacher see us.) Then we bent over, making sure we had some spit in our mouths, pressed our tongues against our palms, and slowly, slowly swallowed the crumbs. The two of us furtively swapped snacks as we walked along. She gave me a piece of shortcake, and I gave her a few soybeans. Other people's food always tastes better. We exchanged smiles. We felt like we'd never eaten such delicious food in our lives. It was absolute bliss.

We stopped for a midday rest at a place called the Culture House, and everyone sat down for a picnic. I opened my bag and generously gave Sheona one of my salted duck eggs. The trouble was my mother had over-salted them and we were parched with thirst all afternoon, and our throats were as dry as dust. At least that stopped us eating any more until we got to the end of the march late in the evening, so we ended up with quite a lot of our rice and biscuits left. Otherwise, at the rate we were eating, we wouldn't have had anything left for the next day.

That night, we slept in a high-ceilinged gloomy ancestral hall, on bundles of rice straw borrowed from the local farmers. We occupied the whole room, the boys slept on the east side, the girls on the west side. Sheona and I squeezed onto the same pallet together. I always took my clothes off to go to bed, so I sat on the pallet, about to unbutton my jacket, when Sheona grabbed me by the hands. 'Don't! Don't let your skin touch the straw!' She was right. The straw had not been beaten flat, so we were going to get prickled all over by the stalks.

In the evening, I drank a lot of water, and woke up for a pee during the night. The huge ancestral hall was lit only by an oil lamp on the dark offerings table. To my sleepy eyes, the memorial tablets on the wall looked like rows of silent ghosts, glaring down at me, as if preparing to shoot out an arm and yank me back into the wall and seal me behind the bricks. I stood in the aisle, my hair nearly standing on end, and suddenly I screamed. The children carried on sleeping like logs. Only a few teachers woke up. 'What on earth's going?' someone asked. I got a terrible scolding, but one of the women teachers struggled to her feet and took me to the latrine. She yawned all the way, and complained, 'You're brave enough to climb trees, but you're too scared of ghosts to go to the toilet!'

'The hall's so scary,' I whispered.

She gave me a hard slap on the back of the head. 'What are you scared of? The place is full of people!'

The next day we went to see the Zhaojue Temple. The monks and lay workers had never seen primary school students like us, all in identical uniforms and neatly lined up, and came out in little groups to see what was going on. We gave them a rousing chorus. 'China will be strong! China will be strong! Eight hundred warriors will do brave battle with the enemy!' Then we sang The March of the Volunteers: 'Arise, ye who refuse to be slaves! With our flesh and blood, let us build a new Great Wall!'

The monks gaped at us. I have no idea if they understood what we were singing. In the dawn mist, they stood still as statues, their blue-grey robes bleached to the colour of ash.

Then we went on a tour of the buildings: the Hall of Heavenly Kings, the Hall of Guanyin, the Wei Tuo Bodhisattva Hall, the Depository of Buddhist Sutras, the Five Contemplations Dining Hall, and the Putong Pagoda. We paid perfunctory respects to the Maitreya Buddha, and the Four Heavenly Kings, and the Eighteen Arhats with their fearsome grimaces. I had never liked Buddhist temples and the smell of incense made me sick, but Sheona studied everything very carefully. I even saw her surreptitiously stroking an arhat's foot when she thought no one was looking.

Then we reassembled and walked back home, but by now we were straggling, not marching. Some of us had blisters and were limping, some had lost the soles of their shoes and had to tie them back on with a bit of straw, and some had finished all their food and were trailing along on empty stomachs. There were less than two hundred of us but we ended up spread out over a couple of kilometres. Two men teachers who had to carry a child on their backs, did not get back to Huaxi Fields until dawn of the day after.

A couple of days later, my scalp was itching and

so was Sheona's, and I could hear a rustling, as if hundreds of bugs were crawling around on my head. Shuya parted my hair and recoiled in disgust. 'Mum! Come and look! She's got lice!' she shrieked.

My mother shampooed my hair, and sure enough, there was a layer of whitish-grey nits floating on the surface of the water in the bowl, paddling with their little legs as if they were having fun. I shrieked too. They really were disgusting.

Sheona's family had no idea what to do, and her mother ran upstairs and asked my mother for advice. Mum didn't hesitate. 'Cut Sheona's hair short, that's the first thing!'

I had always had short hair, and cutting it only made me look more like a boy. But Sheona was inconsolable when her beautiful golden hair was cut short, and she was left with a head of ugly blond bristles. She burst into tears and refused to go out of the house for days.

Meanwhile, my mother went to the herbalists and bought the ingredients for a potion to kill the head lice. Once she'd boiled the soupy mixture, she spread it on, and wrapped my head in newspaper. We waited for the repulsive, stubborn beasts to die. She gave Mrs

Fan a packet too. That medicine must have been quite toxic, because my scalp went red and my face, even around my eyes, puffed up. Nowadays, stuff like that certainly wouldn't be licensed for use on children. Back then, people were careless, and carelessness sometimes killed them too.

The next thing was, my mother got Uncle Fan to bring a large bottle of ethanol from the hospital, and she wiped our scalps with ethanol-soaked cottonwool every day. It smelled nasty and made us feel sick, especially if we'd just eaten.

These shenanigans went on for a couple of weeks before we were completely free of head lice. Sheona swore she would never go camping again, she'd rather drop out of school.

I didn't think it was that serious. I'd already had an idea: I'd shave my head next time. Having a close-shaved head wasn't a big deal. People would just think I was a novice nun.

Chapter 7
The Profs

Let me tell you some stories about two professors living in Pomegranate Gardens.

The first one story is about Uncle Tao and the bear cub.

I remember it was the evening of the Tomb-Sweeping Festival that year. We were standing around Mum's coal briquette stove, watching her make willow pancakes for us. Su and I had gone to the river to collect the bright yellow young leaves. I shimmied up the tree and along the branches like a monkey, doing my best to press the branches as low as possible, so they almost touched the ground. Su quickly reached out, on tiptoe, plucked the tender leaf shoots and dropped them into the basket. When we got home,

Mum washed the leaves, shredded them, soaked them in brine to get rid of the astringent taste, then squeezed them and mixed them with flour to make a batter. As a special treat, she added two eggs. Then she heated the skillet, brushed it with oil, and slowly poured in the batter. There was no need to use a spatula, the batter flowed naturally along the walls of the pan past the handles at each end, and a wafer-thin, hat-shaped pancake took shape. It cooked on a low heat, and was then sprinkled with chopped shallots, and it was ready. The fragrant, bright-yellow pancakes, crunchy-crispy outside, soft inside, were shoveled into the plate. As we ate them, it was almost as if we could taste the coming springtime.

Every year at Tomb-Sweeping Festival, Mum made these 'nibbling spring' pancakes, because it was the custom in our hometown, Nanjing. Mum used to say that no matter how far a person travels, they must hang onto the thread that binds them to their home, and not let it go until they die.

The batter only made two pancakes, and we only got a quarter each. As we nibbled our bit, making it last as long as possibe, pandemonium suddenly broke out downstairs. We ran outside to the walkway to see what was going on, and a strange sight met our eyes: the other kids were standing around a dark furry bundle, shrieking with excitement.

This was better than any pancake. I took Su by the hand and we ran downstairs and squeezed into the crowd. The little creature was covered in dark brown fur, and had a round head, a round belly, short legs, two little eyes like shiny glass marbles, and a leather collar around its neck. The collar was attached to a rope, and the rope tethered it to the locust tree in the courtyard. It was just a baby, probably too young to have any fear of humans, and when anyone reached out to poke it, it jumped at them. That yanked on the rope, and it tumbled in the dirt. It didn't seem to mind, it just rolled over, staggered to its feet and jumped forward again. Then it stuck out its little pink tongue and started sucking the finger of one little boy, smacking its lips like it was suckling its mother's nipple. The boy, a four-year-old and one of the Xu family, couldn't stop giggling.

Sheona squeezed out of the crowd. 'You know what that is? It's a bear cub!' she said urgently.

'What?' I couldn't believe her. 'Surely they only live up in the mountains where there are trees. It's all fields around here!'

'Of course it is! Prof Tao brought it back from Tibet! It was a present from some Tibetans,' she said.

I turned around to see Professor Tao, propped against the courtyard wall, his legs spread wide, hands folded over his belly, watching this mob of excited children, laughing like a naughty boy himself. He had a moustache and beard, and I was surprised to see he was wearing a Tibetan felt hat over a dark corduroy suit and a thin scarf of light gray cashmere. On anyone else, the ensemble would have looked ridiculous, but Uncle Tao was handsome and flamboyant enough to carry it off.

The bear cub really had been given to him by some Tibetans. Uncle Tao was a professor in the Department of Historical Linguistics. He lived downstairs, next door to Sheona and her family. According to my dad, he'd been thrilled when his department transferred to Chengdu and Huaxi Fields because now he was near the Tibetan areas in Sichuan, Yunnan, Guizhou, and Tibet itself. The entire area, with its mixture of ethnic groups, was a treasure trove of languages. Uncle Tao stayed on campus for a year before aiming his sights at the Songpan Plateau and taking his students to do field research into Gyalrong Tibetan. For most of the year, they ate and slept out in the open, among the Tibetans. Uncle Tao liked his liquor, and after just one drink, he would start laughing his head off like a kid. He loved to sit cross-legged and have long chats with his interviewees about everyday stuff. He made friends wherever he went. On this trip, he had been to the Minjiang River, an area deep in dense forest where wild animals roamed. I even heard he had come face to face with a pack of wolves.

Before he set off for home, his Tibetan friends had raided a bear's den. They pulled out the baby bear, and presented it to Uncle Tao. Uncle Tao arrived back at Pomegranate Gardens in a rickshaw, bags under his feet, and a rolypoly bear cub on his knees which everyone mistook for a puppy though, in the event, it was more like a ticking time bomb.

For the whole of April and May, the bear cub and the children got along fine.

At first, everyone was eager to feed it and gave it everything from meat and fish to fruit and greens. Of course, it ate it all up – and had diarrhoea, lost patches of hair, and got infected eyes. Eventually, it got so listless that it could hardly move. If we hadn't gone to Professor Mei, Dad's friend from the department of animal husbandry, and begged him to help, it would have died.

When it had recovered, Uncle Tao called a meeting of all the Pomegranate Gardens children and we agreed some rules: each family was responsible for feeding the bear for one day. Only rice porridge, soft noodles, baby corn, and a little fruit was to be given. Uncle Tao drew up a rota with great care. Next to our names, there was a column for us to note the date we had fed the bear, and another for us to put how much and what kind of food we had given. He stuck the rota at the foot of the stairs. Very sternly he reminded us, 'Do you see this? If any family doesn't do its duty, then there will be public condemnation!'

'Tao, they're not your dissertation students. They're feeding a bear cub!' my father mocked him.

'And why not?' said Uncle Tao. 'It's the only way they'll learn to manage their lives.'

Of course we knew the cuddly cub was going to grow. We just didn't know how fast. In fact, now it was getting lots of the right food, it shot up. Within two months, the fluffiness had gone and it had a thick pelt of bristly hair, a pointy snout, and a mean look in its eyes. When it stood on its hind legs, it was taller than our Su. One day it was our turn to be on bear duty. Tianlu was teasing it by dangling a cornmeal bun in front of it, swinging it back and forth, when the creature got angry, let out a terrifying roar, and charged. Its paw ripped Tianlu's sleeve, and left two bloody scratches on his arm. If it hadn't been tethered with a leather strap, things could have been much worse.

That scared everyone, and after that, the younger children never dared to get close to it. Another two weeks passed, the weather got hotter, and the bear pen stank horribly. Uncle Tao called us kids together for the second time. There was a democratic vote and it was agreed to donate the bear to the local zoo. The next day, the zoo sent an oxcart with an iron cage on board, and two strong men. They muffled the cub's head in a piece of cloth and hoisted it into the cage. As they were about to leave, we all stood in a line to see it off. We'd also clubbed together to buy a basket of young corn, and put it in the cart for the cub to eat at the zoo.

Before six months were up, the bear had disappeared from its new home. When we went to ask what had happened to it, we were told it ate too much. This was wartime, zoos had limited funds and could not afford to keep such large beasts. Of course we asked where had the bear gone but we never got a straight answer to that question. Sheona was very worried that they might have killed it for its meat. I didn't think so, because I'd heard Professor Mei say that wild animals were not good to eat. The meat was too tough and gamey-tasting. Surely, with so many animals in the zoo to choose from, people would not choose tough, gamey bear's meat, would they?

Our neighbours on the same floor as us were the brilliant physicist Xu Fangxun and his family. It was his son who'd had his fingers sucked by the bear cub. Professor Xu graduated from Columbia University in the USA, and then returned to China to teach at Soochow University. When the Japanese army captured Shanghai in 1937, he took the entire physics faculty and students to Chengdu, and the faculty merged with West China Union University.

Uncle Xu was always very smartly turned out. Even if he was only going out with a cookpot to buy soy milk for the family's breakfast, his hair was still impeccably combed and so smooth that any flies that tried to land on his head would have slipped off straightaway. His coat was a dark gray tweed with fine dark red stripes, and he topped it off with a dark red silk scarf tied around the neckline. How elegant he was.

He was a true Shanghainese, my mother said. They always liked to dress with flair whenever they went out. One had to keep up appearances.

I detected a note of jealousy when she said this. Compared with Uncle Xu, my dad never tried to keep up appearances. He often went to his test fields barefoot, carrying a pair of straw sandals in one hand. He was notorious in Pomegranate Gardens for looking like a tramp.

At the beginning of the Anti-Japanese War in 1937, the Chinese army was very poorly equipped, with only a few rounds of ammunition for each gun. Once the guns were fired, there would be silence for ten minutes while the bayonets were attached, ready for hand-to-hand combat. Uncle Xu read the newspaper every day, and when he read worrying news from the front, he leapt out of his chair, paced around the room, then strode across the corridor to find my dad, slapping the newspaper down angrily.

'What kind of a war is this? Eh, Huang?' he demanded.

'It's treating our young people like cannon fodder!'

My father would sigh heavily, 'China's poor. And old habits die hard.' Uncle Xu would shake his head, his eyes popping with indignation.

It was not long before the situation deteriorated in the South-West. Japanese planes came right into the interior of China, and began to bomb Chengdu and Chongqing. The war was spreading, China was sliding into an abyss, and everywhere families had to flee for their lives. Those were desperate times.

Uncle Xu decided he couldn't carry on being an 'armchair' physicist. He set up a Technology Research Department with other physicists and some chemical engineers, to develop ammunition and explosives. They searched around for chemicals to use as raw materials. Once, in the middle of the night, it occurred to Uncle Xu that there might be something useful in the dye shop on Shaanxi Street. He took a torch, felt his way downstairs, and went along to the dye shop, where he thundered on the door. The family inside thought it was robbers, and were so scared when they opened the door that they couldn't get a word out. Another time, he heard that an old warlord near Chengdu had a secret stash of potassium chlorate. Uncle Xu tried to strike a deal with him but for some reason the old man refused to give it up. Xu was getting frantic, and so one night he climbed over the wall and got into the warlord's house. He found his way to the old warlord's bedroom, and plonked himself down on the bed. And then he talked: he talked about what the War of Resistance meant, then about a citizen's duties, and he kept talking for an hour. The old warlord was so moved that the tears coursed down his cheeks. Finally, he got up and found the precious stuff, presented it to Uncle Xu with both hands and refused to take a penny for it.

When they had more or less enough raw materials, Uncle Xu got a copy of *Explosives*, by E. de Barry Barnett, from an old classmate, and threw himself into the next stage. As this point, in his words, he owed everything to the east wind. East wind? The East Wind was a stove that could cook up explosives. There was a lean-to in our courtyard, originally built as a shelter for the bear cub when it rained. Uncle Tao had built it out of his own money. After the bear was taken to the zoo, the shed was empty. Uncle Xu asked Uncle Tao if he could use it, then he bought sun-dried bricks and paid someone to make him a small stove. By the end of the day, he had a stove a couple of feet tall in the shed.

After Uncle Xu got the stove going, it never went out for a month. Every night, we stood on the walkway outside our flat, watching the leaping flames, as Uncle Xu and his colleagues stood around the stove, leafing through the manual, discussing, arguing, and throwing their heads back with laughter. How we hoped that his experiment would work, and they would be able to produce explosives to blow the Japanese to smithereens. We children all wanted to help in whatever way we could, even if it was just adding a piece of coal. But Uncle Xu was adamant: no children were allowed anywhere near. He said that it was too dangerous and there might be an accident at any moment. So wasn't Uncle Xu in danger too? Surely he wasn't the only person in the world who wasn't afraid? We were very annoyed.

Still, we had to admire the ingenuity of the professors. It was such an ordinary-looking stove, but it actually produced a dark powdery explosive that looked a bit like soot. Uncle Xu got some of his students to take it to the front lines for a trial run. Apparently, they buried it by a railway line and used it to blow up a Japanese train. When the good news arrived, Uncle Xu bartered his tweed coat on the black market for two bottles of whisky, and toasted the success by handing out drinks to the neighbours. They all got drunk and sang at the tops of their voices, resistance songs like 'The Song of the Road', 'Graduation Song', and 'Fighting All the Way Home'. Then they sang English songs like 'The White Cliffs of Dover' and 'A Nightingale Sang in Berkeley Square', and finished off with American gospel songs. Mary Fan, who normally kept herself to herself and was considered a bit snooty, opened her door wide and played the piano accompaniment. They sang and sang, and the men pulled their ladies by the hand and danced in the courtyard, and my dad even persuaded my mother to come down and join in. The celebration went on all night.

After his initial success, Uncle Xu was elated. He persuaded a banker friend to invest some money and they built a small munitions workshop in Huaxi Fields where they recycled shells. They collected spent cartridges on the battlefield and refilled them with their home-made explosives. The shells could then be reused. It was a makeshift operation using very basic materials and skills, and the shells they produced only had a range of a hundred metres. All the same, a shell is a shell. Firing one off in close combat could inflict injury, even if it did not kill, and that was certainly a deterrent.

After that, Uncle Xu branched out into detonators. This was dangerous work, and could cause explosions if not done properly. At the critical stage, Uncle Xu would chase everyone away – colleagues, students, and workers – leaving him to focus on adjusting his intruments. But even though he was very careful, one detonator exploded, the window pane shattered, and Uncle Xu was knocked unconscious. He fell to the floor and blood poured down his face. He looked in such a bad way that when his wife caught up with him in the hospital, she thought he was done for and collapsed in a dead faint herself. Meanwhile the patient, lying in his hospital bed, wheezed, 'Don't worry, I'm all right!'

His injuries were not serious – he'd hurt his hand, and he had blood spattered over his face, which made it look worse than it was. Luckily, all the necessary skills were available in Pomegranate Gardens. Uncle Fan was a surgeon and amputated the ring finger and little finger of Uncle Xu's right hand. A month later, Uncle Xu was to be found in his little workshop at the back of Huaxi Fields again. Now he was studying the rifling in gun barrels, in the hopes of improving the range of Chinese-made rifles. He strode in and out of our courtyard, as erect and neatly turned-out as ever.

However, Sheona was very observant and noticed a change in Uncle Xu that had passed me by. One day, she tugged at my sleeve. 'Look, Orange! Look at Uncle Xu's hair!'

'What's wrong with his hair? Has it grown too long?' I said. I stared at him.

Sheona sighed. 'It's hard work getting through to you.'

'You're hard work. Why can't you talk straight?'

She was annoyed, turned her back on me and ignored me. But she couldn't hold it in. After a while, she spoke again, 'Look! You know Uncle Xu never goes out without combing his hair! Look what a mess it is now.'

I thought about this for ages, but I couldn't make sense of it. What was hair supposed to tell you about a person?

I thought and thought but I didn't dare ask Sheona. I didn't want my best friend to think I was daft.

Chapter 8

Air Raid! Air Raid!

As summer arrived, the vegetation grew rampant. There was still plenty of countryside left in Huaxi Fields, and elms, locust trees, olives, camphor trees, willow and chinaberry trees stretched away as far as the eye could see, swathes of dark green mixed with light green and splashes of bright yellow. Cicadas chirred, and the birds sang, belting out their songs as if their lives depended on it, or billing and cooing affectionately, though sometimes it was hard to tell if they were arguing or being nice to each other.

One day on our way to school, we saw two greyish-brown birds in the bushes. They were not very pretty – they had weirdly big heads, and mottled feathers. They were each on a different tree, competing to see who could sing louder, fluttering their wings and pirouetting as if they were about to take off and fly away, but not actually going anywhere.

I thought they were fighting for territory, but Sheona said no, this was a courtship dance, that was why they were spreading and fluttering their wings.

I laughed. 'Is that what your mum and dad did when they were courting, dance for each other?'

Sheona was furious. She went bright red in the face. 'That's blasphemous to compare my parents to two ugly birds!' she shouted.

She ignored me for the rest of the day. I was super bored without her. After school in the evening, I went to the woods, stole a fledgling with a yellow beak from its nest, and gave it to her. She was horrified. 'It'll die without its mother! Put it back!' I raced back to the tree, climbed up, and put it back in the nest.

But at least Sheona wasn't angry with me anymore. She knew I cared.

Summer was always dry, with cloudless skies, and we hadn't had a drop of rain in ages. The dirt roads turned to pale dust which scrunched under our feet as we walked, and then puffed into the air. If you wore a pair of white socks to go to school, they were a dirty grey by the time you got there; if you took them off, the dust caught in your throat and made you sneeze.

We all longed for rain. When it rained again, we could paddle barefoot in the courtyard. We could fill buckets and have water fights. On the flooded river banks, we could find loofahs, calabashes, and half-submerged grapefruits, and sometimes even a starey-eyed fish or two, dead but not yet rotted. We used to throw the fish to the stray cats, and watch them fight over them, glaring at each other, their fur standing on end, making terrible growls in their throat. It was such fun.

The rain made the air cooler too, so the whole family could sleep indoors again, under a mosquito net, instead of having to bed down on straw mats on the walkway (the only place to get even a whiff of warm breeze) and getting bitten to death by mozzies. I felt really sorry for my little brother, whose little face was a mass of bites. It made him look like he had measles. He was too little to know how to scratch, and the itching made him cry. He cried so hard that he almost choked. It was unbearable. 'Poor child! Such thin skin and tender flesh, no wonder the mozzies find him delicious,' my mother sighed.

But before the rain came that summer, we had

other things to contend with: the shrieks of air raid sirens and earth-shattering bombing raids.

Apparently the bombing was personally approved by the Japanese emperor, and in order to have the maximum chance of striking military targets, he ordered it to be indiscriminate.

And so war came to Huaxi Fields. Those were terrible times.

I still remember when the first air raid siren went off. We all thought it was a drill and nobody paid any attention. We were in class, and the maths teacher was spouting on about a maths word problem called 'chickens and rabbits in a cage'. Sheona was quietly drawing pictures of girls on her desk. I was watching a big, fat cicada on the locust tree outside the window, and wondering whether I could climb into the tree and grab it without the teacher noticing. I was worried it would fly away before the class ended.

Suddenly, we heard the wail of the air raid siren. It was far away, but in this hot weather, the classroom windows were open, so we could hear it distinctly. One of the boys, the most fidgety in the class, jumped to his feet. 'Sir! It's an air raid!'

The maths teacher was getting to the crucial bit

and was annoyed at being interrupted. 'What are you talking about? Sit down!' The boy made a face, but obeyed. However, he carried on fidgeting and looking out of the windows on each side, as if he was quite looking forward to something happening.

The teacher picked up a piece of chalk and threw it hard at him.

'If you keep looking out of the window, you'll be the first to be blown up!'

The chalk pinged on the boy's head, and bounced off again and landed on the ground. Everyone burst out laughing.

Since our arrival in Chengdu, there had been nothing to remind us of how awful it was when planes bombed you.

We had forgotten the horrors of fleeing the war zone. Kids remember food and they don't remember fighting, and so that day we just laughed. We had no idea of the hell that was about to descend on us.

The teacher was explaining how to work out how many chickens there were in the cage, knocking on the podium with his bamboo cane for emphasis. Then a second alarm sounded, more terrifying and shriller than the first, reverberating in the sky overhead. The teacher realized something was wrong, stopped talking and listened hard. What was going on outside?

We heard explosions near the school, and we all, teachers and students, rushed pell-mell out of the classrooms and into the sportsground. The school head ran down the corridors, his gown hitched up in one hand, banging on every classroom door with the other, shouting at the top of his voice, 'Run, children, run, get outside immediately!'

We were instantly galvanized into action. We jumped to our feet and ran, overturning tables and chairs in our way. There was such a crush to get through the door that some of the boys jumped out of the window. I was going to follow them, but then I looked back and saw Sheona, dressed in her usual skirt, looking helpless. I went back, grabbed her arm, and dragged her into the corridor.

It had been so dry that the stampede of teachers and students stirred up clouds of dust in the sportsground. The siren wailed after us, pursuing us like some bloodthirsty beast after a herd of rabbits. Sheona lost one of her shoes and bent down to retrieve it, but I pushed her forwards. With only one shoe, she was hobbling, but just then, that was the last thing on my mind.

We crossed the sportsground as fast as we could, and hid among the trees on the other side in small groups, trying to catch our breath. Sheona looked back, annoyed. Her shoe was lying all on its own behind her and she said she was going back to pick it up. Just then, there was a deafening explosion. We fell to the ground, our hands blocking our ears, our hearts pounding in terror.

The next moment, a Japanese plane burst out of the clouds and swooped down, its engines screaming. In those days, Chengdu was practically defenceless against air raids, so the Japanese could fly as low as they wanted. The plane fuselage was so near to the ground that we could see the pilot sitting at the controls, looking ever so smug. The bright red Rising Sun flag was startlingly visible on the wings of the plane.

One after another, more planes roared overhead, coming down even lower in search of their targets, their bellies almost scraping the tops of the trees where we were hiding. Every time one passed by, I made a point of counting. I needed to remember this moment, and how much I hated those planes. But when I'd counted twenty or so, there was a second explosion, and it sounded like it was coming from the direction of our house. I immediately thought of Mum and Su and Kid. I was so worried that I forgot to count anymore.

We lay on our bellies in the dry undergrowth, keeping quite still. The only sounds, apart from the explosions, was the pounding of our hearts. Sheona was gripping my hand tightly. Her palm was wet. I turned my head slowly to look at her. Her face was filthy and there were tear tracks on her cheeks. I quickly dug my nails into the palm of her hand, meaning, *Don't panic, we're all together.* Finally, the raid was over, and the school head blew his whistle for everyone to stand up. Sheona's hand was still gripping mine.

On the way home that day, we found out that two bombs had fallen in Lantern Alley, and the Tingbi Teahouse had been hit. All that was left of it was a smoking heap of timber, scattered with bricks and tiles, and shiny white fragments of teapots and teacups. Another house had had a bomb drop through the roof, the doors and windows had all been blown out, and there was a hole as big as a dining table in the walls. A dead dog was lying beside it, a mangled lump of flesh and blood, brightly-coloured intestines spilling out of its belly. Luckily for the inhabitants of both houses, they had heeded the sirens and got out in time, so no one was hurt.

Pomegranate Gardens had come to no harm, nor had Mum and Su and Kid. Mum said she hadn't gone downstairs when the planes came. 'Your dad's gone to the countryside again. I wouldn't have had time to find somewhere to hide with the two little ones. We might as well stay home and let them blow us up.'

I admired my mother hugely. She was an uneducated housewife, but she could keep her head when it mattered.

Kejun and Shuya didn't approve of her attitude. They thought you should always get out and find a hiding place outside. The way my brother looked at it was, Pomegranate Gardens was a building of several stories, easy to see and hit from the air. If there wasn't enough time to get away, he told Mum, she could take the little ones and take shelter at the foot of the courtyard wall, which would give them a bit of protection.

A day passed, and Kejun got it into his head that he was going to build an air-raid shelter for the family.

Huaxi Fields was in a dead-flat valley. Not only were there no mountain nearby, there was not even a slope. We would have to dig down into the ground. Kejun took command, and Shuya, Tianlu and I all threw ourselves into his project. For tools, we had two spades, a kitchen spatula, a bamboo scoop, and a claw hammer that could serve as a mattock. We set to work: every day after school, we went to the vegetable patch behind the courtyard wall, and dug a hole as big as a round table. Next, we took turns jumping into the hole, and scooping out the soft earth. Whoever was on top was responsible for receiving the scoop and getting rid of the dirt.

But we had gone down less than three feet deep when the hold began to fill with groundwater. It was too bad. The next morning, we had a shallow well. My brother went to take a look and came back furious. He swore in English, 'Shit!'

The project had to be abandoned. Kejun felt he had let Mum down, so he took us to the woods and we chopped lots of branches and took them home. He made them into camouflage wreaths, and told Mum, 'If there's an air raid, you three hold these over your heads when you go out so you won't be seen from the planes.'

'Fine,' said my mother. But the summer was hot and dry, and the wreaths hanging from the wall soon lost their green leaves. All that was left was bunches of bare twigs that looked like bird nests.

Shuya pulled a face. 'These are ridiculous. You can't wear them on your heads.'

Kejun said nothing. He probably thought the camouflage wreaths looked a bit daft himself, a bit like pretentious modern art decorating the wall. One day, when there was no fuel for the stove, Mum pulled one of them down and used that. The twigs were perfect fire-lighting material, so dry that they snapped and crackled as they burned.

The air raids came fast and furious after that. Any time during the day, whether we were in class, out on the sportsground, or eating our lunch, we would hear the ear-piercing wails of the siren and everyone in Huaxi Fields would scatter and hide.

Gradually, we got used to it. We got to be able to judge the likelihood of a Japanese bombing raid, depending on the weather, or the time of day. We also learnt how long it would be between the early warning signal and the air raid siren. We even worked out where we would be least visible to the bomber pilots – in a ditch by the river, in an overgrown cemetery, or in undergrowth.

We learned to keep calm and carry on living and studying through the air raids. Sometimes, during Chinese lessons, the teacher finished the class in the mulberry copse. It provided plenty of shade, but was very hot, and the sound of distant explosions rolled around like thunder, as we intoned the words of the ancient poet Lu You, after the teacher, 'My dying eyes see only dust/My sole regret that China is divided/The day the emperor's troops sweep the North/Remember to come and tell it to my tombstone.'

At moments like this, as we recited these desolate lines, even the naughtiest children would look solemn, and their eyes would well with tears.

Kejun started senior high school that year and was eligible to join the Wartime Air Raid Rescue Team organized by a number of local schools. When the sirens went, they rushed around escorting anyone who needed help to a hiding place, putting out fires, and retrieving people's valuables from the rubble. They also got the wounded to hospital, did simple bandaging, and paid visits to the wounded to cheer them up. Kejun summoned Shuya, Tianlu and me, and told us that in the event of an airstrike, if he and Dad were not at home, the three of us had responsibilities. Shuya was to look after Su. I was put in charge of Kid. Tianlu's task was to make sure that Mum was safe.

Kejun pointed a stern finger. 'You three, if you're

in trouble, go and get the rescue team. If anything happens to Mum or the two kiddies, I'll come looking for you!'

I went and found my mother and asked her how much Kid weighed. 'What a funny question to ask,' she said. 'About twenty pounds or thereabouts.'

I'd better work it out. If I had to carry a twenty-pound child, how far could I run in three minutes? I asked Shuya tentatively, but she just laughed, 'Definitely slower than a rabbit, and faster than a tortoise.'

There was no point in getting angry. She was always trying to squash me.

However, it was good to be prepared, and I had to admire my brother's foresight. One afternoon, we younger ones were home from school, but Dad and Kejun were still out. Mum was busy cooking dinner, Shuya and Tianlu were in the back room doing their history homework, and I was playing cat's cradle with Su and Kid. Suddenly, there was a loud explosion. Shuya ran out of the back room, white-faced, and shouted to us, 'Air raid! Run!'

It turned out to be a surprise raid. The Japanese were getting very cunning. They made good use of the cloudy weather in late autumn to fly in the clouds, and then dive without warning and catch us off guard. At times like that, the air-raid warning system was useless.

Mum was in the middle of dinner, so she quenched the fire in the stove with water, and came to get Su and Kid. But Tianlu firmly grasped her by the arm. 'Mum, come with me!'

By that time, I had Kid in my arms, and Shuya was carrying Su piggyback. The six of us stumbled downstairs, crossed the courtyard, and headed to the river bank, where there was a vegetable patch, and a gourd frame, which was a good place to hide.

Shuya got there first with Su. I couldn't hold onto Kid, he was too heavy for me and slipped out of my arms. He burst into loud tears and, in my anxiety, I grabbed his arm and dragged him with me until we got down to the river. I discovered then that his shoes and socks had come off as I was pulling him along, his little feet were bare, and they were covered in mud up to the ankle.

When Shuya had got her breath back, she suddenly yelled, 'Hey, where's Mum?' I got up to go and look back along the road. There was Tianlu, giving my mother a piggyback. He was staggering along under the weight, making as much speed as he could. We waved frantically from under the gourd frame. 'Here,

Tianlu, this way!' He headed our way, and managed to stumble the last few steps, then flopped down, and his shoulders heaved as he struggled for breath. He was scarlet in the face and looked done in. Mum was a small woman, but she was a grownup, after all, and Tianlu was only just fifteen.

Mum sat on the ground and bemoaned her useless feet. (They'd been bound when she was a small girl, then unbound, but the bones hadn't healed and she still had difficulties walking.) 'Look how useless I am, I can't even walk properly. I almost did our Tianlu an injury! How awful if I'd hurt Tianlu!'

'Don't keep going on!' said Shuya impatiently. 'We wouldn't have left you behind. If we had, Dad and Kejun would have had us for breakfast, wouldn't they?'

Tianlu was still struggling to get his breath back, but he waved to Shuya to shut up. Then he got my mother by the shoulder and, like a real man, he pushed her firmly down onto the ground so that he was protecting her with his body.

It was not until then that I noticed, to my surprise, that Tianlu had grown quite tall. He was taller than Shuya and he looked like a grownup guy. No wonder he could give my mother a piggyback.

When had he grown so tall without me noticing?

That raid was the closest we came to getting killed. From where we lay on the river bank, we could clearly see the bomb hatch under the plane fuselage. When the wing tilted, the plane would shit out a long string of silvery bombs from its hatch. We also saw flames leaping upwards into the sky in the distance, and roofs belching smoke, and so many planes that for a short time the sky was dark with them. Kid screamed so desperately that he cried himself hoarse and lost his voice. Su trembled in Shuya's arms. The terror of that day made her mute for several days after.

Pomegranate Gardens was also bombed. Fortunately the bomber pilot's aim was off, and only the courtyard wall took a hit, and a bit collapsed.

When we got back to Pomegranate Gardens, my father was there, looking terrified. He stood in the walkway and looked at the damaged wall, repeating over and over, 'If it had come any closer…if it had come any closer…'

And if we had not managed to get away, carrying Su and Kid and Mum, the consequences would have been awful. And that was why Dad took us down the street (just Shuya, Tianlu, and me) and thanked us from the bottom of his heart. Then he bought us two bowls of dumplings each, one spicy and one sweet.

A schoolmate of Tianlu was caught in the raid, and had her leg and half her buttocks blown off. Uncle Fan wouldn't let Tianlu and his friends go and see her in the hospital. He said they were too young to visit someone that badly wounded. The girl screamed in pain for two days and nights, and then died.

It was not until two years later that Japan attacked Pearl Harbor and the United States formally entered the war. An American air base was built on a piece of wasteland less than fifty kilometres south of Huaxi Fields, and its pilots launched counterattacks against the Japanese bombers from there.

We saw American planes (they were called 'Black Widows') taking on the Japanese right over our heads. Black Widows were big and powerful. The Japanese ones were small but agile, and they were like terriers. Once they sank their teeth into an American plane, they wouldn't let go. We never heard the machine-gun fire, all we saw were blinding flashes. Every now and then, when Japanese plane was hit, there would be a big fire ball, and the plane would hurtle earthwards, trailing a long plume of black smoke. When it hit the ground, there would be an earth-shattering explosion, followed by a glowing mushroom cloud.

Occasionally, an American plane was shot down, and the pilot ejected, and a parachute, like a cottonwool ball, floated down to earth. It always looked like it was going to land on our heads, but never did, and we never saw where it landed. Whenever an American pilot ejected, we watched with our hearts in our mouths. To us, these pilots were true heroes, heaven-sent to save us.

Over time, the air raid sirens ceased their wailing over Huaxi Fields, and life returned to its former calm. But still waters run deep, and the effects on us were lasting. Two years of hiding from the air raids had taught us that we could live, eat, and go to school because countless soldiers had built a great wall to protect us, and some of them paid with their lives.

Chapter 9
Flight of the Bumblebee

Sheona and I finished primary school. I got a place in Huadu Girls' High School. Sheona wasn't going with me. She was going to a church school. She said her mum wanted her to go there.

'The thing is – you see, I'm a child of God,' she said.

She said goodbye mournfully, and gave me a silk handkerchief embroidered with pink roses. I gave her a cloisonné brooch which I'd bought in a junk shop on Shaanxi Street. It didn't cost much. The price of rice had shot up, and bank notes were hardly worth the paper they were printed on. People survived by selling their old stuff. When you walked around the market, the stalls were full of musty-smelling calligraphy scrolls and paintings, antiques, fur coats, and pretty pieces of jewelry, all going for a song.

We made a big ceremony out of saying goodbye. At that age, we loved doing things that had a bit of drama attached to them. But we were both still living in Pomegranate Gardens, so there was nothing to stop us gossiping and getting up to mischief together during school holidays.

My new school was only a kilometre and a half from Pomegranate Gardens, and with my long legs, it was no more than twenty minutes' walk. But my dad wanted me to be a boarder. One reason was that Su was getting too big to share my parents' bed. She needed to move to the bed in Shuya's and my room. The second reason was that my dad felt I was too much of a tomboy. I needed to live with a group of girls so that they could civilize me.

On registration day, I was still wearing the unisex Youth Militia uniform that I'd had at primary school. My hair was cropped too – Mum had cut it because the weather was hot and we sweated a lot – and my ears stuck out on either side. When I clattered into the dormitory with my washbowl and bits and pieces, there were screams of horror from the dozen or so girls who were in there folding their bed quilts and sorting their things – they thought I was a boy.

I was so embarrassed and annoyed that I could hardly wait to get home at the weekend and tell Mum. She was very sympathetic. She took me shopping and bought me two pieces of fabric, one dark blue, of the kind that everyone wore back then, and one light blue. That evening, she ran up two student gowns for me, with a slit up the legs and fitted at the waist.

I was thrilled. The next morning I put one on and rushed off, first thing, to the arched bridge over the stream on the campus of the West China Union University, so I could see my reflection swaying in the clear river water. What I saw was a girl with long legs and long arms, a very small head, a skinny waist, and disproportionately large hands, and short hair that stood up like a cockscomb in the breeze. For the first time in my life, I was not happy with my image.

My sister was not happy with me either, because our mother had been going to buy a padded jacket for Dad with the money she'd spent on my new gowns. Shuya laid it on thick, 'Poor Dad, spending all winter in the fields in the freezing cold without a thick jacket!'

I was so ashamed that my new clothes prickled my skin. But the gowns were made and we could not take the material back. I promised myself that I would study really hard and not let my father down.

There were a total of four dorm rooms in my school, each with seventeen or eighteen girls. They were all arranged in much the same way: three rows of wooden bunkbeds, six in each row, and two aisles so narrow that you had to walk sideways. There was a simple shelf at the foot of each bed to hold our toiletries. Our suitcases lived under the bed, and we each had a wicker box to keep bits and bobs in. A single lightbulb hung over each of the aisles. It gave off a feeble yellowish glow – it must have been a 15 or 25 watt bulb. It was so dim that if I read too long in bed, my eyes got puffy and sore, and started to weep.

The dormitories were arranged around a small courtyard which was about the same size as another room. We girls went to the sluice room every day to fill our washbasins and carry them back to the dormitory. We washed our faces and wiped ourselves down, and when we'd finished, we flung the dirty water out into the courtyard. The brick cobbles were always running with water, which froze in winter and was a haven for mosquitoes and army worms in summer. These were greyish-yellow with faint stripes, and crept slowly along like caterpillars. There were so many of them that you soon got used to them. They were quite harmless. But I remember once when a girl in my dorm brought her lunch back at noon and wanted to keep half for dinner. She covered the bowl with a lid, but somehow an army worm still managed to wriggle inside. The girl didn't see it until she'd started eating that evening. She jumped up with a shriek, flung her bowl to the floor, and rushed into the courtyard to vomit. After that, if we ever wanted to leave food in the dormitory to eat, we had to tie the lid down securely with newspaper, because the sight of an army worm in your bowl put you right off your food.

I hated having to get up to pee at night. The only toilet in the school was in the far corner of the sportsground, and to get there from our dormitory, you had to go along a walkway around the courtyard. It was dark, because there were only two light bulbs, one on either side, which swayed in the breeze, and flickered over the pillars and doors and windows. The shadows they created could easily be hiding ghosts and monsters. Once you were out of the gate, you had to cross a sportsground, where parallel bars and balance beams stood in the sand. On the windy nights, the wind whistled over it, blowing up eddies of sand, and making the branches of the poplar and willow trees around the edge shake demonically. The effect was hypnotic. On still nights when there was a moon, the ground turned an eerie white and there was deadly silence. It felt so unreal, I always worried that I might put my foot down and go right through into another world. So I never drank any water after four o'clock in the afternoon. If I really needed to go, I would hold it in until another girl needed to use the toilet too, and go with her.

About one month into the term, one afternoon after class, I was in the dormitory reading my novel. It was a Russian novel translated into Chinese, and had been doing the rounds in our room until finally it was my turn to read it. The pages had gone yellow with age, but there was still a queue of girls waiting for it in the dormitory opposite.

The old gatekeeper stood in the middle of the courtyard and shouted at the top of her voice, 'Orange Huang! Your brother's here to see you!'

I shut my book and went out to see. It was Tianlu. 'You here?' I said in surprise.

'Why not?' he retorted.

I grinned. What a silly way to greet him.

I invited him in. He poked his head in to make sure there were no other girls in the room, and then stepped cautiously through the door.

He had grown so tall that he almost scraped his head on the lintel.

He headed straight for my bed and put a package on the pillow. Inside, there was a large piece of sponge cake, a few green-skinned tangerines, and a lightweight padded jacket.

First, he unwrapped the cake and handed it to me. 'Eat up. I only had ten cents. This was all I could buy.'

He almost sounded apologetic that it was so small, and I was touched.

I crammed it down my throat. Ever since I started boarding here, I'd been starving hungry.

He looked really sorry for me. 'Orange, you look like you haven't eaten for three hundred years!'

But my mouth was so full of cake that I couldn't answer.

He held the jacket out to me. 'Mum wanted me to give it to you. She said it's getting windy and cold. She's worried you'll catch a chill and get laryngitis. You've got to wear it.'

So my mother had sent Tianlu!

He gave me all the news: Kejun, who had started in the third year of senior high school, was in four or five school clubs, and sometimes sat in on lectures at one of the five universities in Huaxi Fields too, so he was hardly ever home. And Shuya had a boyfriend. This I already knew from last weekend when Sheona had whispered it to me. She said she'd seen Shuya learning to ride a bicycle on the university sportsground, with a dozen boys sprinting along behind, all competing to steady her handlebars. 'Your sister's like a queen!' Sheona said enviously.

If Shuya was a queen, I imagined she'd be leaving home soon. The same with Kejun. Mum often said that you reared the bright ones for other people. Only the ones who were a bit dumb really belonged to you. My mother could hardly read and write but there was nothing you could teach her about human relationships. She was always spot on.

Having gobbled down the cake, I started to peel one of the tangerines. As soon as I pulled off a small bit of the thin skin, the juice spurted out and the room filled with the fragrant, sweet-sour smell. Delicious.

Tianlu looked at me with a wry smile. He obviously

thought that girls like me were all greedy pigs.

I let that go. After all, he had brought me some food.

Tianlu looked idly around the room as I ate the tangerine. The first thing he spotted was the book I had just put down on my shelf. 'Are you reading *Mother*? By Gorky?' he asked.

At that age, I wasn't too interested in class work, but novels were very exciting. I wiped my sticky fingers on a towel, and picked it up very carefully. 'Have you read it?' I asked.

'No, but I've heard of it.' A lot of his classmates were crazy about Russian novels, and some of them had poetry collections too, he told me. He'd leafed through the poems, but couldn't make much sense of them. 'It's like going down the stairs, two or three characters a line. Weird.'

'You daft brush! That's Mayakovsky!' I yelled.

He grinned sheepishly. Compared with me, who was up and down like a yoyo, he seemed so grownup, sitting quietly on the next-door bed, perched half-on, half-off and gripping the edge with both hands, probably worried about leaving her sheets crumpled. He seemed pleased to see me. He was even looking at me with fondness. Dignified and sensible, that was the impression he gave.

I'd only been at school a month and had no best friends yet. I had no one like Sheona, who I was always whispering secrets to. But I was a chatterbox and a fidget, and my head was full of strange imaginings. It was such a treat to see Tianlu. I told him everything I had been bottling up: the lessons, the director of studies with the amazing frizzy perm, the awful food, even the embarrassment of not daring to go to the toilet at night. It all came spilling out.

'Well, it sounds like a good school,' he nodded. 'Apart from the toilet.'

I jumped up. 'What's good about it? Sheona's school is ten times better than this one! They get pork steaks for lunch. And hot baths every week.'

'But you're not a Christian,' he said, unperturbed.

'Of course not.'

'And you're not a blonde, blue-eyed foreigner.'

'Of course not.'

'In other words, you'll never go to a school where you eat steaks and have hot baths.'

I felt like a pricked balloon. There was no point in saying anything more.

'You'd better go,' I told him. 'If my classmates

come back and find you here, it won't look good.'

'I can't go yet. Uncle (that was Dad) told me to be sure to go over your homework, especially the maths. He says you mustn't get behind with your maths, if you drop even a bit behind, you'll never catch up. That was what happened with me.'

They were so annoying, Tianlu, and Dad, both! It was as if they'd guessed that in my test yesterday I only got seventy percent and made a complete fool of myself!

I refused to show him. I said that the test was next week, and the work had been very basic, not difficult at all. When it got more difficult, I'd ask for his help.

'Shall I show you our piano room? You can report back on that after you get home.'

He thought for a moment. 'Fine.'

I had no problem taking him to the piano room. My piano lessons were going well, and I felt good about them. Of all the high schools in Huaxi Fields, the Huadu Girls' High School was the best for music. Girls who went there learnt to sing and play all kinds of instruments, and had to be proficient in at least one of them. Although I was not much interested in music, I had done piano with Sheona's mother since I was a child so I had a head start over the students who had only just started to read the notes. I was quite happy for someone to watch me play the piano.

We walked out of the courtyard's moon-gate side by side. Tianlu was so tall now, and he had a really long stride. In fact he bounced along as if he had springs under his feet. I had to take two steps for every one of his and, quite naturally, I reached out and grabbed his arm. He was so startled, he went red from ear to ear, and looked around guiltily. Then he brushed my hand off and whispered, 'Orange, you're in high school now!'

So what? Tianlu, you'll still be my brother, even when we're old! I thought to myself, but I didn't say anything. It was too bad. Why did people get so stick-in-the-mud when they grew up? So boring.

I saw the senior girls sneaking glances at him as we went by. I might be dense but I couldn't fail to notice how they were reacting. There was a little group walking towards us. They looked up and suddenly saw the tall figure of Tianlu coming towards them. They came to a halt and the colour began to mount in their faces. They looked flustered, half turned away, whispered to each other, chewed their braids and then glanced back quickly.

Aha! So my brother was a good-looking guy! He'd put all these girls into a fluster. That made me proud, and I marched along beside him with my head stuck in the air, quite the high and mighty.

It was too bad that Tianlu was such a shy, well-behaved young man. Having so many girls staring at him made him nervous. He followed me, head bent, his eyes on the ground, sticking close by my side. I began to laugh. I could not help it, and soon I was bent double. Tianlu was so embarrassed that he hissed in my ear, 'You're crazy!'

He was probably sorry he ever agreed to this trip to the piano room. A big lad like him, plonked down in the middle of a girls' school, he must have felt like a fawn surrounded by tigers. For whatever reason, that was Tianlu's first and last visit to my school. In fact, after that, when my mother sent him to fetch me home, he wouldn't come in, and Su had to come in and get me.

The distance that day from our dormitory to the piano room seemed like miles. The two of us walked across the sportsground and past two rows of classrooms with carved wooden eaves. Then we went through a hidden courtyard whose walls were heavy with wisteria and tiptoed past the teachers' office window. Finally we arrived at the piano room, its door painted with musical notes.

The door was unlocked so that students could go and practice at any time. Practicing piano was actively encouraged in our school. I led him in and opened the piano lid, putting my finger on middle C. 'What would you like to hear?'

Standing in this girls' piano room, he was still embarrassed. 'Why not play something your teacher's taught you?'

'That's boring.' I was swanking a bit. 'Classes have only just started, the teacher's teaching fingering.'

'I don't understand. Anyway, play what you want.'

'No, you tell me a piece.' I was being mischievious.

He hummed and hawed for a while, and finally had an idea. 'Yesterday I heard Sheona playing and it was lovely. It was weird, like insects buzzing around. It was mesmerizing. I could hardly breathe.'

'"Flight of the Bumblebee"!' I yelled.

I played a few notes on the piano with one hand. 'Is that it?'

'Right!' he exclaimed in excitement. 'It's lovely.

isn't it?'

I got up and found the Rimsky-Korsakov sheet music in the piano cabinet.

'Flight of the Bumblebee' was an orchestral interlude originally written for Rimsky-Korsakov's opera *The Tale of Tsar Saltan*. The son of King Saltan was fitted up for a crime he hadn't committed and was exiled to an island. There he was turned into a bee, so that he could fly back to his father and denounce his enemies. Mrs Fan told me the story and made Sheona practice it with me. She did not think it was difficult to play; the challenge was to play it fast enough. Too slow, and it sounded more like a blundering fly than a bee.

Well, I'd really shot my mouth off now. One way or another, I had to make this bee fly, otherwise Tianlu would just laugh at me.

But the truth was that my playing was nowhere near as good as Sheona. I put my hands on the keys, and with some difficulty played a fast descending chromatic scale. Then I was sensible enough to stop. It was hopeless. I couldn't make my fingers gallop over the keys, let alone get the naughty little bee airborne. I could not even hoist a blundering fly off the ground.

I sat there without speaking. I felt near to tears.

'It doesn't matter.' Tianlu reached out and gently put the lid down. 'Shcona started classes at four. It's not the same thing at all.'

'I never liked piano,' I said baldly.

'No one likes everything.'

'But I still want to learn.'

'Then learn. You'll make progress.'

'But you'll laugh at me!'

He thought for a moment. 'No, I'll go back and tell Uncle that you're working very hard at school.'

'Really?'

'It's the truth. You are working hard.'

I looked hard at him, trying to tell if he meant it or was making fun of me.

'It's true. When you understand that you're not good enough, that's progress.' I relaxed and smiled broadly.

He reached out and tugged me by the hair. 'Don't be angry, little bee. One day you'll fly over these keys.'

'Right,' I said. 'For definite.' I really meant it too.

I saw him as far as the school gate. He had not gone more than a few steps when he looked back at me. His eyes told me that he believed in me. I could do anything.

'One day...' Those were his exact words.

Chapter 10
The Flying Tigers

We boarders normally went home at the weekend. After spending all week in our cramped and old-fashioned school, I was always desperate to get home, to see if the pomegranate tree in Pomegranate Gardens had fruit on it, whether Professor Mei's hybrid hens had laid double-yokers as he promised they would, and whether the canna flowers at the foot of the wall were out yet, so I could suck honey-sweet nectar from them.

Shuya once wrote about me in a school essay: if, on any Saturday afternoon, you saw a girl with a sweaty face and wild hair, streaking like a goat along the dirt road through Huaxi Fields, 'it must be my little sister'.

I wasn't going to let her get away with that. It was

only one and a half kilometres from school to home. Even if I was running, I wouldn't break a sweat.

'You don't know anything,' Shuya retorted. 'Exaggeration is a rhetorical technique! No wonder you get such bad marks in your Chinese tests.'

I could never get the better of Shuya. She always knew how to wind me up. 'You'll never get a boyfriend. Your tongue's too sharp,' I hissed.

One Saturday, I charged into the courtyard, took the stairs two at a time, and ran along the walkway to our front door. Su was always the first to come and open up. I always shouted at her, 'Don't come near me!'

Su stood and watched as I took off every stitch of clothing I was wearing, carefully checking every seam and every wrinkle to make sure there weren't any bedbugs hiding inside. That was Mum's rule. We'd had an outbreak of bedbugs in the school dormitory. The caretaker tried every which way to kill them, though she never completely succeeded in getting rid of them. Mum was so afraid that I'd bring them home, she made me take off everything I was wearing at the door, and then she boiled my clothes up in a big cauldron.

Finally, I could go in. The first thing was to eat. Mum always put something to one side especially for me – a bowl of *liangfen* noodles or two *baba* cakes or, if there was nothing else, a bowl of brown sugar water, which was always comforting. Su and Kid used to watch goggle-eyed, but my mother was sorry for me because I boarded at school, and she was convinced that I wasn't getting enough to eat or warm clothes to wear.

Once I'd eaten and drunk, I wiped my mouth and went downstairs to find Sheona. Tianlu wanted to listen to 'Flight of the Bumblebee', and I was still upset that I hadn't been able to play it. I wanted to see how Sheona got her fingers up to speed.

I heard someone playing the piano in the Fans' living room. It didn't sound like Sheona – her playing was graceful and fluid, proficient but a bit laidback. It made me think of dragonflies skimming the surface of a pond. As Mrs Fan would say, it had no soul.

It wasn't Mrs Fan playing either. She made the piano sound like a rushing, raging torrent. This person sounded a bit rusty, and there were some wrong chords, but there was strength there – I could see those hands thumping the keys.

I did not want to disturb whoever it was, so I tiptoed past the window. I had just poked my head through the front door when Sheona spotted me and exclaimed, 'Orange, Orange, come in!'

I stood in the doorway of the piano room: the piano-player was someone I'd never seen before, a good-looking young guy in his mid-twenties, with blue eyes like Sheona's, a thin face, a prominent nose, and a scattering of brown freckles on either side. He had a wide mouth and when he smiled, it stretched almost from ear to ear, revealing two even rows of shiny white teeth.

Sheona happily pulled me over to the piano. 'Let me introduce you to my cousin, Mark, he's a Flying Tiger fighter pilot. He's on leave from Kunming and he's come to visit us!'

What? A Flying Tiger fighter pilot! My eyes nearly popped out of my head. Chennault's Flying Tigers had been in the newspapers countless times because of their impressive contribution to China's war effort. They'd been fighting heroic battles against Japanese planes in the skies above China.

I was so dumbstruck that I even forgot to say hello to the hero. I could only gawp at his blonde hair, blue eyes and wide chin. He had on a tatty sheepskin jacket, which seemed to be fighting a battle to hold his bulging muscles in, and baggy trousers, and scuffed leather shoes. I'd always thought that the Flying Tigers were half-human and half-god, or at least super-strong like King Kong, capable of swatting a Japanese plane out of the sky with a single slap. I wondered where Mark's special powers were hidden. Which part of his body became a knife or a sword when he needed them?

Mark was the perfect gentleman. He got up and came over to me, his hand outstretched.

'Pleased to meet you, Miss Orange,' he said.

How did he know my name?

Feeling slightly dizzy, I reached out my own hand. His hand was huge. There was a dense brown fuzz on the back, and his palm was fleshy and calloused, like a bear's paw. It swallowed mine whole, along with my wrist, which looked doll-like by comparison. He must have been afraid of doing me an injury by squeezing, because he let go straightaway.

He said something, smiled and shrugged.

I felt really freaked out. I hadn't a clue what he was saying. His accent was so thick.

Sheona put me out of my misery. 'He says he already knows who you are, from my letters,' she whispered in my ear.

I must have looked dazed still, because she

added, 'I talk about you every time I write to him.' I immediately began to wonder how Sheona described me to him. Did she say I was a tomboy, and climbed trees to pick mulberries, and jumped in the river to collect freshwater mussels, and came home on Saturday with bedbugs?

The thought made my face burn. I couldn't stay a minute longer. I turned and fled, clattering back up the stairs to our flat.

Tianlu was on the walkway, wringing out the wet laundry for Mum. Sudsy water trickled over the floor bricks, the tiny bubbles catching the light. 'Sheona's got a visitor,' I gasped. 'He's a Flying Tiger!'

'Eh?' Tianlu stood with the clothes in his arms, completely gobsmacked. 'Really? You mean, one of Chennault's Flying Tigers?'

He stared at me for a full five seconds, then threw the wet laundry into the basket and was down the stairs in leaps and bounds. Then he stopped. He walked slowly up the stairs again and peered over the balcony. 'You can't see from here,' I told him. 'He's inside the Fans' house.'

'So what can I do?' said Tianlu. 'I'm not a kid anymore. I can't just run over and hang around in the doorway.'

'No problem,' I said and tugged his sleeve. 'Come over with me.'

He pulled away. 'No, that's no good. Girls can stand around and gossip, but boys can't do stuff like that.'

I hated when he talked about girls do this and boys do that. I was about to thump him when I saw Su watching us curiously. I spared him my fist but not the tongue-lashing. 'Tianlu, I'm like a roundworm in your gut. You can't hide from me. I know you want to see the pilot because you want to join the air force and fight in the sky.'

'How do you know?' he asked flustered.

'You love planes. You've got lots of pictures of planes in your schoolbag. I've seen them.'

'You've been snooping in my bag!' He was angry and flustered.

'Admit it, I'm right, aren't I?'

He looked at our open door and waved at me to shut up. 'Don't talk rubbish, and don't let Mum hear!'

But Tianlu got to meet his hero in the end. He was still standing on the walkway when, a moment later, Mark appeared with badminton rackets and a shuttlecock. In the middle of the courtyard, he bent down and drew a line in the dirt, and started a game with Sheona. His huge hands were really scary – they made the racket and shuttlecock look like toys. He took off his jacket and played in his army vest, so you could see the muscles swelling and contracting with every movement. When he lifted his arm to serve, the knots of muscles scurried along like squeaky little rats under his skin.

Tianlu was peering over the railing, looking down intently. The look on his face was both solemn and respectful. I reckon that, given half a chance, he would have cheerfully offered to become the shuttlecock and dance on Mark's racket.

Sheona was no match for Mark. She laughed and screeched and only lasted ten minutes. Then she dropped the racket, and bent down to catch her breath. Then her mother took a turn, and Uncle Fan stood watching with a smile on his face and a pipe in his mouth. Mrs Fan's technique was a bit better, and her serves were on the mark. But she stood stock still, too plump and heavy to put on a spurt when she received the ball. Even I, a badminton ignoramus, could see that Mark was feeding her the ball, but it didn't do any good. She was useless.

I poked Tianlu in the arm and said, 'Go on! Go

and play! You're way better than Sheona.'

He jumped backwards and went scarlet in the face.

'You're a coward,' I taunted him.

He nodded miserably, looking ashamed of himself. What a sight!

The next day was Sunday, and Sheona went house-to-house first thing in the morning to invite everyone to dinner that evening: her mother wanted to lay on a Chinese-style party for Mark.

We children went crazy with excitement. The adults immediately started to make preparations, with every family figuring out how to make their best dish. My mother was going to make egg dumplings. Her recipe took twenty eggs! She sent Kejun on his bike to a market five kilometres away to buy pork. Then Shuya and I got busy helping Mum. We worked all afternoon and when we finished, we laid the gleaming yellow egg dumplings on two porcelain dishes, and sprinkled them with a handful of green garlic shoots and leaves. Our mouths watered.

Professor Mei killed two of his precious hens and the family cooked a big pot of red-braised chicken. The birds were the hybrid offspring of his Rhode Island Reds. They were really good layers, and we were used to hearing their cheerful clucking in the courtyard all day long. I don't know how he could bear to kill them.

Uncle Tao's family provided a big basket of Sichuan cold noodles flavoured with shredded cucumber, chopped egg yolks, grated carrots, peppercorns, and shiny peppers, in a medley of green, bright yellow, orange, and red. Mrs Tao was from Chongqing, and her cold noodles were very good, but she rarely got a chance to show off her prowess these days because white flour was so hard to come by.

Sheona's mother was not a cook. They even had to ask my mother to help them with pickling their cabbage every year. But Mrs Fan had a stock of tinned food she had managed to get hold of somehow – tinned pork, beef, haricot beans, and jam. She even conjured up two bottles of Scotch whiskey.

Tianlu worked the hardest of all of us. As soon as he heard about the dinner, he started running up and downstairs helping in any way he could. He sprinkled the water over the courtyard and swept it, killed the hens for the professor, rustled up tables and benches, arranged them for a cold buffet in the courtyard, and laid them with bowls and chopsticks borrowed from every family. Shuya told him sniffily, 'Tianlu, you're just going to end up being a waiter all evening.'

It was an unusually bright moonlit night, with a gentle breeze that wafted the scent of the osmanthus trees over the wall to us. My dad and Professor Tao sat over their drinks discussing the war as usual. My dad tentatively asked Mark about American participation in the war now that the Japanese had attacked Pearl Harbor, but Mark shrugged, blushed, and said he wasn't sure how to explain it. There was a chorus of encouragement from the professors and he finally got to his feet and gave a smart salute. That took us all by surprise, and we kids burst out laughing. Tianlu thought this was very disrespectful, shot us a furious glare, and aimed a kick at me under the table. Meanwhile Mark was using the bowls and chopsticks to demonstrate the battle lines. He talked about Europe, Germany, Roosevelt, Churchill, and so on. My English was quite basic, and I didn't really understand much, but I could see his excitement, especially when he talked about battles with the Japanese fighter planes over China. He made everything come alive, jumping to his feet and demonstrating combat tactics in the air.

Tianlu was finding it hard to follow too, but he

was straining his ears, his eyes fixed on Mark's mouth, as if he could actually swallow down the words. His eyes shone brighter that evening than I'd ever seen them before, and even his forehead, nose and teeth glowed golden in the moonlight.

After dinner, everyone was still in high spirits, and there was a sing-a-long. In those days, everyone used to sing, it was a favourite pastime, no matter whether you were happy or sad. The profs led off with 'China Must be Strong' and then tackled the challenging heights of the drinking song from Verdi's opera *La Traviata*. Then we children sang 'Two Old Tigers' (to the tune of Frère Jacques) and 'The Newspaper-Boy's Song', to a round of applause. Uncle Tao was quite tipsy, and actually climbed onto the table, and launched into John Keats's 'Ode to the Nightingale'. Uncle Tao had been to Oxford University and his passionate recitation, spoken in his lovely British English accent, made our hearts beat fast.

Then Tianlu organized a group of us to clear up, wash the bowls and chopsticks, and return them to their owners. Then the tables and benches were taken in, and the courtyard was swept clean.

By then it was late at night. I was almost asleep

on my feet, but Tianlu was still fired up. Before we went upstairs, he told me mysteriously that he had something to show me.

'I'll give you a prize if you guess what this is,' he said with a cocky smile.

I was not in the mood for guessing games. I was yawning my head off, and my brain was one big fug.

He looked disappointed at my dopiness, but he still pulled a scrap of paper out of his pocket and opened it. There was something scrawled on it in English.

'Mark's given me the address of his base. He says I can write to him!'

That woke me up. I yelled with excitement and flung my arms around his neck, nearly sending him flying. He forgot his new-found reserve with me, and grabbed me round the waist and waltzed me round the yard. He put me down and said very earnestly, 'Orange, we'll both write to him. You write a letter and I'll write a letter, and then we'll go and post them together.'

'I guess we'll have to write in English. I don't think Mark understands Chinese, does he?' I said.

'Sure.'

'I don't write English very well.'

'Nor do I, but we can help each other.'

Ah, so Tianlu was only getting me involved because he was scared to do it on his own.

But no matter. I would work really hard at my English so that I could write to Flying Tiger Mark. This was going to be a big deal for both Tianlu and me.

Chapter 11

Shuya Leaves Home

Before the winter vacation, we had our last tests of the school year. On the day of the Chinese test, I got diarrhea – I must have eaten something that disagreed with me. I had to go to the toilet twice during the test, which used up a lot of time. I must surely have messed that up, I thought; I had no chance of passing. According to the school regulations, if you failed one-third of the work, you had to repeat the year. If you failed half, nothing could save you, you'd be out on your ear. I had never been a high achiever at school, but Chinese was my best subject. If I failed the test, I'd look like an idiot.

I was on tenterhooks for two days while we waited for the results. There were no more classes to keep me in school, but I didn't dare go home.

The results went up on the morning of the third day, pasted on the wall at the far end of the assembly room. It was an enormous sheet of white paper with the names of every student in the school and, below them, our marks in each subject in red or black pen. The red marks were the fails. You could see your name from a distance and if there were a lot of red numbers underneath, there was no point in totting up the total, you simply packed your bags and left.

I squeezed through, my heart hammering, dreading what I was going to see. I screwed my eyes into slits and squinted, terrified that all those red numbers were going to leap off the paper and stab me in the eye. I felt like I was going to faint.

I'd failed my Chinese test. But I'd done much better than I expected in all my other subjects. There was the row of numbers: black, black, black. I had even done well in maths, the subject I was most worried about.

The Chinese teacher called me to her office. She could not understand how I had managed to mess the test up. She was a woman in her forties, a spinster, with a long face and long legs, who strode along swinging her arms like a man. She wore her hair pinned in a crown braid on top of her head. Not a single stray hair escaped from morning till night.

'Orange, this is terrible. However did this happen?' she said reproachfuly. 'You're the class representative!'

I hung my head and blurted out what had happened. I don't know if she believed it or not, or just wanted to believe it, but her expression softened, and she even sounded sympathetic. 'Silly girl, why didn't you tell anyone?'

Probably because I wasn't sure I'd failed until the results came out, I thought to myself.

She looked stern again. 'Well, just this once we'll let it go. If it happens again, even the Almighty won't be able to save you.'

I smiled inwardly. The Almighty certainly would not be saving a 'silly girl' like me a second time, and I did not want his help. I had failed once, but it would never happen again. I had some self-respect.

Clutching my school report, I hurried home in high spirits. As I went up the stairs to our flat, I heard my sister and mother arguing. It turned out that my sister wanted to sign up for the Sichuan Women's Battlefield Corps during the winter holidays. They would start from Chengdu and go along the Sichuan-Shaanxi Highway to Xixiang county on the Hanshui

River where there was a field hospital which took in the wounded who had been evacuated from the front line. The Corps duties were to boost patients' morale, and to 'sow the seed of patriotism', doing war propaganda and educating the local villagers.

My mother was chopping pickled vegetables on the chopping board and shouting at my sister, 'You really are a fool, and a troublemaker! The women in the Corps are all college students. You're only a kid in school, what are you playing at?'

On the other side of the table, Shuya shouted back, 'Don't call me a kid! Orange and Su are kids, I'm not! I'm in senior high school! I'm seventeen!'

'Senior high school is still school, not university!'

'Right, so you tell me, when the Japanese kill the Chinese, do they only get college students and not high-schoolers?'

Silence.

'The government's called on the whole population to fight the Japanese, Dad told you that, and so did Kejun!'

Silence.

'Mum, the whole population. And that includes high-schoolers and college students. We all have a responsibility. And anyone who stands in our way is an enemy of the people!'

Mum was defeated. The way Shuya put it, it would be an outrage not to allow her to go and do propaganda work.

I wanted to go and see the world too. I asked Shuya if the Corps accepted junior high school students.

She smirked at me. 'And how old are you?'

'You know how old I am. I'm going to be twelve after the New Year.'

'The youngest member of the Corps is fifteen. No one's going to accept a twelve-year-old, are they?' Shuya said scornfully.

Fine, so they won't. But why did she have to be so cutting? I was indignant. I waited till she was packing her bags and stole the tin of face cream that she had stuffed into one sock, and hid it under the mattress. I imagined the cold and the freezing winds in the countryside. With no face cream, she'd come back with a face as wrinkled as a dried persimmon.

Shuya left, brimming with enthusiasm. For the first two days, Mum was still grumbling at my dad for not putting his foot down, and letting Shuya go, just like that, but then she let it drop. To tell the truth, there were so many of us, the housework was never-ending, and Mum was exhausted. It was simply impossible for her to tuck every one of her children under her wings and protect us.

The next day, Sheona turned up in a brightly-patterned Chinese-style padded jacket. 'Orange! Hey, I've got something interesting that I can put your name forward for.'

'Eh?' I put down the paper plane I was folding for Kid.

'Huaxi Civil Aid Corps. Have you heard of it? Join it with me, then we can be together.'

I never really expected anyone to accept a kid of my age. I was so excited that I almost cried. But when I got there, I discovered that the corps was made up of women and girls who went to Sheona's church. They were nice enough, but everything was Jesus this and Jesus that, and I couldn't stand all the prayers and Bible readings.

'You never told me it was all church-goers,' I complained to Sheona.

'That doesn't matter!' she said carelessly. 'It's all in aid of the anti-Japanese War effort, anyway.'

She was right, of course. And beggars couldn't be choosers.

We got together in the church every afternoon to sew jackets for soldiers, stitch soles on cloth shoes, and make simple cloth bags for carrying schoolbooks, dried food, and needles and thread. It was very well organized, with all the work shared out in an orderly way: some cut fabric, some padded jackets with cotton waste, others sewed seams or sewed on buttons; everyone did something different. There was even a sewing machine in the room. You pushed the cloth under the sewing foot, then pedalled the treadle with both feet, and the cloth whirred along and out came a sleeve. I could hardly believe my eyes.

I went home and told my mother, who was suitably amazed. 'Is it easy to use?' she asked. I solemnly promised to take her to the church to see it one day.

I swore to Sheona that I would learn to use a sewing machine.

She smiled and said nothing, perhaps not wanting to discourage me. When I had nothing else to do, I would hang around by the machine to watch how it was threaded and how the cloth was pushed through. Once, the old lady who was working the machine went out to go to the toilet. Without a moment's thought, I sat myself down and stepped on the treadle. There was a clunk, and the needle broke. I went pale with terror, and my legs went rigid. I literally could not move. Luckily for me, the old woman let me off, but there was a lot of grumbling. 'Oh dear, oh dear, with the war like it is, wherever will I get more needles?'

When Tianlu wrote to Mark, I begged him to ask if the Flying Tigers could get hold of a box of sewing machine needles. A long time later, we received a small package from Yunnan – needles! I was ecstatic. I took them around to Sheona's house and asked her to pass them on to the old seamstress in the church.

Instead of learning how to use the sewing machine, I was assigned to do embroidery with Sheona. Back then, we used to embroider a rousing slogan on any garments sent to the front line, like, 'Bravely kill the enemy!', or 'Long live patriotism!' to show we were cheering them on. The supervisor at the church reckoned that girls had good eyes and deft fingers, but were not strong enough to stitch soles on cloth shoes, so we were given embroidery to do.

But I hated embroidery. After half an hour, my head was swimming and my bum was sore. I couldn't stop fidgeting. Sheona's characters were neat and clear; mine were wonky, as if a bug was crawling across the jacket. Sister Wu, the head of our embroidery team, took me off the job and put me on ironing duties. The jackets with embroidery ended up quite wrinkled, which spoiled the effect, so they had to be ironed flat. Ironing was more up my street. I liked getting the iron hot and pressing it against the damp garments. Then there was a sizzle and a pop, and a gout of steam. The fragrant, clean smell of freshly-ironed cotton went straight to my head. Ironing was a simple, straightforward business.

Once someone donated a bolt of heavyweight satin, ice-blue in colour. It was so soft, absolutely gorgeous. It was clearly not suitable for making front-line supplies but no one could agree on what to use it for. Then I had a bright idea. Why didn't we use it to make purses and tobacco pouches, sell them in the market, and use the money to buy cotton cloth?

The ladies called me a 'clever little thing'. Some of the more skillful seamstresses immediately set to, scissoring, stitching and embroidering, and in no time at all, they had produced a pile of pretty purses and tobacco pouches.

But I soon regretted my stupid idea, because the task of selling them in the market landed on us – me, Sheona and a couple of smaller children. The view of the church ladies was that children were appealing, and could sell things for a good cause, while no one would bother to buy them from adults.

What could I say? I'd dug myself into that hole.

There was a very cold snap after New Year. The sun was as pallid as an unrisen flatbread, and the sogon grass shrank into the gaps between the roof tiles. The road surfaces froze at night and thawed by day, so the potholes were full of icy mud. No one went outdoors unless they had to – porters, sedan chair bearers, and men and women with baskets on their backs or pushing barrows. People selling New Year couplets, salted fish and bacon, and rice noodles were out in force, but business was slow. It was war time, China was exhausted, prices were sky high, and no one had money to spare.

We four set off, our heads swathed in scarves, wrapped up in our padded jackets, trousers, and cloth shoes, each of us carrying a small basket. We walked up one street and down the next, holding out our baskets with their pretty knick-knacks, but we were too embarrassed to shout out, or even look any anyone in the eyes. Once, I plucked up courage to tug the sleeve of a passerby and ask, in a pathetic little voice, if he wanted one. He was in a bad mood, no doubt because he did not have the money to buy things, and having us pounce on him made him even crosser. He looked down at me in disgust and then flicked me away as if I was an annoying bit of dirt.

I had never in my life been so insulted.

Sheona had an even worse time. She failed to sell anything. In fact, she was treated like an object of curiosity by country folk who had never seen a foreigner. As soon as they saw her, the porters and carters pointed, and poked her, and she was followed by a crowd of snot-nosed kids, who threw dirt at her and shrieked, 'Look, a foreign girl! A foreign girl!'

Sheona, however, kept her cool, perhaps because she was used to being stared at, or because Christians were taught to be forbearing. The next time she went out, she braided her blonde hair and stuffed the plait firmly inside her headscarf. She wore a mask to try and hide her high nose and pale skin, but that did not work either. It actually attracted more curiosity than her western face. People got out of the way when we approached. We could not understand why until a nice old lady came up to us and asked, 'What's wrong with the girl?' We suddenly realized that people thought Sheona had some infectious disease.

Sheona was really down in the dumps by now. She took off her mask and stuffed it into the basket. Then she said, almost in tears, 'Orange, you and I had better go separately, otherwise you won't be able to sell a single purse.'

'But if I do that, I'll have the two little ones as well, and I'll be worrying about them, so I still won't sell anything,' I said.

We went back home, Sheona and I, and sat looking gloomy. We poked around in the baskets at all the little bags. We dare not go back to the church to tell them that we hadn't sold a single bag. It was too embarrassing. We felt bad for the frontline soldiers too.

The room on the other side of the partition was the boys' room. My brother was not there but the door was open and I could see Tianlu running in and out, busy doing something. First, he fetched a pile of old newspapers from my dad's desk and then we heard him grinding ink. After he had finished that, it sounded like he was folding and cutting paper, and then the smell of fresh ink wafted out.

It was quiet again. There was something about the business of grinding ink and writing characters that was very soothing.

Sheona said quietly, 'Tianlu is so different from Kejun and Shuya.'

'Not surprising,' I said. 'He's not family.' Sheona pressed even closely and whispered in my ear, 'Don't you think he's very, very nice to you?'

I jumped to my feet and pushed her down onto the bed. We rolled around like puppies and laughed until we could hardly draw breath.

A few minutes later, Tianlu appeared in the doorway. He knocked and asked nicely, 'Orange and Sheona, could you come and look at this?'

We scrambled off the bed and dashed next door. On the bed, four big sheets of newspaper were laid out. Each had one big character written on it in elegant calligraphy. The black ink was still shiny and wet. The four sheets together read, 'War Effort Charity Sale'. There were also two long narrow strips of newspaper, like traditional couplets, with more writing: 'For every bag you buy, we can make a winter jacket' and 'Every extra bullet, one more enemy dead'.

It turned out that my mother had been worried about us going to the market, and so she asked Tianlu to follow and keep an eye on us in case there was trouble. Tianlu had tagged along twice, and quickly realized that we had no chance of selling anything. So he'd made these banners for us, so we could set up a stall in the market. His idea was that we should make it plain from the start that we were collecting for charity. That way, people would be encouraged to buy the purses and pouches and would know where their money was going.

'You always have to explain the reason,' he said. 'That's the way to get results.' We nodded enthusiastically, so overcome with admiration that we couldn't think of anything to say.

He picked at the ink stains on his fingers, looking shy. 'I haven't written it very well. I hope it'll do,' he said.

'It's brilliant!' we chorused.

I wondered why I had never realized before just how resourceful Tianlu was. He didn't say much, but he didn't miss a trick. And he was very thoughtful.

We were all fired up by now, but it was getting late, so the charity sale would have to wait until the next day.

I was like a cat on hot bricks all evening, trying to work out how much money we could make on the bags. I kept doing the sums on my fingers, until eventually I fell asleep over them.

As soon as it got light, my mother woke me. Outside, a pale mist shrouded Pomegranate Gardens. It looked as if the pomegranate tree was wrapped in white gauze, and the trees and river in the distance were hardly visible. Mum must have seen how nervous we were and said cheerfully, 'Don't worry, an early mist means a fine day.'

Sure enough, by the time we'd had breakfast, and Mum had made a steaming hot bowl of paste to take with us, the mist had gone, a wintry sun was shining, making everything glitter, and it looked as though a rare warm day was in store.

Our little band set off in great spirits. Tianlu led the way, carrying a small square table made of bamboo, our main 'prop'. I came behind, holding the banners in one hand and the bowl of paste in the other. Sheona was nicely balanced, with the two baskets, hers and mine, one on each side. Tagging along right at the back was Su. She had insisted on coming, and had begged so pathetically that I agreed that she could carry the small cardboard box that we would put the cash in.

Tianlu was carrying the table on his head. It was quite a long way and the table must have been heavy because we hadn't gone far when his neck began to wobble. We rapidly made a decision and unloaded our stuff by the side of the road. First we found a suitable bit of wall and then I, as the lightest, stood on the table, brushed the paste on the wall, and stuck up the four big characters one next to the other. Then we moved the table along and I stuck up the couplets on either side. Then we set up the table in front. We made an artistic display, layering up the purses and tobacco pouches neatly, one on top of each other, until they made a pagoda. The impression was that we were selling exquisite, costly objects. In the centre was our cash box, a pretty little thing, covered in red paper box with a gold border pasted on, glittering in the sunlight. Finally, Sheona and I stood one at either end, like guardian spirits in a Buddhist temple.

Tianlu was absolutely right. Laying everything out nicely created a sense of occasion, completely different from before. People kept coming to read the words on the couplets aloud, and admired them. Some of the stall-holders asked how much the bags were. They seemed to feel they were expensive, but after some thought, they generally took a satin purse or tobacco pouch and dropped a bit of money into the cash box. There was a young man who looked like a college student, who bought nothing but gave us a ten-yuan note, and went away smiling. Then there was a middle-aged man with a big head and a mandarin jacket, who bought a tobacco pouch and gave us twenty yuan.

The pagoda of bags on the table shrank, then collapsed into a square pagoda base.

Around noon, we heard a clip-clopping of horses' hooves coming from the main road. We all looked up and saw an officer in uniform sitting ramrod straight, his orderly leading the horse by the reins, coming straight towards us. As they passed our table, the officer reined in his horse and his eyes swept over our display. Then he reached down and picked up a pouch, weighed it in his hand, and nodded approvingly at us.

'Well done, kids!' he said. We bowed respectfully, our hands at our sides, flushed with excitement.

He bent over and whispered to his orderly, who opened a briefcase he was carrying, carefully counted out ten bank notes, saluted us with a click of his heels, and then fed the money, note by note, into the cashbox.

We stared stupidly at him, and no one remembered to say thank you. Then the officer rode away with a smile, the sound of the horse's hooves growing fainter until they all vanished from sight at the end of the road. Sheona pulled herself together and exclaimed, 'Orange, a hundred yuan!'

Su was thrilled. 'Sis, a hundred yuan!' she echoed.

We three girls shrieked and bounced up and down with excitement, then spun around like spinning tops.

A few days afterwards, we had sold everything and in a burst of enthusiasm were preparing for the next round of fund-raising activities, when Tianlu suddenly came running in. 'Hey, do you know who he was, the man who bought our purse that day?'

'Who?' I asked.

'I checked the newspaper! General Deng Lixiang's just been in Chengdu, giving a lecture in the university. It must have been him, General Deng. He fought in the Battle of Changsha. He's a famous war hero!'

It was the middle of winter and Tianlu had a drop hanging from the end of his nose, and was stamping his feet from the cold. But he was wild with excitement, and full of regret that he'd missed a fantastic chance to tell the General how much he admired him.

'Orange, Orange, that was General Deng!' he exclaimed.

'Right, General Deng.'

'The war hero,' he repeated.

'Right, the war hero.'

He chewed his lip, apparently deep in thought.

Suddenly, I thought of a question. 'Tianlu, who do you think he gave the purse to, his wife, or his daughter?'

Tianlu looked at me as if he'd never understand how girls' minds worked. How could I be jumping from something so serious to a bit of gossip? He sighed and looked disappointed in me. 'Orange, when will you grow up?'

In my opinion, I'd already grown up, and could do anything. The Huaxi Civil Aid Corps ladies regarded Sheona and me as their charity sales experts. In their view, we were capable, intelligent, resourceful, and reliable. Lately, we had started to sell calligraphy brush caps made of brass cartridge cases, and rag dolls made of scraps of material, and pipes artistically whittled from bits of tree roots. We were doing well. Sheona even suggested, 'We two could open a shop together. We would make good money.'

But I had no intention of opening a shop. That was not what my parents had sent me to a private girls' school for.

That winter holiday, while we were immersed in fund-raising events, Shuya was still away, involved in a different kind of war work. Apparently, she and her corps had marched through Moon Gorge (which was rugged and hard-going) all the way to the border with southern Shaanxi province. This was wild, lawless country where Shuya and the other women did not understand the dialect or the customs. It had certainly been no picnic. The day before the new term began, she came home covered in dust and with her clothes almost in tatters. She arrived half-starved and wolfed down a large bowl of rice, three sesame cakes, and two fried eggs, hardly pausing for breath. Finally she began to talk. She told us that she had discovered for the first time on this trip just how hard life was for Chinese farmers and how tough the war against Japan was for them. She said she had seen families where old and young shared one pair of padded trousers in winter, and when you looked inside the cooking pot there was only water and weeds in it. She had seen how in the hospitals, the wounded and sick died in terrible pain because there was such a shortage of medicines and supplies. She talked and talked, 'China is so poor. What will the future be like if the war goes on like this?'

Kejun leaned over and patted her arm. 'Relax, China still has our generation, and we're ready to throw ourselves into the fray and destroy the Japanese.'

Tianlu backed him up. 'Kejun's right, it's our duty as Chinese to sacrifice ourselves for our country.'

I listened, my heart beating fast. Kejun and Tianlu's words and the expressions on their faces were so determined that they sent a scary shiver down my spine.

I didn't say anything, but deep inside, I felt horribly apprehensive.

Chapter 12

A Girl in Love

On Saturday afternoon, I went home as usual, carrying a small bag which contained a few dirty clothes and a book of English poems. I never used to take dirty clothes home, because I knew my mother had more than enough work to do, and as a junior high school student I should be looking after myself. But, a few days before, we'd had a very cold snap again, and the pipes froze and then burst. The cook had to get water by filling buckets from the river, so there was no way I could wash my dirty clothes at the school. As for the poems, to be truthful, they didn't mean much to me. I understood the words but not the sentences. I had the book with me so I could show Tianlu that I was working hard to improve my English and we could write to Mark together.

I wasn't at all sure why I was making all this effort for Tianlu. It was weird, because I used to find him so annoying when I was a kid.

We'd had the first month of Chinese New Year, and the smell of spring was in the air. Wild flowers were beginning to come out – bright yellow sprigs and clumps of them, clothing the arid winter earth, and brightening everyone's mood. Along with the flowers came the bees, and little white butterflies, and the birds hopped and fluttered cheerfully, and filled the trees with their chirping and chattering.

As I walked, I watched the bees flying up and down the road and thought of the piano piece, 'Flight of the Bumblebee'. I suddenly had a eureka moment: when bees flew, it was different from the way butterflies flitted. Their wings vibrated faster, their movements were more defined, focussed, and fiercer. All that should be matched in the music too. When you were playing, it should be like so...like so...

I got excited just thinking about it! I slung my bag onto my back, freeing up my hands, completely focussed on spreading all ten fingers over this imaginary keyboard. My arm whooshed to the left, then whooshed to the right again. They ran down the scale. An arpeggio. Touch a key, raise a finger. A lighter touch on the black keys – that was better. I had to convey the feeling of a bee swooping to sting someone!

Suddenly, there was a loud laugh from behind me. This mad cackle burst out, like wind chimes shaking uncontrollably in a gale.

I whirled around, to see Shuya a dozen metres behind me, rocking with laughter. I was furious, and embarrassed too. I was angry that she had been trailing me silently all that time, pleased as punch, watching me make an ass of myself. If she hadn't been walking along with a boy, and if she hadn't had her hand around his shoulder, I would have got into a fight with her rightaway.

Good heavens, was this her boyfriend? Was Shuya in love?

I ignored my sister's smirks and took a good look at him. What a handsome guy! I may have been a messy, devil-may-care little squit of a schoolgirl, but even I could tell that. He was medium height and wore a black Sun Yat-Sen jacket with a stand-up collar and a gray plaid scarf around his neck. Slung over his shoulder, he had a soft leather schoolbag. He was pale, and his gaunt features made him look malnourished.

But his expression was composed, and he looked at me tolerantly, as if to say, 'Ignore your sister, she's loony.'

In short, this boy was not a macho type like Kejun. His good looks reminded me of a pond in midsummer, cool, clear, soft, and smelling of water weeds and lotus leaves.

For a moment, I was stunned. Then I turned and took off for home. I was going to report this to Mum.

Shuya called after me, 'Orange!' But I ignored her. I took the stairs in leaps and bounds and rushed in and yelled at my mother, 'It's incredible! I saw him!'

My mother was startled. 'What? What's incredible? And why all this shouting? Will you never learn to behave like a proper girl?'

I bent over, my hands on my knees, and tried to get my breath back and my words in some sort of sensible order.

Mum rubbed my back sympathetically, then smoothed down my hair, all the while admonishing me. 'Take your time, there's no hurry.'

Eventually, I stuttered out, 'Mum, did you know Shuya's courting?'

She looked at me for a long moment, then laughed, 'That's a big word for a little girl, "courting"!'

'Mum! If she's courting, she might leave us!'

She smiled. 'But the two of you have been sworn enemies all your lives! Wouldn't you be happy if she goes away?'

What did she mean? I was beginning to get annoyed with her for being dopey. Then, after a moment's thought, I came to a different conclusion. Mum had not been surprised. It could only mean one thing – she already knew.

'Mum!' I was aggrieved that she hadn't told me.

She reached out and mussed my hair. 'You're a good girl to come and tell me, Orange. You're always on my side. Now you can tell me what you think of him. What's he like?'

'He's OK. He has nice eyes.'

My mother burst out laughing. 'You're still such a baby! And what else is good about him?'

I thought for a moment. 'He's more polite than Shuya.'

'Well, that's something.'

'She had her arm on his shoulder. She must really like him!'

'Mind what you're saying! Don't talk like that to anyone else!'

'Really! I've never seen her with such a big smile

on her face.'

'I told you to mind what you're saying. You're to keep your mouth shut outside this house, understand?'

Fine, if she wouldn't let me talk, then I wouldn't. I hadn't seen anything anyway. I shut my eyes and conjured up the boy in my mind. Yup, he was a good-looker, just right for my pretty sister.

Pretty soon my dad knew too, but not from me. It was my mother who told him. Dad had a different way of looking at it. He didn't ask what he looked like. He was only bothered about the boy's family background and his education. Shuya said that his name was Cheng Yusheng, and he was a first-year student at West China Union University School of Medicine. She'd met him when she was away with the Sichuan Women's Battlefield Corps during the winter holidays. Yusheng's family lived on some pastureland near Chengdu. His father traded in salt and tea, so the family had a caravan of horses to transport their goods between Yunnan and Sichuan. She made a point of saying that as soon as war broke out, the Chengs had turned their horses over to the government to transport supplies and munitions. The family had received a special commendation for war work.

My dad listened silently. He said nothing, not even 'oh', or 'good'. Mum gave Shuya encouraging looks, urging her to say more, but there was no response from Dad. My sister had no idea what he was thinking and lapsed into silence.

Why was Dad being so silent? Did he approve or not? I felt anxious too, and just for once, I felt a smidgin of sympathy for Shuya.

The days flew by, and in no time at all, it was the Tomb-Sweeping Day again. The school gave us three days' holiday. Cheng Yusheng invited Shuya to go and stay with them. He dangled the prospect of horse-riding in front of her.

'What do you think?' Shuya asked Mum when she got home.

Mum sat my little brother down on the walkway, and tied an old bed sheet around his neck. Then she bent over, and started cutting his hair. 'It's up to you to decide,' she said.

It was obvious that Mum was against the idea, but didn't want to put her foot down. She wanted Shuya to work it out for herself. Grownups were so tricky!

Shuya wanted to go, but she didn't dare to go against Mum, so she turned to Dad for help. I thought my dad would turn her down flat, but he put down the current affairs magazine he was reading, and to our astonishment, said, 'Alright, go and see. It wouldn't be a bad thing if you spent a bit more time together.' My mother was still on the walkway, but she overheard and came rushing in, still with the scissors in her hand. 'What are you thinking of? She's just a girl and they're not even engaged. If anyone else finds out, whatever will they think?'

My dad calmly explained to Mum, 'Nowadays, we have to take free love and free marriage seriously. When a couple are courting, it's only by spending time together that they really get to know each other. Shuya is a high school student and Yusheng is at college. They're both mature and educated young people. Are you worried that they won't be able to practice self-control?'

My mother insisted, 'Shuya is still a child until she leaves for university. I'd be very worried if she went.'

My dad thought for a moment, then offered a compromise. 'Orange can go with her.'

I'd been skulking in a corner of the room eavesdropping, and when he said that, it was like an apple fell out of the tree and serendipitously landed on my head. 'Wow!' I exclaimed, and rushed over and gave him a hug and a big kiss on the top of his head.

Shuya frowned at me in disgust. From her glare, it was obvious she was dead against the idea. I ignored her. She wouldn't dare disobey my father, would she?

Before we went to sleep that night, Dad sat my sister down for a talk. I caught a few words. 'For girls nowadays, marriage matters but a career matters too... it's all right to have a boyfriend, but don't rush into a lifetime commitment...in another year you'll be going to college...' It all seemed very distant to me. I listened for a while but I was tired, and soon I was fast asleep.

The next day, Cheng Yusheng picked us up to take us both to his home. It was a dozen kilometres away, and we left after breakfast. We strolled along in the spring sunshine, in no particular hurry, looking at all the wildflowers and the bees buzzing excitedly over them, stopping to drink the water which Yusheng provided when we were thirsty. It was still morning when we arrived in the pastureland. What a pity we couldn't walk more through this lovely scenery.

Yusheng's father had gone with the horse caravan to Tengchong in Yunnan because he needed to collect an important consignment, and they didn't know when he would be back. His mother was a plump, kindly woman. She wore thin silk trousers, and had bound feet with little embroidered shoes. It was comical the way she swayed like a duck when she walked. Shuya was worried I would get the giggles, and squeezed my hand hard to stop me from laughing. When we started calling her 'Mother Cheng', she looked embarassed, and her cheeks went red. I immediately warmed towards her. My mother always said that people who blushed had good hearts. If she was right, then if Shuya married into the Cheng family, at least she wouldn't be bullied by this mother-in-law.

The lunch that Mother Cheng prepared for us was a feast. There was spicy boiled beef, chopped pepper fish, chilli-fried chicken, and all kinds of mushrooms that the family had brought back from Yunnan. In all the years we had lived in Huaxi Fields in Chengdu, our family never had more than two small meat dishes with our meals. My eyes nearly popped out of my head as dish after dish arrived on the table. I didn't know where to start.

After lunch, Mother Cheng was worried that we might be tired from our long walk, and insisted we took a siesta. My sister and I shared a big bed made of carved and gilded wood, with four handsome bed posts at each corner to hold up the gauze mosquito net. Before we got into bed, a big board was laid out with a low marble-topped table holding a mahogany fruit bowl, and snacks like walnuts, jujubes, cracker peanuts, and shredded dried beef. I was thrilled. I lay down on the bed, chewing some of the jerky, one leg stuck in the air, and told Shuya, 'You better decide to marry Yusheng. If you marry him, I can eat lovely food every day.' My sister pounced on me and clamped her hand over my mouth, hissing furiously, 'I'm not getting married, you greedy pig!'

After our siesta, we were each given a bowl of lotus seed and white fungus soup to drink. As we held our bowls between our hands, my sister and I couldn't help but exchange glances. This was not their usual fare, Yusheng told us quietly, but we were guests, and his mother had ransacked the larder to find all the best goodies to cook for us. And he was benefiting too, he said, looking at my sister with a fond smile.

The stables were impressive, spacious and well-ventilated. There was a row of stalls, piles of grass and fodder, and feeding troughs swept clean and neat. Yusheng told us that during his grandfather's time, his family had had as many as forty or fifty horses. The

Shandan horses of the Qilian Mountains were sturdy and strong, and could cover great distances. It was a pity that the stables were empty and the horses all away. There was just one filly tethered on some grass outside. She was a liver chestnut with black tips to her ears and tail. Her belly was round from all the grass she had eaten, and her coat shone in the sunlight as if it had been oiled. She stood among the wild flowers on the hillside, looking skittishly at us and idly flicking her long tail, as beautiful as a painting.

'This is the only one here at the moment,' said Yusheng. 'We can ride her.'

He went back to the stables and brought out a very fine saddle with silver ornaments. He soothed the filly and put the saddle on her back and fastened the girth tightly. Then he untied her rope and held the filly still so my sister could put her foot in the stirrups and climb up. The filly seemed to find someone getting on her back very strange. She pranced and reared, and butted Yusheng's arm with her head. My sister had one hand on the saddle and one foot raised to put in the stirrup when the filly swerved to one side. My sister's foot landed into empty space and she almost lost her balance. She turned pale with fright. She waved her hands at Yusheng and protested, 'No way, I'm not riding. She doesn't know me. You get on her.'

Yusheng looked embarassed. 'She's only young, she's still growing, she couldn't take my weight. If I did her an injury and my dad found out, he'd be furious.'

I saw my chance and butted in, 'Can I ride her? I'm a child.'

'You can if you're brave enough,' said Yusheng.

Of course, I was brave enough. There was nothing in the world that I was scared to try. I didn't even need Yusheng's help. I stood close to the saddle, grabbed a hank of the filly's mane, put my foot in the stirrup, and with one spring I was on the filly's back and looking down at Yusheng.

The world looked very different from on top of a horse. It was much smaller and Yusheng and my sister had turned into miniatures at my feet. The pastures stretched away into the distance and the clouds in the sky seemed so near that I could almost reach out and pull off a piece. I flapped my arms and legs to make the filly gallop, but Yusheng had a firm grip on the rope and was shouting in panic, 'No, Orange, no!'

It turned out that the filly had not been broken in. In fact, this was the first time she had been saddled.

It was all right to sit on her but if I really made her gallop, there might be a terrible accident, and that might be the end of me.

Yusheng held the halter carefully, and we made a slow circuit of the field. He kept trying to persuade me to get off. He promised that next time when the horses were home, he would fetch us over to ride a horse that had been properly broken in. I lay forward on the filly's neck and reached down to pinky-swear with him.

'And don't even think about breaking your promise,' I said. 'Otherwise Shuya will be nasty to you.'

For two days, my sister tagged along behind me. She got on the filly three times, for less than three minutes, and each time she shrieked and screamed, and made a fuss about nothing. I really could not understand it. Why was she deliberately acting like a baby with Yusheng? I was the complete opposite. I got on and my bum felt like it was glued to the saddle. The feeling of being so high up was amazing. How I wished I could swap with my sister – she could go and study at my girls' school, and I could stay at Yusheng's and ride horses.

The pastures in spring were so beautiful. It felt like

another world. The new grass was as soft and delicate as a baby's skin. It rolled away to the horizon and down into valleys, up and down, in endless billows. It was carpeted in wild flowers – purple, pink, yellow, blue – that swayed in the breeze, a dazzling array of colour when you were close to, but fading and merging with the green in the distance. The sunlight was diffuse, its rays pierced the gaps in the clouds, like glittering golden arrows landing on earth. I breathed in deep, filling my lungs, expanding my diaphragm, and the smell of green grass and fresh soil made me sneeze. In all our years spent in Huaxi Fields, I had never seen such a vast and magnificently beautiful land.

After the war ended, I moved back to Nanjing with my family and left Chengdu. I never returned to the grasslands, but it was not because Yusheng went back on his word. It was just that there are too many variables in life, and we humans can't always control what happens to us.

Chapter 13

Rice, Wheat, Cotton, Corn

Just at the height of the spring planting season, the government launched a recruitment drive among the Huaxi Fields students. My father's students, from University of Nanking Agricultural College, responded to the call, signed up, and went off in droves to southwest front, where the situation was grim.

Dad was heartbroken to see his precious students leave. He went home and thumped the table and yelled at Professor Mei, 'What is the government thinking of? Why are they sending these young people to the front? This is so short-sighted! This brutal war's going to end one day, and when that happens, four hundred million Chinese people will need to be fed and clothed! They'll look to the government for cotton and grain!

Where do they come from? Agriculture! Agriculture! We must develop agriculture! Wherever else they go, the army should not be recruiting from amongst our students.'

Professor Mei sucked on his pipe and said slowly, 'With the war dragging on so long, our forces are terribly depleted. They're in urgent need of good students. It makes sense. Warfare nowadays uses aircraft, tanks, and artillery. They don't need cannon, they need educated fighters. And where do they recruit them from if not the universities? Besides, your students weren't press-ganged. They signed up of their own free will. They want to serve their country. If I were younger, I'd grab any chance to go and fight for justice.'

'You're right. I know that,' Dad said. 'But the country's in a terrible state, and it's been a struggle to train up the few students I have. And soon we'll need them. They'll be the backbone of national reconstruction. It's such a shame.'

Professor Mei lapsed into silence, then sighed, 'Pray for these young people.'

The Agricultural College test fields were at the far end of Huaxi Fields. They covered a sizeable area. It was a busy time right now, the end of spring and early summer – pests had to be removed from the young wheat, and the rice and cotton seedlings needed planting out. The orange and lemon trees were just setting tiny, grape-sized fruits. Everything needed fertilizing, hoeing, weeding, debugging, selecting, and pollinating. And right when they were needed, there were hardly any students to do it, and no money to hire local labour. No wonder my father was frantic.

Dad's eyes lighted on his own children. Kejun, Shuya and Tianlu were seventeen and eighteen by now, and could do at least half a day's work. 'I need help in the fields. You and you,' said Dad, pointing at Kejun and Shuya, 'you can do an hour in the morning before you go to school and two hours after.'

'What about me, Uncle?' asked Tianlu.

'You stay home. Your mum needs help too.'

Tianlu always called my mother 'Mum' and my dad 'Uncle'. It was confusing but by now we were all used to it. Tianlu was handy around the house and more than willing to help out with the chores: he did food shopping, bought firewood, fetched water, did the laundry, and kept little Kid happy. Things that annoyed the hell out of us, he was quite happy to pitch in and do. He could carry full water buckets a foot tall, balancing one in each hand, and get them up the stairs without spilling a drop. A year ago, he was a weedy under-sized boy. When he suddenly shot up, it seemed to have given him confidence. He talked more, and was a lot more lively. He followed my mother around all day long, smiling cheerfully and busying himself with this and that. As Mrs Xing downstairs used to say, he was a better son than Kejun.

'Hasn't he grown, Mrs Huang!' she would say admiringly as she watched Tianlu tagging along behind Mum.

And Mum would smile and say, 'Well, that's thanks to everyone.'

Tianlu was a little afraid of my father, so when Dad told him to stay home, he did not dare object. But I was not afraid of Dad, and I was a junior high school student, why shouldn't I be included? So I asked him, 'When I get home at weekends, could I go and do some watering and weeding?' My father took a long look at my stick-like arms, and said, 'Give the war another three years and we'll be calling on you.'

Three years? I would be fifteen by then! And if the war really went on that long, what would happen to China? And to our family? It wasn't something I wanted to think about.

Kejun was in the third year of senior high, and had grown into a young man. He was slim and broad-shouldered, with thick eyebrows and large eyes, with a determined look in them. He was popular with teachers and his classmates, always reasonable, and made an impression wherever he went. He went to the test fields with my father, rolled up his trouser legs, and got down to work: he could carry full buckets on his carrying pole, transplant the seedlings as fast as any of the more experienced workers; in fact, he could turn his hand to anything. Of all of us, I think he was my father's favourite, the one in whom he saw most promise.

When I got back on Saturday afternoon, I went down to the test fields to see Kejun and Shuya. The grains in the wheat ears were beginning to fill out, and their green was paling into yellow, a sure sign that they were getting ripe. Soon there would be a bumper harvest, and after that, the baskets would be heaped high with fine white flour. The first person I saw was my father, dressed in one of the coarse tunics that the peasants wore hereabouts, his trousers rolled up to the calves. He was walking slowly along the ridge that marked the field boundary, bent double, giving the neat rows of wheat a close inspection. He had a large pair of scissors in one hand and the two pockets Mum had sewn into his tunic were bulging. Every now and then, he would climb down off the ridge and peer at an ear of wheat, comparing it to the plants on either side. He was concentrating hard but still could not make up his mind: he looked left and right, then stepped back a couple of paces and looked again, screwing up his eyes with concentration, as if he was a carpenter measuring a plumbing line. I knew he was inspecting every plant in the field so he could choose the champion specimen, the best of the best, to propagate.

Shuya was following my father, looking as intently as he was. She was wearing a short blue cotton jacket over her trousers, and a pointy bamboo sunhat tied tightly under her chin. It looked as if it had been oiled with tung oil and seemed to weigh heavily on her. She had a delicate, willowy frame, nothing like the robust peasant girl labourers. She held a small basket in one hand, and whenever my father chose a wheat plant, he would carefully cut the very top section of the bristle with his scissors. Then he turned around and signalled to my sister, who got a small paper bag out of her basket and blew on it to open it. They placed the specimen carefully into the bag and folded the top over tight. Then my sister took a label out and scribbled something on it with a pencil, and tied the label onto the plant with its length of string.

They looked like they made a good team, deftly selecting, cutting, wrapping and labelling. It was such a peaceful, beautiful scene that it could have been a painting.

When they got to the end of the field, my sister climbed up onto the bank while our father went on to another field to see how the cotton was growing. My sister took her hat off and I saw how sunburnt her face was. Her lips were cracked and flaking, and the backs of her hands were covered in red weals from the wheat bristles. They must have been very itchy because she kept scratching them.

'Where's Kejun?' I asked.

She jerked her chin in the direction of the cotton field where, quite far away, I could just about make up some squatting figures, though I was not sure which one was my brother.

'Are you coming home? Shall we wait for him?' I asked her.

'No, I'm itching all over. It's killing me. I want to go home and sit in the shade.'

I took her hat for her, and insisted on carrying the basket with the paper bags too.

I'd lived with Shuya all my life and I'd never before felt like doing anything for her.

The early summer sun was setting in the west, leaving half the sky tinged with purple and blue. The last glittering rays slanted down through the cloud layer, and the line of poplars along the field boundaries looked like they had been drawn by children with crayons. The colours were so gorgeous that I felt my eyes blur. A late-coming, yellow-beaked swallow swooped overhead and some early bats ventured out and flitted past. There were even double-winged, big-eyed dragonflies, whirling round low to the ground in great clouds. They reminded me of the Japanese planes that had dropped so many bombs on our heads last year.

If only the world could be this calm and happy forever! If only Dad and Kejun and Shuya could spend their time doing the stuff they loved and fulfilling all their desires.

But this peaceful scene was an illusion. Not far away,

just beyond Huaxi Fields, guns blazed and smoke hung over a land littered with the corpses of the dead, and the starving. That was the reality of existence in China.

Before the wheat ripened that year, something terrible happened. One morning, Dad went out as usual to check the fields. He climbed up onto the field boundary, and almost fainted at the sight that met his eyes: a large part of the wheat field that he had nurtured so carefully for the last six months, the precious plants that he had selected and snipped and labelled and bagged, his precious wheat varieties, had been cut down. All that were left were a few solitary stalks, standing forlorn and disconsolate.

Dad turned around and raced back home. He banged on Professor Mei's door and dragged him out of bed. 'What did I tell you? What did I say? The year before last, someone got the best cotton bolls and you said it was a good thing, because that way they got to know about good varieties, and you wouldn't let me investigate. Now look what's happened! My wheat! Most of my wheat! It's just gone, Mei!'

Professor Mei, his whiskers standing on end and his clothes awry, just muttered, over and over, 'Really? Bizarre! Bizarre!'

My father paced round and round the room in his distress. 'You only get one chance a year to select the best varieties, and if you don't do it, that's a whole year wasted. And it's not only me, it's my students too. They sweated blood to breed those varieties. Now they've gone to fight, and the seeds are all gone, they might as well not have bothered. All their hard work has gone for nothing. When they come back from the war, what can I tell them? And if they die on the battlefield, I can never make things right for them!'

Professor Mei sighed, 'The villagers need to be educated, they need education.'

'And there's another thing,' my father went on. 'They know nothing about scientific farming methods. In a couple of years, one hundred percent of all those improved varieties will have reverted, and we'll be back to square one. It's awful, too awful.'

Too awful it might have been, but one thing my father could not do was to conduct a house-to-house search for the stolen plants.

He decided to re-plant the field. It would be better than nothing. The quality was definitely not up to the first lot though. Even my sister could see that. She came home and told us that when they went around with scissors and a paper bag, the samples she collected were not as big and round as before.

Second time around, my father did not dare leave the field unguarded. He ordered that for the few days before the wheat was cut, there should be someone keeping watch night and day.

Daytime was fine, people were always in the fields working, and could keep an eye on the wheat. But doing guard duty by night was hard work. There were mosquitoes, you couldn't sleep, and you might even have to grab a stick and fight off the villagers. My father could not ask the students. He had to organize his children to do it. He sent Shuya back home, and Tianlu and Kejun went out to the fields.

Their first watch happened to be a Saturday and I was home. After they left that evening, my mother couldn't settle to anything, even sitting still. She was in and out of the house every other minute. Eventually I said, 'Mum, what's the matter?'

'I'm scared,' she said. 'Scared they'll get beaten up by someone.'

I piped up boldly, 'Why don't I go and take a look and see if they're all right?' Mum thought a bit, then agreed. She got out a bit of dried cattail and gave it to me. 'Go and take a look, and tell them to light this to keep the mosquitos away.'

I wrapped the cattail up in newspaper and added a box of matches. I'd just gone out of the door when Mum called me back and gave me a thin quilt to take. 'The dew's heavy at night. They might catch cold.'

I went through the courtyard gate, and out into a silent world. Overhead, there was a canopy of stars. The road was like a pale belt flung straight out in front of me, only bending when it passed behind the inky-black shapes of some farmhouses. Frogs croaked in the fields, a few dogs barked, and I heard a shrill cry coming from a big tree. It sounded like a child screaming but it was probably an owl. I suddenly remembered that evening a few years ago, another starry night, when Tianlu had gone with me to my piano practice at Ginling College, and we passed the cemetery, Tianlu waving his stick around telling me he was going to beat up the ghosts. I was scared as anything, but I'd only just started primary school. Now I was in junior high school and I knew there were no such things as ghosts. When people died, they turned into dust. Maybe ten, twenty or a hundred years afterwards, you might find a few bones left when you dug them up. I thought about the war, and all the ordinary people who'd died, and all the soldiers. If you scattered their bones over the ground, how much space would they take up? Then I thought of Dad's improved wheat varieties. Could they really make our country great and pull the villagers out of poverty?

So many thoughts were going through my head that I forgot to be afraid.

As I walked through the sleeping village, I wondered about the stolen wheat seeds. Had the thief come from this village? Would they try again tonight? I began to daydream: a door would creak and a man would sneak out of one of the hovels with a bag on his back. He would set off for my dad's test fields at a run, but I would be at his heels, and before he could jump down off the field boundary, I would give a shout, and Kejun and Tianlu would grab hold of him. Then we would truss him up and take him to Dad. How happy he would be.

The thought made me laugh. I got a better grip on the quilt slung over my shoulder and carried on walking.

I could just make out a light in the far distance, and wispy smoke rising into the air and wafting to and fro, like the long 'water sleeves' of opera actors. In the starlight, I could see two figures hunched over a fire, muttering to each other. It was so quiet that their voices carried quite a distance, though I still couldn't hear exactly what they were saying.

I called out their names and stumbled towards them. The quilt was bouncing up and down, and getting in my way, and by the time I plonked myself down beside them, I was puffing and panting.

'Orange! Why can't you learn to walk properly?' Kejun said disapprovingly as he took the quilt from me.

'Mum wanted me to bring this.'

'And this,' I took out the paper bag with the cattail and the matches. Then I realized they already had a fire lit, they were burning some black stuff. 'What's that?' I asked.

'Old rice husks. They're better than cattail, the smoke can kill any number of mozzies.'

'Who says?' I said, slightly annoyed that I had brought the cattail all this way for nothing.

My brother jerked his chin at Tianlu. 'When he was a kid and they were sitting out in the evening in the summer, they used to burn this stuff.'

'Where did you get it from?'

'We stole it.'

'Tianlu!' I exclaimed. 'You're both supposed to be

keeping the thieves away, and you're a thief yourself!'

Tianlu looked unhappy. 'He's pulling your leg. Why are you blaming me?'

'I was joking, sorry!' Kejun said. 'We bought a big pile for fifty cents, from that house over there. They had enough to fill half their firewood shed.'

I said nothing. I felt bad. Why had I picked on Tianlu? And why was he always so nice to me? Whatever I did, he forgave me.

It was weird the way these thoughts suddenly popped up in my mind. A bit scary.

I got a twig and poked the fire, just to create a diversion really. But Tianlu stopped me. 'When you burn rice husks, you need to make a slow-burning, smouldering fire. You want lots of smoke but no flames. That way, you smoke the mozzies.'

'You know everything,' I muttered.

Tianlu said nothing but Kejun laughed. I don't know what was so funny.

I went red in the face. Lucky they couldn't see.

After a while, I left them and set off home. Tianlu got up and said he'd see me on my way, but I insisted I would be fine.

The sky was clear and cold. I stopped for a

moment and strained my ears. I could hear the pitter-patter of dewdrops in the rice paddy. The stars seemed very far away, and further still, I could vaguely see a silvery strip. Was that the Milky Way? I imagined the star-crossed lovers, the Cowherd and the Spinning Maiden, gazing at each other across the Milky Way. I searched the skies for them, looked as hard as I could but I couldn't be sure. The sky was too big and my eyes were too small.

Chapter 14

The Book That Flew Across the Hump

Before we broke up for the summer holidays, we had one more set of exams. This time I did quite well, and didn't fail a single exam. The headteacher told everyone I was the student who had made the most progress in the whole school.

But there were two girls in my class who messed up half their exams. They sat in the head's office crying their eyes out and their parents had to be fetched to take them home. Apart from them, two others were leaving the class. One, a girl with a lisp, had the bed opposite me in the dormitory, and her father was an army division commander. He was off to Yunnan to relieve the garrison there, and from there to Burma. The girl was going with her family. And then there was the girl who'd been promised as a child bride since she was tiny, although she was still living with her parents. Her future family were not happy about her continuing her education and threatened to annul the contract if she didn't leave. Her parents could not decide what to do, but eventually felt that the marriage was more important, and pulled her out of school. The family servants came to fetch her, and practically had to tie her up. She kicked and fought, but it didn't do her any good.

With four fewer, the dormitory seemed very empty. 'Don't worry, there'll be more coming to fill the spaces,' my classmates told me. But I was sad. Friendships, love…why wasn't anything in this world forever?

The day after I got back home, a Sunday, I heard a shout from Sheona downstairs. I went down, and as soon as I got to her door, she grabbed me and pulled me inside.

'I haven't seen you for a week!' She hugged me and kissed my left cheek, then the right one. She felt warm, and I could smell a perfume, sweet and cloying. I took a look, and saw she had two creamy white magnolia flowers in her hair.

'I kept two for you!' she said, giving me two tied

together with thread. 'Put them in and let me look.'

But it was hopeless. My hair was too short and they kept falling down and hanging from my ears. She laughed her head off, then took them out and stuck them in my buttonhole.

'Why aren't you in church?' I asked.

'I told a fib. I said to Mum and Dad I wasn't feeling well. I know I shouldn't lie but I really wanted to see you. God will forgive me.'

I told her my school had broken up. We could spend every day together now.

'I'm on holiday but my mother's on holiday too, so I'm at home but I'm not free. I'm going to have to fight to get time to spend with you,' she said.

We lay on the bamboo recliner bed and told each other what had been going on at school. We talked about her schoolmates, my schoolmates, her teachers, my teachers. It sounded like they had a lot more rules in their school than we did. They had to pray several times a day, which must have been boring. Besides, we had PE classes, we could skip and play shuttlecock. She only had domestic science, etiquette, and needlework. 'Look what I did to my finger on the sewing machine,' she said, 'The needle went right through. It hurt so much, and I thought it was going to get infected!'

She had a big scab on her finger tip.

Mrs Xing came in with two bowls of liangfen noodles for us. When she saw us sprawled out on Sheona's mother's big bed, she shrieked, 'Ai-ya! Don't lie with your legs wide open like that! What a way to behave! Girls should sit properly and lie properly! Whatever would your mummy think?'

Sheona mimicked her cheekily, 'My mummy's gone out!'

We both began to laugh like crazies. Sheona whispered in my ear, 'Isn't it nice when Mum's out!'

Mrs Xing's liangfen noodles were tender and slippery. She had flavoured them with red chilli pepper and yellow mustard and green coriander. When we had finished, we looked at each other's red-stained mouths and went off into fits of laughter again.

Suddenly Sheona asked, 'Do you think Mark likes chilli pepper yet?'

'Don't you eat chillis in America?'

She shook her head.

I thought for a moment. 'He's in Yunnan. They eat chilli pepper in Yunnan, so he must like it by now.'

'I think so too. Next time he visits, we'll invite

him over for liangfen.'

Sheona had an idea. She got up and went to the bookshelf, and took out a big fat book in English called *This Above All,* by Eric Knight. The cover was a picture of a handsome soldier and a woman in a nurse's uniform. They were holding hands and looking lovingly at each other.

'Is it a novel?' I asked.

'It's a best-seller in Britain. It's about a soldier and a nurse, a war-time love story. It's really good. When Mark was sent to India, he bought a copy and sent it to me.'

So this book had gone over 'The Hump' just like Mark. The Hump was the world's most difficult and dangerous flight path. What a wonderful present.

'Do you want to read it?' Sheona asked.

I was doubtful. 'I don't think my English is good enough. Look how fat it is.'

She pushed it into my hands. 'I've finished it. You borrow it. If there are things you don't understand, come and ask me.'

I couldn't refuse. I took the book upstairs, and proudly showed it off to Kejun and Shuya.

'This book came over the Hump!' I told them.

My brother gave it a cursory glance, then said scornfully, 'It's for girls, it's a love story!'

As soon as Shuya heard it was a love story, she grabbed it off me. She stumbled over the title. 'This – this – whatever does this mean?'

Kejun thought for a moment. 'You could translate it into Chinese as "Higher than anything",' he said.

'Yes, because love is higher than anything else,' Shuya said, sounding coy. Just the mention of the word 'love' made her go all gooey and starry-eyed and she hadn't even read the first page of the book.

I never did get the novel back off her. Her excuse was that she needed to read it to improve her English. She borrowed my dad's English dictionary, and every now and then stopped reading to look up a word. Dad had brought that dictionary all the way from Nanjing, and he treasured it. I don't know what he would have said if he'd found out that his beloved dictionary was being used to read a romantic novel.

It took Shuya more than two weeks to read it. Every day she sat glued to her stool from morning till night, ignoring everyone, including our mother. She hated the mosquitoes so, after we'd gone to bed, she pulled the lamp to her side of our bed and got under the mosquito net, and kept on reading. It was hot in summer, and one night she left the light on too long and too close to the mosquito net, and the net started to smoulder. Luckily, I got up to pee, and smelled burning and yanked the net away from the bulb. Disaster was averted, but Shuya knew my mother would be furious with her so she swore me to secrecy. She sewed up the hole herself, then made it really obvious by sewing a scrap of patterned material on top. But our mother was much too busy to notice a little thing like that in any case, and my sister got away with it.

One day, Sheona asked me, 'Have you read *This Above All*?'

I had to confess I hadn't read a single page. 'Shuya's reading it,' I muttered.

Sheona's eyes sparkled. 'It's perfect for her!' she exclaimed. 'I mean she's got a boyfriend now, hasn't she!'

What was it that made girls go all silly as soon as anyone mentioned boys and romance? I just didn't get it.

'So what's the book about?' I asked my sister when I got home.

She looked like she was in a dream. She blinked

at me vaguely for a long time, then flung herself down on the bed, the open book clasped tightly to her chest, and pronounced dramatically, 'Orange, you wouldn't understand. It's about the most beautiful, most romantic thing in the world! It's about longing and yearning!'

That was too much. I thumped the table and laughed and laughed till I nearly choked. Shuya looked at me with loathing, 'You numbskull.'

A little while later, she added pityingly, 'When will you ever grow up? Will any boy ever like you? When will you ever get a taste of love?'

And she gazed misty-eyed into the distance. Suddenly it occurred to me that I hadn't seen her handsome hunk of the grasslands, Cheng Yusheng, for ages. This summer holiday Shuya hadn't once mentioned his name.

What was going on? Was love really so lovely? To me it was all one big riddle.

Chapter 15
The Translators

That summer, all the universities put up enrolment lists, and Kejun was offered a place at Yenching University to study journalism.

Dad was not at all happy about that. He'd always wanted Kejun to follow in his footsteps and study agronomy. The way he looked at it, China was an agricultural country with a large population, a shortage of arable land and an uncertain climate. The spectre of famine had stalked China for thousands of years. Farming practices absolutely had to be improved for China to take its proper place in the post-war world, so agronomy was the way to serve our country and its people. Uncle Fan downstairs had a different opinion: in his view, Kejun was clever, thoughtful, and dependable in a way that few young people were, so medicine was for him. He declared, in his strongest Sichuan accent, 'What do you need to save the country and the people? A scalpel! You Chinese believe the Bodhisattva rescues people from pain and suffering, don't you? Well, nowadays doctors are Bodhisattvas!'

Sheona clapped her hand over her mouth to stifle a laugh.

But no matter how much Dad and Professor Fan wanted my brother to follow in their footsteps, he was going to take up journalism. He wanted to fight this war with his pen and make the best contribution he could in his own way.

Kejun was very methodical. As soon as he'd enrolled in the journalism department, he got hold of the curriculum for the four-year course and read it from start to finish. He immediately spotted a problem: photography was a key element of the course. A journalist who could not take pictures was useless, not a proper journalist at all.

But photography was the domain of the rich back then. Just getting hold of a Leica camera was a near impossibility for ordinary folk. And then there was everything else you needed: film, darkroom, enlarger and chemicals – developer and fixer. It was all terrifyingly expensive.

Kejun always wanted to be the best at everything he did. That was the kind of person he was. When he was little, his classmates always beat him in school races. So he went home and begged Mum to make him two heavy sandbags which he tied to his calves and practised running to and from school. A year of that, and he came first in the city-wide primary schools 800 metres race. Now he'd signed up for journalism, he absolutely needed to take pictures as well as write.

He borrowed my father's bike and spent two days riding around the city, poking through all the markets, second-hand shops and out-of-the-way nooks and crannies where someone might have a stall. Then he came home, got a bit of paper and did some sums. He seemed very relieved. 'The prices are not too bad,' he said. 'These people used to have a lot of money but they lost it all when they fled the war zones and in Chengdu they're barely scraping by. They've been pawning their belongings, and taking whatever they can get for them.' And he ticked off on his fingers the kind of things he had seen going for a song in the markets: art and antiques, Buddhist figurines and porcelain. 'Everyone's having such a hard time,' he said with a sigh.

He had a reporter's instinct for a story even before he started the course.

But no matter how cheap a camera was, it was way beyond our reach. By that time, the war had bled the country and the people dry. The price of rice went higher every month while university teachers only received about eighty percent of their salaries. Luckily, our parents got a reduction on our school fees, and we also got food subsidies from the government. Otherwise, we would have been in dire straits, with only Dad's salary to keep us.

My brother shut himself in his room and racked his brains for a way to make the sums add up. Then he had an idea: *This Above All*, the novel my sister was reading, was a huge best-seller. Why not translate it into Chinese? If he could translate it and find a publisher, he could earn substantial royalties.

He put his plan into action the very next day. He got Shuya to go with him and they approached a local magazine publisher. Kejun introduced himself and his plan, and then Shuya told the story of the book. My sister was articulate, spoke passionately and made the story come alive. She'd just read it from cover to cover, and she knew the plot and the characters off by heart. She performed her role brilliantly. The editor was won over. He made up his mind to serialize the novel as soon as possible. He was confident that after that, they could publish it in hardback and paperback throughout unoccupied China, as well as Hong Kong, Southeast Asia, and even occupied areas such as Beijing and Shanghai. They were looking at sales of 10,000 copies, or maybe 50,000, or even 100,000. A publishing sensation in the making!

'What a wonderful story! What wonderful characters! This is just the right time to publish a novel like this. It will really boost morale. It's exactly what's needed!' The editor shook Kejun by the hand, his voice trembling in excitement.

Kejun was over the moon. He came home and poured each of us a bowl of cold water. 'Imagine it's wine, and wish me luck!' he said. My sister was as excited as he was. She picked up Kid and whirled around the room with him in her arms, shrieking, until our mother yelled back at her, 'You're crazy!' Tianlu said nothing, just got busy setting up the writing desk for Kejun, and laying out pen and paper and anything else he might need, like glue and paper clips.

Then Kejun chased Su and Kid out of the room and locked the door, leaving just the four of us inside. I was pleased as punch to have been included. After all, I was only a junior high schooler, but I was ready to work day and night if I could help out.

Kejun divided up the tasks: he had the best English out of the four of us, so he was the translator. Shuya knew the book inside out, and wrote fluently and had beautiful handwriting, so she became the proof-reader, making corrections and edits. Tianlu was methodical and had good writing too, so he was in charge of making the fair copy. As Kejun emphasized, 'Transcribing's crucial. If the handwriting's not clear, the editor won't be able to read it.'

'What about me?' I asked plaintively, after all the work had been divvied up.

'You can pour the tea,' said Shuya, glancing at me.

I was mortified.

Kejun patted my head. 'You've got an important job to do. You look words up in the dictionary. For instance, if I say, "perfume, what does that mean?" you look under "P", quick as you can, and tell me what it says. You'll save me loads of time, which is great.'

Hey, that was good. I liked the sound of that. And for once, I'd be in charge of Dad's big English dictionary.

That afternoon, Dad came home to find us shut up in the boys' room, quiet as mice. That was so unusual that he knocked and came in. When we told him what we were doing, he was pleased. 'It's a good learning experience for you all to be doing something practical.' Then he added, 'But a romantic novel? It's fine for you to dip into it, but don't get too engrossed. It won't help our country or our people.'

'Why do you have to bring everything back to our country and our people, Dad?' muttered Shuya, rebelliously.

Dad looked at her, surprised. 'Well, what else would you all be thinking about in times like these?'

My sister made a face. She couldn't think of anything to say.

Dad relented. 'It's really hot! Open the window so you get a breeze. And I'll ask your mother to make you some cold mung bean soup. That'll keep you cool.'

'That's more like it, Dad!' Shuya said happily. Dad smiled and went out to talk to Mum.

We had the first draft ready in a week, and Kejun and Shuya went to hand it in. Tianlu and I waited at home, on tenterhooks to hear how it went. We chatted as we waited, and Tianlu told me Kejun had translated the first chapter really well. It read better than anything the famous translator Lin Shu had done. Any reader would be drawn right in and wouldn't want to put it down.

'Who's Lin Shu?' I asked him. 'What novels did he translate?'

Tianlu ticked them off on his fingers: *Uncle Tom's Cabin*, *La Dame aux Camélias*, *Robinson Crusoe*...He mentioned a dozen or more.

I'd never seen Tianlu reading any of these books. I reckoned that he was just repeating what he'd heard, and told him so. He flushed. 'It's true. I haven't read all of them, but our Chinese teacher's talked about them.' His Chinese teacher, apparently, was a bachelor in his forties who always had his nose in a book. He read his way through whole bookshops, so Tianlu said.

'Amazing, right? Imagine how much he spends on books!'

'Sure, he sounds amazing, but why's your book-loving teacher still single? Surely not because women don't like a bookworm?'

Tianlu was evasive, and finally admitted. 'He's bald. The top of his head's shinier than a light bulb.'

I rolled around on the bed, laughing my head off. The idea of an old guy with a shiny bald pate raving on about *La Dame aux Camélias* was just too funny.

Tianlu frowned. 'You know what? The way you're laughing makes me think that girls always judge people by their appearances.'

I retorted, still chortling, 'Boys do that even more! See how many boys in your class are crazy about Shuya!'

He gave me a severe look and pressed his lips together.

'You're going red!' I teased him. 'Admit it, you like her too!'

He sighed and looked at me sadly. 'Orange, why don't you grow up?'

I sat up and went to the table. There I found a pen and made a sketch of a bald man. First, a circle for his face, then his eyes, nose, and ears. Then I wondered how to draw the top of his head. How did you draw a bright shine?

I could feel Tianlu looking at me as though he wanted to say stuff but I ignored him and refused to look up. He was so boring. We were talking about Shuya, and next thing, he's blaming me for being childish.

When Kejun and Shuya came back, they were jubilant. I heard the joy in my sister's voice when they arrived and she called out a greeting to Mrs Xing. They'd brought a bag of red bean ice lollies and handed them out. They even persuaded Mum to try one. I didn't need to ask, it was obvious they'd made a big hit with the translation.

There was a man with them I'd never seen before. He was quite short, with skinny arms and legs, and small features. He gesticulated a lot when he spoke, and made strange faces. It was hard to tell how old he was, maybe twenty, but he could have been thirty. There was an aura about him that was hard to describe, but was powerfully attractive. It was as if he was giving off heat, the way the sun did, and if you were drawn into his orbit, you'd never get out again.

My brother introduced him to Tianlu and me, 'This is Mr Li. He's the literary editor of *Tide* magazine – they're going to serialize *This Above All* – and he's a poet too.'

The man greeted us, bowing over his cupped hands in the old-fashioned way. 'Victory Li, I've just changed my name to Victory.'

I couldn't help laughing. 'But we haven't got

victory yet!' He turned deadly serious. 'It'll come one day, it'll come.'

'Mr Li is our editor,' Shuya put in. 'He thinks this novel is very timely. People need novels like this to cheer them up. Right, Mr Li?'

Li raised his brows. 'Very timely indeed! The more we're in a dark place, the more we must lift our arms towards the light! Have you read Gorky's poem *The Song of the Stormy Petrel*? Listen, it goes like this:

'High above the silvery ocean,

Winds are gathering the storm-clouds.

And between the clouds and ocean,

Proudly wheels the Stormy Petrel,

Like a streak of sable.'

He stretched out his short arms, raised them high, and flapped them as if he was flying. 'The people's war is the ocean, the storm clouds are the hated Japanese enemy, and we're the stormy petrels flying towards victory.'

Mr Li's recitation was a bravura impromptu performance. We had never come across anyone quite like this, so passionate, so boundlessly heroic. Tianlu stood there dumbfounded, forgetting to suck on his lolly. I could see it dripping all over the floor. Kejun showed no signs of surprise, no doubt because he'd already experienced the poet's fervour in the magazine office. Shuya, meanwhile, held the lolly between her teeth so she had both hands free and could applaud him.

'That's great! Great!' Her eyes shone.

So this was what poets did, I thought to myself. They roused their audiences by declaiming verses like a stage performer. There was a Chinese teacher who took the senior classes at our school, a man in his fifties. He used to get intoxicated by Chinese classical poetry, shaking his head back and forth as he recited it. The difference was that our teacher got carried away all on his own. Mr Li was different. There was something demonic about him, as if he could suck someone's soul away. I was a bit worried Shuya might lose hers.

Mr Li asked Kejun if he could see his copy of *This Above All*. He burbled about how fascinating the book was. What could be more sublime that a story of love on the battlefield? So moving! He thanked us on behalf of all hot-blooded young people in China for this very proper task we had undertaken. For China today, this novel was like a call to arms, or rather, a battle cry. In fact, it was a more effective rallying cry than any government call-up, because it was imbued with the power of literature, it was a call to believe.

He went on and on for so long that I'd finished the last drop of lolly by the time he stopped. The words poured out in an unstoppable torrent, like an avalanche sweeping all before it.

He finished by making a suggestion. 'Objectively speaking, *This Above All* is a bit abstract as a title, not very romantic. How about *Love and Death*? Or *Farewell My Love*?'

My brother looked awkward. 'But the English book title is *This Above All*, surely the translation should be faithful to the original?'

'You can be flexible.'

My sister supported him enthusiastically. 'I think so.'

But Kejun was sticking to his guns. 'We should give it proper thought. Why don't I ask the English professor at Yenching University?'

Li waved his hand deprecatingly. 'It's just an idea. You don't have to change the title.'

He opened the book, flicked through to the last page, and then flicked back to the beginning. He didn't look at any of the words, I noticed. It occurred to me that, like me, he probably couldn't read the English. But then I felt guilty. I shouldn't be so petty-minded.

Shuya insisted that he stay for dinner. Mum

bustled around, frying up some bacon and steaming a large bowlful of eggs. But Mr Li hardly seemed to notice what he was eating. He was busy talking to my dad, analyzing the situation at the front, the Wang Jingwei government's collaboration with the Japanese occupiers in Nanjing, the failure of the German army at Stalingrad, Japan's support for Myanmar's independence, and the dissolution of the Comintern. He talked about Yan'an and about Mao Zedong's *On Protracted War*, which he promised to send to my dad the next day. 'It's very incisive about the war, extremely profound,' he declared.

After he left, my dad paced up and down with his hands clasped behind his back, then stopped and said, 'This man is very interesting. Is there anything he doesn't know?' Then he asked, 'What's the background of the magazine? Does it have links with Yan'an?' No one answered. Kejun and Shuya looked bewildered by Li's tirade, as if they needed time to digest it.

The serialization of *This Above All* was a runaway success. When the first issue of *Tide* came out, it sold out within three days. It was re-printed, and sold out again. For the second installment, the editor-in-chief decided to bite the bullet and print 10,000 copies straight up. The newspaper boys went out selling, and were surrounded by readers clamouring for their copy as soon as they were spotted in the street. The editor-in-chief was so happy that he invited all the editors to dinner that night, and he made sure that Kejun and Shuya got an invite too.

'It's just like it was when Zhang Henshui serialized his novels all those years ago! He was such a popular novelist.' Mum sighed nostalgically.

Actually, the novel was a hit because of the translation, and the translation's success meant that my brother had enough to buy his camera.

I still remember the day, just before the end of the summer holidays, when he bought an old Leica in a mouldy old leather camera case and brought it home. He roamed around the compound in a high state of excitement. He snapped my mother, he snapped Su and Kid, and he snapped a pair of Professor Mei's crested silkies, a cock and a hen. Then he took pictures of the busy-lizzy and canna flowers, and the persimmon fruit that were as big as a fist by now. At Shuya's special request, he did some close-ups of her, and swore that she would look classier than any filmstar.

Then he and Tianlu blocked out the light in their

room by covering the window with an old army mat, and wrapped red paper round the lightbulb, to make an improvised darkroom. He chased us all out of the room, but kept Tianlu to help him. They were at it all night, using up bottles of developer and fixer, but the photographs they developed were out of focus and blurry.

No one minded except Shuya, who had been on tenterhooks to see her portraits. She was furious. 'You're such an idiot!' she yelled at him.

Kejun looked shame-faced. He tried to explain that things often didn't work out the first time around.

'Fine! Carry on trying!' she said, and pulled down the red paper to rub on her lips and use as lipstick.

But Kejun didn't dare take any more pictures. He'd only bought two rolls of film and had used up one. The camera hadn't cost much but films were pricey and he was worried about wasting a lot of money.

Then, when he started his course and had learned a little bit about photography, he took the unexposed roll of film to a photo studio, and got the technician to divide it into three or four smaller rolls. He thought that would be a good way of eking out what little film he had. If he took bad photographs, or messed up the developing of one mini-roll, it wouldn't be the end of the world.

So Shuya got her filmstar pictures in the end. We kept them in the family album for years. Before my mother died, she used to take the album out and look at them for minutes on end, smoothing them out with her fingers, sometimes muttering to herself as she did so.

I'll never forget those photos: Shuya had her hair in two long shiny braids, her fringe curled with curling tongs, nice and even and curving over her eyebrows, setting off her porcelain skin and oval face. Even in black and white, you could see how satin-smooth and plump her skin is. Flawless. What's interesting is that in the photos, her head was tilted at a forty-five degree angle, and her eyes were focussed on a point at the top right corner of the picture. She was not gazing romantically into the distance. She had her eyes wide open in wonder, ready for anything life was going to throw at her. If you looked closely, her eyes were sparkling, like stars falling on the lake.

My sister was seventeen, as stuck up as a princess and as merry as a magpie. She had no idea how fragile life is, how sometimes a star falls to earth with a big thud and turns to dust.

Chapter 16
The Bookshop

The Heaven and Earth Bookshop was on Clearwater Road. The owner was an overseas Chinese who had apparently made his money as a rubber plantation owner in Malaysia. When he got to fifty, he handed over the property to his children to manage and came back home to China. One of his forebears had passed the imperial exams and he had inherited his love of learning. Besides, he enjoyed the company of book-lovers, so he put some of his money into a bookstore. In fact, he had so much money that he didn't need to make any more with the bookstore. It was just a bit of fun for him, a way of making friends. The Huaxi Fields students used his shop as a library and went there in their free time to browse the books, drink tea, and chat, sometimes for hours on end. The Heaven and Earth Bookshop was always bustling.

The first time I went there with Shuya was during that summer. Kejun had been paid for the translation of *This Above All*, and generously divided the fee between us, depending on how much we'd contributed. Tianlu refused to take his money. He said he'd just spent a few days copying the manuscript, and it was good practice for him. Besides, he was fed and clothed, and he had nothing to spend the money on. Fine, said Kejun, he'd save it up for Tianlu.

Shuya and I took ours. We didn't have any scruples. After all, he was our brother, which Tianlu wasn't. I wanted to spend mine on books. I'd begun to become obsessed with novels by authors like Lin Yutang, Ba Jin, Mao Dun, and even plays by Cao Yu, like *Thunderstorm* and *Sunrise*. I loved them all. These novels and plays taught me so much about how people lived in China. They opened one window after another in my mind: infighting within feudal clans, standoffs between workers and capitalists, and how the oppressed could stand up for themselves. I gradually began to sense that the country and society I lived in was a turbulent place, and something brand new was on its way, something lumbering towards us on a giant's feet, or rolling across the sky like great clouds, or a tidal wave, something that would turn our world upside down.

Not long before, I'd picked up a book by Lu Xun too, one that Mr Li had recommended to Kejun and Shuya. It was called *Weeds*. I flicked through it, but I didn't understand much. 'You're not supposed to understand it,' Kejun told me. 'Lu Xun didn't write for children.' I breathed a sigh of relief. I was beginning to worry that it was because my reading level wasn't good enough.

Mr Li had also told Shuya about this bookshop where you could read the books for free, so she was good enough to offer to take me there.

Obviously, being able to read books for free was an irresistible draw for a highschooler like me.

We set off from Pomegranate Gardens. We had to ask a few times, and it took us a while to finally spot the carved wooden sign on Clearwater Street: Heaven and Earth Bookshop. The black-painted door was so small that we almost missed it, it looked like the entrance to someone's home. We pushed it open, went inside – and found ourselves in a different world. It was the middle of the day, but all the lights were on. There were serried ranks of tall bookshelves, and everywhere young people, standing, sitting, propped against the walls, or huddled in pairs whispering together. Ones without the money to buy a book they'd read and liked very much, just found a windowsill to rest their notebook on, and were bent over, copying the whole book out! Others strolled around and gawped, without reading or buying anything, and the shop assistants simply left them alone. The funniest thing was two girls of about seven or eight sitting cross-legged in the corner, engrossed in a game of cat's cradle. Perhaps they were here because it was nice and cool indoors, or because it was a fun place to be.

'No wonder this place is so full. It's very relaxed!' Shuya whispered to me in surprise.

She pulled me by the hand and we walked around the shop looking for a place to settle ourselves down. There was a small tea room to the left of the cashier. We walked through and came to a half-open door, beyond which someone was reciting in dramatic tones. My sister came to a sudden stop, and exclaimed joyfully, 'Oh my God, it's Mr Li!'

Without a moment's thought, we went straight

in. The room was small and airless, and crowded with people sitting on benches. Their faces shone with sweat, and there were patches of sweat on their chests and back too. There were also two men who looked a bit older than the students. They were dangling lighted cigarettes between their fingers, and the smoke curled up and hung above everyone's heads. The air was so foul that as soon as we went in, I felt like I was suffocating, and had to hold my breath.

Mr Li, in a grey T-shirt and a pair of very baggy black trousers, stood on a high-backed chair at one end of the room. The sweat was dripping off him as he talked about the book in his hand. He was holding it open and I spotted a bright red flag on its cover, and a picture of someone in a fur-trimmed hat on a horse. Maybe because we were in midsummer, just the sight of the fur hat made me feel weird. My scalp prickled.

Victory Li was reading a passage with great eloquence, 'Life gives us a huge gift of infinite nobility. That gift is youth. The springtime of youth is brimful of effort and expectations, aspirations, and ambitions to seek knowledge and to struggle, full of hope and confidence.'

'The springtime of youth.' That was the first time I'd heard the expression and it struck me as an odd thing to say.

It took me a few moments to understand the connection between springtime and being young. So that meant school students, right? I knew what hope and confidence were but what did struggle mean? Fighting the Japanese? Could be, but then again, maybe not. Anyway, I thought the words he was reading came across as very fresh, quite different from the language in English and American novels, and from Ba Jin's and Lin Yutang's novels. I had a glimmer of understanding. How I wished I understood more of it. My heart was going pitter-patter with excitement.

When he'd finished reading the paragraph, Mr Li looked up from the book and sighed. At that moment, he suddenly saw Shuya and me in the doorway. 'Ah-hah!' he cried enthusiastically, jumped off the chair and came over to us. 'It's the Misses Huang! I'm so glad to see you here! Come in, someone move up and give them some space on a bench!'

Two bespectacled young men kindly gave up their bench to us. Mr Li pulled us over and sat us down. This meeting, he explained, was a reading group organized by the bookshop. Every week, a speaker was invited to talk about their favourite books. This week it was his turn and he was talking about a Soviet Russian novel *How the Steel Was Tempered*. He gesticulated energetically and laughed. 'Don't get the wrong idea. It's not a book about how to make steel. It's a novel about a Red Army soldier named Pavel Korchagin. How brave and magnificent his life is. It's a great book, and Pavel korchagin is a great hero! Hold on a moment, please. I'll read you another paragraph.'

He hurried back to his chair and jumped up on it again. Striking a pose, he opened the book at a dog-eared page. 'Listen, everyone, this is the most brilliant passage in the book.'

He paused, his eyes lighted on at my sister, and then swept the room. When he was sure we were hanging on his words, he read in solemn tones. 'The most precious thing in life is life itself, and we each only live once. We should live it so that when we look back, we don't regret having wasted it. When we're dying, we should be able to say that our whole lives and all our energies have been dedicated to the noblest cause in the world, the fight for the liberation of humankind.'

He closed the book, thrust his hands into the air, and his voice blazed out. 'What is the liberation of humankind? It means that everyone has enough to eat and clothes to wear, we have equality, and the world is united. And what it means today, is that the Nationalists and the Communists should join hands, fight together to drive out the Japanese, and build the democratic society we dream of! Today in the twentieth century, the old era is past and gone and a new dawn is in front of us. The great Soviet Union is our role model. Pavel Korchagin is our role model. At this great and solemn moment in history, we must not spare our efforts! We must fight!'

By now, he was pouring with sweat, actually dripping, as if he'd been fished out of the water. His hair stuck to his forehead like a piece of black plaster. From half across the room, I could feel the energy and heat radiating from his body. It was crazy.

As we left the bookshop, Shuya was elated. 'What do you think of Mr Li?' she burst out.

I thought for a moment. 'He's like a fireball,' I said.

'You're so right!' she gushed, and clapped her hands. 'He's living poetry! Just what poets should be like.'

I didn't answer. I was thinking all the way home. Were poets like silkworms, their bellies full of silk thread which they vomited out when they opened their mouths?

Shuya was in a high state of excitement for days after that. Victory Li was all she talked about, to Kejun, to Tianlu, to Dad.

'You should all go and listen to him. He's so interesting! He's unique! And that book, it's so well-written, I'm going to buy a copy!'

And she really did buy a copy of *How the Steel Was Tempered*. Our whole family took turns reading it. Kejun thought it was really good. 'Touching', was how he described it. Tianlu asked my sister, 'Do you think someone like Pavel Korchagin really exists?' My dad had only read the beginning when he got an invitation from the Chongqing government to discuss setting up an agricultural project with international partners. By the time he came back, the harvest had begun and he never had time to sit down and finish it.

I swiped the book one day and lent it to Sheona who read it but told me that she couldn't understand why, since Pavel and Tonya were so in love and Tonya was such a beautiful and good-hearted girl, they couldn't be together. Surely love was more important than this thing called revolution?

I didn't know what to say to that. Love and

revolution were both such faraway things, they were completely beyond me. Besides, the Russian names were so long and tongue-twisting. Even at the end of the book, I couldn't remember who was who and what they were to each other.

Shuya persuaded Kejun and Tianlu to join the bookshop reading group. Their first day, Mr Li was there again as visiting speaker. He was talking about P. B. Shelley's famous *Ode to the West Wind*, and recited:

'O wild West Wind, thou breath of Autumn's being,

Thou, from whose unseen presence the leaves dead

Are driven, like ghosts from an enchanter fleeing...'

My brother muttered *sotto voce*, 'I'm glad he didn't read the last line, "If winter comes, can spring be far behind?" It's such a cliche, everyone quotes that.'

My sister jabbed him hard in the ribs. 'Don't be so mean, just listen properly!'

Kejun and Tianlu went once and refused to go again. My brother said that he prefered calm discussion and intellectual analysis of the current situation and the war, and the atmosphere of the reading club didn't suit him at all. Tianlu said it was a waste of time. After the summer holdiays were over, he was starting his last year in senior high school and wanted to put all his energies into getting into University of Nanking to do chemical engineering. He was going to rebuild China by helping to build up its industry. He said that was what Dad wanted for him too.

'But you're not Dad, you can make a choice about what you want to do,' Shuya told him earnestly.

'No, I've got to follow his advice. He can't be wrong,' Tianlu insisted.

'But Tianlu, we're not a feudal family.'

'I know. It's what I want.'

Shuya looked at him sorrowfully. He was obviously a lost cause.

My sister had to drag me along with her to the bookshop, since no one else would go. For the whole of the last half of the holidays, I tagged along as her pageboy, footman, servant, what have you. But some of the shine rubbed off on me too. Every time we stepped in through the door of the tiny back room, everyone rushed up to Shuya, ready to admire and wait on her – and I found myself swept along in her wake. I began to fantasize that all young women were universally welcomed and waited on.

We got to the last day of the holidays.

Summer was going out in a blaze of heat. Although the sun was hidden behind a thick cloud layer, it was stuffy and humid, and even the cobbles on the roads and the brick walls on either side seemed to sweat. The cicadas screeched mournfully in the trees. Far in the distance there were distant rolls of thunder, like artillery fire, which made me feel uneasy.

'It feels like a storm's coming,' I said to Shuya.

'What are you worried about? The more violent the storm the better, so Gorsky said in his stormy petrel poem, It's the storm! The storm is breaking! Let it break in all its fury! She squared her shoulders, lifted her head high, and pranced along on the balls of her feet as if she was dancing.

I tried to imitate her and lifted my arms as I walked, but I couldn't keep my arms and legs moving in time. I looked like an idiot.

We didn't see Mr Li that day. Shuya asked the shop assistant but she said that his magazine was going to press so he couldn't get away. A senior sociology student from Cheeloo University gave a lecture on religious studies in Tibet instead. It was all too deep for me. I couldn't understand a word of it, and I saw my sister fidgeting too, maybe because Victory Li wasn't there.

Halfway through the lecture, the storm broke. There was a crack of thunder and the rain came down in torrents. Looking out of the window at the roofs opposite, it was like the onslaught of a massive army, wave after wave of water, then a great fog descended.

The rain was so heavy that the customers in the bookstore couldn't leave for a while, and they all gravitated towards the bookclub. The room was already packed and the rest had to stand. The speaker mistook this for enthusiasm and gave himself an extra half hour for his talk.

Finally the talk finished and by then, the rain had eased off a little. Filthy water was pouring down the middle of the street, carrying with it a mass of dead twigs and leaves. Miniature waterfalls cascaded down off the corrugated roof tiles like someone was peeing. Those who couldn't wait for the rain to stop rolled their trousers up, tucked their heads into their jackets, and sploshed through the water. School was starting tomorrow and Shuya still had some holiday homework to finish, so she decided to go too, and too bad if we got home looking like drowned rats.

We were wearing skirts, so all we needed to do

was roll up our waistbands a bit and we were ready to go. We decided to take our espadrilles off so they wouldn't get soaked, and tucked them under one arm. Just as we were about to step out into the rain, Cheng Yusheng suddenly appeared, holding a yellow oilcloth umbrella over his head and a folded patterned paper umbrella under one arm.

'Hello, Shuya!' he said. 'I knew you were here and I saw the rain, so I brought you an umbrella.'

My sister looked astonished. 'I thought you'd gone to Yunnan with your Dad. How come you're back? How did you know I was here?'

'My classmates said they'd seen you here,' Yusheng said earnestly. My sister said nothing. She didn't seem pleased to bump into him.

I thought they'd be there for a while, so I went back inside and started browsing the bookshelves. Not two minutes later, I could hear them arguing. Shuya's voice was determined and rather indignant, while Yusheng was speaking very quietly, as if explaining something. The raindrops spattered loudly on Yusheng's umbrella, which made it difficult to hear what they were saying even though I strained my ears. Finally Shuya poked her head inside and summoned me angrily, 'Orange, come on!'

I ran outside, hands over my head, and rushed into the rain. Shuya strode after me. Yusheng called anxiously after us, 'Why don't you take the umbrella!' But my sister ignored him.

Halfway home, we stopped and looked at each other. We were soaked through, our faces were running with water, and our hair plastered down. We looked like crazies. My sister stared at me, and must have seen how ridiculous we looked because she hooted with laughter. I couldn't help it, I had to laugh too. The pair of us looked terrible, but we were having so much fun.

'Have you split up with Yusheng?' I asked her.

She stopped laughing and looked angry. 'He had his classmates keep an eye on me!' she said.

'But it might just have been a coincidence,' I said.

'What coincidence? I know him. He's narrow-minded, and boring.'

I thought of the carved and gilded bed we'd slept in at Yusheng's house, the skittish filly, and the gloriously beautiful pastureland. The thought that we would never be able to go to that lovely place again if my sister broke up with Yusheng made me very sad.

Shuya leaned close, gripped my shoulder, and

said importantly, 'Orange, I'll tell you a secret, but you're not allowed to tell anyone.'

'OK.'

'Mr Li was in Yan'an.'

My mouth dropped open but I really didn't have a clue what she was on about.

'He didn't say but I guessed. Only someone from Yan'an would have such spiritual energy and talk about the liberation of humankind.'

'So he's like Pavel Korchagin, you mean?'

'That's right, like him. The most heroic, loveable and self-sacrificing kind of person in the world.'

Her eyes blazed and her expression was filled with fervour and determination.

The dark clouds had dispersed, and the sunset sky was suffused with purples and blues. The air was clear and cool, and so sweet you wanted to take deep breaths of it. Water rushed along the roadside ditches and through the paddy fields. The cries of frogs and insects rose from the paddy, and a dripping wet dog leapt onto the field boundary, and barked frantically at some imagined enemy.

At that moment, I suddenly had a fantasy that Shuya was about to disappear, about to fly up into the sky and turn into a beautiful cloud, and I'd only be able to see her from my window for ever after. I reached out and grabbed her arm.

'Shuya!' I cried.

She patted my hand. 'Home. School tomorrow.'

Chapter 17
Sports Gala

Every autumn, the students of Huaxi Fields turned out en masse for their sports gala.

Students of all five universities, high schoolers and primary students, and even kindergarten children, put on a display.

Our PE teacher was Ms Zhong. She was a Singaporean Chinese, short and dark, and wore white sailcloth shorts with white tennis shoes, and went bare-legged all summer, which created quite a stir. She showed us how to do high jumps, taking a run with a bamboo pole and launching herself into the air. When she landed, her pony-tail flew up above her head into the air, as if she'd suddenly acquired a real pony's tail on top of her head.

With a teacher like that, we were definitely going to improve. Our yearly sports display was proof of how good she was.

We were a girls' school, so muscle sports were not really our thing – we would never do as well as mixed schools. So we focussed on calisthenics and, this year, Ms Zhong choreographed a peformance based on folk dancing. The whole school would take part (that was one hundred and ten girls, less than that and we would not have sufficient impact), and we all wore pleated white skirts, black cloth shoes and bells around our ankles. We went on stage holding up our skirts, formed up in squares, and executed a variety of movements, stepping forwards and back in pairs, kicking and turning, all to the accompaniment of a trumpet wrapped in a piece of red silk and played by Ms Zhong, who also called out instructions in English in a commanding voice. We were an impressive sight.

First we practised: we lined up on the sports ground, and listened excitedly as Ms Zhong took us through her choreography. As girls, we enjoyed putting on a splendid show like this. Never mind the dance steps, just performing in those pleated skirts was hugely exciting.

For our first rehearsal, Ms Zhong mixed the age groups and lined the girls up according to their heights. I was in the middle towards the back. My partner was a senior. She had the figure of a young woman, her chest and waist and legs forming graceful curves. Facing her, I felt stupid, a beanpole with bony shoulders, a flat chest and a gormless look in my eyes. I just couldn't compete.

I had no problem with learning the steps. I had a good sense of movement. Whether it was stepping forward or backwards or to the left or right, I made it back to my original position. Not so my partner. A couple of turns and she was completely lost. She was so flummoxed that Ms Zhong had to step in and lead her back to her place. Quite soon, though, the girl figured out what to do: when the command rang out, she fixed her eyes on me, and followed me wherever I went. Problem solved.

Once we had learned the steps, we had to add leg kicks and hand movements, and that was where I messed up. I lacked coordination. In fact this was something my sister had always made fun of me about. I always stretched out my hand and stepped out with the wrong foot when I was doing morning exercise in primary school. As soon as Ms Zhong shouted, 'Stand straight! Pull in your stomachs! Kick!' I would panic and put out my right hand instead of my left, and kick in the wrong direction. Gymnastics was a collective effort, and as soon as I messed up, other girls near me would follow what I was doing and mess up too. Our lines became a shambles and Ms Zhong started to lose her temper.

'Orange!' she shouted at me. 'Concentrate on your hands!'...'What are you doing with your legs? Don't kick your partner in the bottom! What's this all about?! A bright girl like you, how come you're so clumsy?'

The more she shouted, the more confused I got. Eventually, she came over to me and tried to put my arms and legs into position for me, but by that time I had gone stiff as a post all over.

She heaved a sigh. I didn't dare sigh along with her. What I really felt like doing was bursting into tears.

She made me stay behind and gave me some extra tuition. She stood in front and I stood behind her. She held out one hand and I imitated her exactly. She counted the beat aloud and got me to do the dance steps, starting slowly, then speeding up. As she put me through my steps, she held a slender piece of wood, sanded smooth and varnished, and every time I got a step wrong, she would strike me on the ankle. I ended up the lesson with red and swollen legs.

But I was so grateful for the extra help she gave me. She could have made me drop out of the performance altogether but she didn't; she stuck with me and got me through. If she'd lost patience and sent me home, I would have been the only girl excluded from the school performance. Then I would have been mortified. I wouldn't have dared show my face in the school again, let alone in my class.

My younger sister Su was taking part in her primary school sports display for the first time. She was so excited that she was counting down the days. One of the pieces that they were doing was a 'big-head doll' dance and Su was picked to be the doll. She threw herself into it and practised every day after school, waddling around pigeon-toed with a basket over her head. One day, there was a disaster: she couldn't see where she was going and knocked the stack of rice bowls off the cooker. As they crashed to the floor, Mum came running and spanked her hard, twice. Su burst into howls of tears, her head still inside the basket. 'You stupid child!' Mum shouted. 'Now what are we going to have our rice in?'

'I'll buy some more,' sobbed Su.

'Buy more? What with? Even if we sold you, it wouldn't be enough to replace those bowls!'

My father came out, put his arms around Su, and made peace between mother and daughter. But we still had no bowls for lunch that day. Mum put the rice cooker in the middle of the table and we all dug our chopsticks in. 'Why don't we eat with our hands like nomads do,' Shuya suggested sarcastically. Su felt she was being got at, put down her chopsticks and began to bawl again. We almost split our sides laughing.

Tianlu was down to do shotput. He assumed that because he had strong arms from carrying water for Mum – he could easily balance a heavy bucket in each hand – throwing a lead ball should be no problem at all. Kejun told him it wasn't the same skill, he'd be using different muscles. Tianlu took this advice to heart and went off to the river bank, where he searched around and picked a large round smooth stone of about the same weight as the shotput ball. He took it back to Pomegranate Gardens and went out to a patch of waste ground behind it every day to put himself through his paces. At the beginning, he could only throw it six or seven metres from standing, but his technique improved.

He learnt how to turn, and use his back muscles, and increased his throw distance to more than ten metres.

'Considering you're only in high school, you've made very good progress,' Kejun told him authoritatively.

Shuya had always done gymnastics in school, and she signed up to do two gymnastic routines: balance beam and vault horse. She was pretty certain about both of these, but on the first day, there was a mishap: there was a bit of a breeze and her hair blew across her eyes so she couldn't see. She missed her step and fell, and scored zero. She wept with embarrassment and annoyance, and would have refused to try the vault horse if Tianlu had not been there to encourage her.

Maybe being annoyed with herself drove her on, but she did exceptionally well on the vault horse, and a news photographer who was there took a great shot of her. So the next day when it came out in the newspaper, Shuya was in the limelight. The picture captured the split-second when she let go of the apparatus with her hands: she was in a white leotard, with her arms outstretched and her legs at ninety degrees to her body. Her short black hair had flown up and outward, and she seemed to be soaring into the blue sky like a great white bird. What dynamism!

But it was Kejun who really dazzled the spectators. At senior high school, he had been an all-rounder in sports, and as soon as he started in Yenching University, the sports teacher spotted him and asked him to join the university football team. The teacher had a master's in PE from somewhere abroad. He was not particularly athletic himself, with his black-rimmed glasses and gentle manners, but he was a good teacher and mentor. He'd apparently written a book about teaching athletics too.

He made Kejun play attacking midfielder because he was quick off the mark and had good ball control. He never missing anything that was going on around him, and always passed the ball exactly where he wanted it to go. He somehow controlled the rhythm of the game. He was like a fish in water, darting here and there and slipping through gaps. He had a natural grace. By the time Yenching University had played the University of Nanking and West China Union University a few times, he was the one that everyone had their eyes pinned on, even though he was relatively new to the team. Women and girls in particular. They flocked to watch him as soon as a game was announced, and mobbed him at the end, pouring him drinks, and giving him their hand towels to mop his sweaty brow. Every match began to feel like a carnival.

This year, Kejun had signed up for javelin, long jump, and the 400-meter relay. It would be the first time he had tried javelin, but the main thing was to join in. The long jump was his strong point, and he was working hardest at that. As for the 400-meter relay, it was hard to say. It depended on what happened on the day, anyone of the four of them in the relay might make a mistake. He was cool about that, and was trusting to luck.

On the day of the opening ceremony, our whole family was there. Even Mum got dressed in her best clothes and brought Kid with her. She got Mrs Xing from downstairs to go along with her, and they walked the whole way to the sports ground – a kilometre and a half – to see the fun. Mum especially wanted to see my dad, because he'd been chosen to referee the track and field events, and had a position at the edge of the track. 'I have to watch the old man seeing fair play,' she said.

Yenching University's Journalism Department made sure to give the sports events full coverage.

They built a rudimentary broadcasting stage on one side of the square, with microphone, loudspeaker, and a gramophone for music, a motley collection of equipment. Their students were taking part in every event, and the journalism students were really fired up. At first they wrote their reports and read it over the microphone, but then they all crowded onto the stage, shouting and cheering into the loudspeakers in support of their fellow students. Later on, they got rice bowls and used them as drums, banging away as hard as they could to drive on their side and put their opponents off their stroke. Some of the other schools withdrew as a result, their principals protested strongly to the dean of Yenching University, and the broadcasting stage was dismantled.

During the three days of the sports events, Kejun was probably the busiest of anyone, because his camera finally came into its own. Except when he was competing, he ran all over the sports fields with the Leica hung around his neck, taking pictures, retreating into his darkroom to develop them, interviewing the winners, and writing his reports. The most beautiful report he wrote was about the opening ceremony. It read, 'The Yenching University teams snaked along towards the sports fields, a majestic sight. The cycling team led the way, holding aloft the orange university flag. Then came the band, followed by our finest men and women athletes in track and field. They were in full voice, marching in unison, and supported by every department of the university. What an impressive array of talent! What thundering war cries! The heroes of Yenching University are among the best there are. They are the champions, they can see the prizes already within their grasp!'

One of the female students from Yenching University broadcast his report for him. There was hissing and booing from the spectators, and students from all the other universities bellowed back, 'Boasting! Boasting!!'

Everyone was fired up by now, and the fun was about to begin.

The all-important 10,000 metre race took place on the last of the three days. Yenching University and University of Nanking were competing for the championship. The athletes on both sides were professionals, lean and lithe, with shaven heads, and pumped-up muscles on arms and thighs. Kejun was cheering for Yenching University, my dad for Jinling.

Father and son stood side by side at the edge of the track, trying to out-shout each other every time a sweat-soaked, panting athlete ran by. By the time the match was over, both were hoarse. In fact my dad had lost his voice completely and couldn't teach the next day. My mother made them pots of herbal tea and forced them to drink it, for three full days.

Chapter 18
Sad Times

All through history, happy times have ended in sadness. There's even an ancient Chinese proverb that goes, 'Extreme happiness brings sorrow in its wake'.

In the autumn of 1943, when China was in dire straits, there was a smidgin of good news, and it came from a far distant country that few of us knew much about: Italy. At the end of August, the newspapers reported that the Allied forces had landed in Sicily, which was under fascist occupation. Kejun got out the world atlas, looked it up for us, and showed us an island in the middle of the Mediterranean just off the mainland of Italy. 'The Allied landing craft are pretty powerful, and one small island's not going to be able to resist. But the Italian mainland's another matter.

Let's not get too optimistic too soon,' my brother said.

Kejun was at university by now. He spoke with such authority that the rest of us received his pronouncements with unquestioning admiration.

However, less than two months later, he was proved completely wrong: in early September, the Allied troops landed on the mainland and met little opposition. Five days later, Italy surrendered. In mid-October, it even declared war on its former ally, Germany.

The newspapers were full of jokes about the Italian army. According to one, the fiercest resistance encountered by the Allied forces when they landed was from a panther that escaped from the local zoo and attacked two American soldiers. Another went like this: an Italian fortification raised a white flag after the British fired a few shells at it. The Italian army commander told his British counterpart with great seriousness, 'We're out of ammo.' Behind him there were some boxed-up munitions, but no one could find the tools to open them up.

Kejun chortled as he read. 'These Italians are too funny. They can paint battles on their frescos, but when it comes to real bullets, they run away. If only the Japanese were more like the Italians, we'd have run them into the sea long ago.'

But we knew only too well that the Japanese weren't like the Italians. They were murderous and determined.

A couple of days after our grand autumn sports gala ended, the British RAF, which was stationed in Huaxi Fields, heard how successful it had been, and wanted a bit of the action. They pulled together a football team and challenged the five universities to a game, Royal Air Force v Universities United. The news of the challenge got the male students all fired up. China's national pride was at stake. Surely the cream of the universities would have no trouble wiping the floor with a scrap team made up on the spur of the moment by a few pilots!

All the PE teachers got together and hurriedly selected the best of their talent for the Universities United team. Kejun was in, and chosen for the starting lineup. After three or four days' hurried practice, the teams gathered on the campus of West China Union University. The RAF players drove up in their green military trucks, and all you could see was a lot of fair heads leaning over the sides, smiling and blowing kisses and whistling at the prettiest girl students.

There was a carnival spirit before they'd even kicked off. By contrast with the swaggering British, the eleven Chinese players looked extremely nervous, although they'd prepared themselves well.

The football stadium had three tiers of seats, all crammed with spectators. Even VIPs like the mayor of Chengdu were making an appearance. A number of newspapers had been tipped off, and their reporters scurried around conducting interviews. The day had started quite cool, but they were soon pouring with sweat.

Sheona and I were not beefy enough to push our way into the stadium, there was too much of a crush. So we beat a retreat and found a basketball goal stand some way off, which we climbed up. From the top, we could see the whole game. Sheona made a big fuss about hauling herself up there, and kept patting her chest and saying she'd never done anything like this before, just to see a football match!

'Oh, is that right?' I said. 'All the girls are here to see these handsome English guys, and I bet you are too!'

She blushed and protested, 'Not me. I'm only here to see Kejun play.'

I didn't know whether she was telling the truth or

not, but I felt a warm glow inside.

I don't remember the details of the game that day. What I do remember is the final score – 5:3 to Universities United. The stadium erupted in wild cheers at the end of the game, and all the students, boys and girls alike, threw their arms around each other, leapt into the air and screamed. The losing team didn't seem the slightly bit put out at being beaten. They did a circuit of the field, greeting the students with big smiles on their faces, and being cheered by the girls.

Unfortunately, Kejun was injured during the game. A hulking great British player tripped him up and he went flying and landed hard, grimacing with pain. Some reserve players rushed onto the pitch and he was carried away. In the hospital that night, Uncle Fan diagnosed a fractured ankle. He put it in plaster and wrapped the plaster in layers of gauze. Then his classmates carried him back to our home between them. For two weeks after that, Tianlu pushed him along on his bicycle to daily lectures, and picked him up from Yenching University in the evening. After two weeks was up, the plaster was removed, the swelling gradually subsided, and Kejun could get around on crutches. The upside of the accident was that he became the campus hero. All his classmates competed to do things for him and he never had to lift a finger for himself.

In the meantime, we had another casualty in Pomegranate Gardens. Uncle Tao arrived back from a field trip on a stretcher. He was the one who had brought the bear cub from Tibet. Playing with that bear was one of the happiest memories of my childhood. This time, what he brought home was a lot more fearsome: malaria.

A month before, Uncle Tao had led a small expedition to the Daliang Mountains to collect data for the study of the headman system among the Black Lolo tribe. When he came to say goodbye, Dad said anxiously, 'It's such a wild area, all that dense forest. Do you really have to go?' But Uncle Tao was not going to be deterred. 'The Daliang Mountains may be dangerous, but not nearly as dangerous as the front. How many of our compatriots are spilling their blood fighting on the battlefield? There's nothing to worry about.'

But it was a long and risky journey. They took a boat from Chengdu down the Min River to Yibin, then up the Jinsha River to Pingshan county, and from there to Leibo. Then they hired two Lolo men to act as guides, and set off through the virgin forest to the Lolo tribal lands.

And there, Uncle Tao was struck down by malaria. He shivered uncontrollably, burned up with fever, his arms and legs twitched, and he drifted in and out of consciousness. His Lolo friends made a stretcher for him and with great difficulty managed to get him down from the highlands and back to Chengdu.

His family got the best doctor from the Union Hospital of West China Union University, National Central University, and Cheeloo University to treat him but the drugs he prescribed were no help at all. His wife's family, who were originally from Sichuan, then found a famous Chinese-medicine doctor who made up a foul-tasting herbal medicine. They forced it down the patient's throat, but soon after, Uncle Tao vomited it all back up again, and the house stank with its bitter smell.

Within a few days, Uncle Tao was at death's door. He'd been such a larger-than-life character, always ready with a joke, but now he lay in bed, so thin that he barely made a hump in the bedclothes, his skin sallow and his cheeks sunk into deep hollows. He shook so violently that his bed banged on the floor, and when he was feverish, his eyes opened wide and he looked like he was breathing fire. Every time I looked in through their window, all I could see was Auntie Tao dabbing away her tears with a handkerchief.

One day at dinner, Mum said to Dad with a sigh, 'I can't see Tao making it through…He was fine here in Huaxi Fields. What did he have to go away for?'

My father put down his chopsticks, jumped to his feet and said sternly, 'Don't talk nonsense! People have always, ever since ancient times, sacrificed their lives for science and truth! Tao is a wonderful man, he decided what he wanted to do, then he went and did it, he threw himself into the battle for knowledge, he – he – '

Suddenly, Dad choked up. He left the table, and went into our room, slamming the door. We heard muffled sounds coming from the other side.

My mother was startled. She sat at the table, with a dazed look on her face. A little while later, Uncle Fan came to see us and told us that only quinine could help Tao.

'What's quinine?' asked Dad.

'It's an anti-malarial drug made from the bark

of the quinine tree, which grows in the tropical rainforests. We don't have it.'

My father grabbed his arm. 'Fan, where can we get hold of some?'

'The China Red Cross Ambulance Corps apparently have stocks, donated by overseas Chinese in Indonesia. They make it there. Last year, an expeditionary force went to Myanmar, and the ambulance corps went with them and every soldier got a dose.'

'Where's the Ambulance Corps now?'

'Guiyang.'

'It's too far, it would take too many days to make the round trip. Tao doesn't have that long,' said Dad.

'Listen, I heard there's an Ambulance Corps team who just relocated to Yibin. That's less than three hundred kilometres from Chengdu. The team leader is Lin Zhibai from the Union Medical College – he's a good friend of mine.'

'Great! Fan, please can you write a letter to Prof Lin? I'll take on finding someone to go to Yibin!'

To get to Yibin, there was a boat from Chengdu down the Min River. It took no more than two days because it was downstream. But on the way back would take a day longer because it was upstream. A round trip of five days to get the quinine.

Dad said he'd get someone to fetch the drug, but the next question was who? He was only a university teacher and he had no clout. This was a private matter, after all. Kejun was still out of action with his ankle, Shuya was a girl and it was risky for girls to travel on their own. So the task fell to Tianlu. My father gave him his instructions, stressing, 'Be as quick as you can, no hanging around. Only you can save Uncle Tao's life.'

But the trip took Tianlu more than five days – seven in fact. To start with, all went well: he got on the boat, arrived in Yibin, found the Ambulance Corps, showed Uncle Fan's letter, was given the quinine, and put the oiled paper packet carefully away in his inside pocket. So far so good. But they were hit by rising floodwaters on the way back, and the boat was forced backwards and smashed against a cliff. It capsized. Luckily, Tianlu was a good swimmer and after some time, he was rescued by a passing boat. Eventually, he managed to make it back to Chengdu. He got to Huaxi Fields and rushed straight to the Tao's house. But the precious medicine that he brought with him was useless. Uncle Tao had died three days before he arrived.

Tianlu sat on the stairs and burst into tears. Uncle Fan put his arms around him. 'Listen to me, boy, even if you weren't held up for two days, it wouldn't change anything. It was God's will.'

Tianlu still felt guilty. He kept insisting that it was his fault. He was depressed about it for a long time, and refused to talk to anyone, just buried himself in his schoolwork.

Mum was haunted by the image of the boat capsizing and Tianlu falling into the water. I heard her complaining to Dad a few times, 'He's only eighteen. How could you send him on such a dangerous trip? You were crazy! This could have ended in disaster.'

Our dad pressed his lips together and refused to answer. Perhaps he too regretted it.

What was clear was that both our parents were terribly sorry for Tianlu. I could tell that from the way they kept looking anxiously at him.

As the weather got colder, we residents of Pomegranate Gardens heard more sad news: Mark had crashed while flying a cargo plane over the Hump. The plane was loaded with high-octane fuel, a precious commodity needed for fighter planes. So when it crashed, his comrades saw an enormous plume of smoke rising from the ravine.

An officer of the Nationalist Army came with one of Mark's fellow Flying Tigers, bringing his personal possessions all the way from Kunming in Yunnan to the Fans' home in Chengdu. The American told them that this was what Mark had wanted. Mark had said his aunt would get him home.

Mrs Fan, her expression rigid, stood holding his kitbag, which was half as tall as she was, and muttered to herself, 'Okay, I'll do it. Mark shall go home. There's still his favorite windmill on the farm in Kentucky.'

The young American solemnly saluted and left. Mrs Fan stood alone looking out of the window for a while, then sat down and began to play the piano. Through the afternoon, through the evening, and on until midnight, she played music that was alternately mournful and rousing, and we all sat at home listening, and shedding tears for the Flying Tiger who had been so kind and friendly, Mark.

A couple of years later, when the Anti-Japanese War was won and the Pacific Ocean re-opened to navigation, the Fan family got tickets straightaway and took Mark's kitbag back to the United States. They had worked here for half their lives, as a teacher and a doctor. Their daughter Sheona had been born and raised in Huaxi Fields – and suddenly they were gone. What did they feel, Uncle Fan, Mary Fan, and Sheona? I have no idea.

The day after we heard the news, Sheona came upstairs in search of Tianlu, and handed him a silver-painted model of a fighter plane.

'Mark left this model for you in his will.'

'Mark left a will?' asked Tianlu in surprise.

'Yes, they have to write their will before they fly, because the Hump is such a dangerous route.'

The model fitted into the palm of his hand. It was exquisite, right down to its nose painted with the head of a shark. When Tianlu was writing letters to Mark, he once said he wanted a photo of Mark with his shark-headed airplane. But there were no photos among his possessions, probably because Mark didn't have time. Getting a photo was quite a business in those days.

Tianlu asked my mother for a piece of the twine she used to make shoe soles. He knotted it around the plane, and hung it inside his mosquito net. Every night he fell asleep looking at it. He probably dreamed of Mark, of the brown freckles that covered his nose, his hairy hands as big as bear paws, and the muscles that bulged in his arms when he played badminton. But he surely never dreamed of Mark's death because he had never been to the Himalayas, or seen the Gaoligong or the Hengduan Mountains, and could surely not imagine a cargo plane with a cruising height of less than 5,000 metres, roaring over the Hump whose peaks topped more than 5,000 metres, on a hair-raising, deadly journey.

Chapter 19
Catching a Spy

A pall of sadness hung over Pomegranate Gardens after Mark and Uncle Tao died. Every time I went in and out of the compound, I couldn't help glancing at the Taos' house, somehow hoping to see his cheerful, laughing figure in his Tibetan felt hat mis-matched with a corduroy jacket, leaning against the door. Sometimes, I remembered the time Mark visited and the Fans threw a party for him, and Uncle Tao climbed up on the table, and gave a passionate recitation of John Keats' *Ode to the Nightingale*.

'Why is it always the ones we love best that die first?' I said to Sheona. She looked down and thought about it, then muttered, 'Maybe God loves them too.'

'You believe that God brings happiness to

humankind, don't you? But he doesn't. He takes away the people we love most!' I protested.

Sheona went pale with horror. 'Orange! Spit those nasty words right out!'

But I refused to. If God took away all the good people, then I had no respect for him.

With Kejun studying journalism, lots of newspapers had begun to appear in our flat. There was the Ta Kung Pao, the Central Daily News, and the New China Daily, as well as the Wartime News, which came out twice a week, and hardly anyone had heard of. Kejun said it was like the New China Daily, in that it was run by the Communists, and mainly covered the successes of the Eighth Route Army, news from their base in Yan'an, and speeches by well-known pro-Communist progressives. He also said that after he read these newspapers, he felt that China was not a country reduced to ruins by war. There was vigour and vitality among the ruins, and new things were sprouting from the ground upwards. China had a future full of promise.

This was all a bit deep for me. In fact, there was a lot that he said that I didn't get. I liked reading the funny articles. Once, I saw a report that the police had caught a Japanese spy in a hostel in Chengdu. The man spoke proper Sichuan dialect, wore a long Chinese gown, ate spicy Sichuan food, played mahjong, and sat over his tea in a traditional tea house. He had a wife and children, no different from any other man in Chengdu. He owned and ran the hostel himself. That made it easy for him to make friends with any travellers who dropped by from all over the country, and he could collect intelligence for the Japanese army.

I pointed out to Kejun that there was an inn in Lantern Alley that might have a spy in it too. The manager had a foxy face.

Shuya overheard. 'If it was so easy for you to tell who was a spy, they wouldn't be a proper spy, would they?'

'So what do spies look like?' I said rebelliously.

'What do they look like? Just like you and me! A spy has to look like anyone else, so they can go unnoticed, right, Kejun?'

My brother agreed.

But I didn't believe them. I was sure that a spy had two pairs of eyes, eyes within eyes, so they could see stuff to report to their masters.

After that, I made sure to look carefully at

everyone I met when I was walking home from school on Saturdays and going back to school on Sundays. I paid special attention to the way they looked at me. Did they avoid my eyes? Did they look suspicious? I really wanted a spy to make a slip-up so I'd catch them out. I'd get any passers-by to help me truss them up and take them to the police station. It would be my very own small contribution to the war effort.

That winter, the news from the front was horrific. After the Chinese expeditionary force crossed into Myanmar and was defeated by the Japanese, the latter chased after them back over the border, and occupied Wanding, Mangshi, and reached the Tonghui Bridge on the Nu River. We only stopped the invaders by blowing up the bridge. But the Japanese were buoyed up by their successes, and moved large quantities of artillery up to their side of the river. If they could force their way across this natural barrier, they could attack upstream towards Chongqing. The Chinese expeditionary force was determined to resist, and there was a battle across the river, which ended in heavy losses on each side.

Meanwhile, Japanese military leaders like Tojo Hideki were desperate to finish the war with China. They shipped all the guns and munitions they had from

Japan, moved troops up from all over the occupied south and sent lots of agents to infiltrate Sichuan. The plan was to attack from Wuhan and Changsha and take Chengdu and Chongqing.

As the war clouds gathered ominously overhead, the situation grew more tense on the ground. We all felt as helpless as we had a few years before when the Japanese first invaded.

Around that time, a new cook arrived at the school. As soon as I saw him, I thought he looked very sinister: his head was huge, his body was very small, his face was sallow, his teeth were blackened and his eyelids droopy, so he peered at you through the slits. He had a funny walk too. He was bow-legged and so pigeon-toed his feet looked as if they were going to hit each other. He waddled and wobbled as if he might fall over at any moment.

'Mr Dong,' that was how the school head introduced him to us. In spite of his oddities, he was a good cook, and we used to gobble down the tasty dishes of noodles and mincemeat, and braised tofu that he put in front of us.

When I got home the Saturday after he'd arrived, I told Sheona all about him. 'He's a Japanese spy, for sure,' I finished.

'What?' She looked at me, confused but excited.

'Well, think about it. What other reason would he have for suddenly turning up at our school?'

Sheona's clear blue eyes were fixed on me now.

'Look,' I pursued, 'he's bow-legged and pigeon-toed, just like Japanese people we've seen in films.'

We didn't have feature films in Chengdu back then, only wartime propaganda films. The Japanese soldiers in them were always short, bow-legged and pigeon-toed, with moustaches and sort of triangular eyes.

Sheona looked doubtful. 'But that sounds like a lot of Chinese too!'

'Rubbish! No, it doesn't!' I retorted.

Now she was anxious. 'Orange, are you angry with me?

Of course, I was. How could anyone compare a Chinese with a Japanese?

'I'm sorry,' she said diffidently. 'I just mean some people, very, very few people. The thing is, I've never actually seen a real, live Japanese, so I was only saying...' She trailed off. She wasn't making any sense but I decided to forgive her. After all, she was American so she probably couldn't tell one Asian from another.

But I was still worried about this weird-looking Mr Dong. I watched him closely. I discovered that whenever he heard anyone call his name, he would tremble all over and jump to attention, his hands hanging by his side, and sneak a look at whoever it was through those over-hanging eyelids, maybe to see if they were friendly or were going to tell him off. If it was the hatchet-faced principal, he would bare his stained teeth in a hideous grin. If it was one of the junior girls, his eyelids would droop again and he would amble off, completely ignoring them.

Once I tried to get a closer look at him. There was an empty bit of ground in front of the cookhouse and I kicked my shuttlecock across it. Little by little, I kicked it closer to the shack where he slept. He carried on with chopping the vegetables and while he wasn't looking, I slammed the shuttlecock right through the door of the shack. Then I shrieked in mock surprise and ran after it.

But no sooner had I stepped over the threshold and before my eyes could get used to the dimness, he had flung down the knife and, in one stride, grabbed me by the collar like an eagle snatching a chicken, and hauled me out.

'You stupid child! You numbskull! You thought you could sneak in behind my back? You watch it, next time I'll give you such a beating. You see if I don't!'

Did he think I was trying to steal his things? But he was a cook! What on earth did he have worth stealing in his rotten old shack? What was he keeping such a close eye on?

And there was something else: the way he had pounced and grabbed me, it was quite different from his normal self-effacing demeanour. He was behaving like a proper kungfu artist.

Now I was even more suspicious.

Then I discovered another of his secrets: every afternoon, at about two o'clock, after lunch was over but before he needed to start preparing dinner, he would hurry out of the school looking very furtive. Where was he off to? We'd begun afternoon classes by two o'clock and sometimes I'd see his stooped figure scurrying past the classroom window. I was desperate to follow and see where he went, but it was no good. I had to stick it out to the end of class, and when I rushed to the cookhouse, of course, there was no one there. The door was wide open, the firewood was piled by the stove, the washed vegetables were lying wetly in the bowl, and the dilapidated shack next door where he lived was fastened with a rusty iron lock.

He must be up to some evil tricks, he was obviously a spy! What else could he be? I would have to blow his cover as soon as possible, otherwise he might do terrible things to who knew how many innocent citizens of Chengdu.

While I was home the next weekend, I made up my mind to tail him so I could see what he was up to.

I begged Kejun and Shuya to be my bodyguards. I mean, I might run into danger. What if he saw me? What if he got out his Mauser, and 'bang, bang!' I'd be dead? No one would know! Besides, if we found out that he really was a spy, one of us would have to keep an eye on him, while the other went and reported him. I couldn't manage it all on my own.

Kejun was busy sorting out newspapers, making clippings of useful articles and binding them into a folder. They were piled all over the place, on the dinner table, and on the ground. We couldn't move for newspapers. Every weekend, he spent an hour or two doing this. He didn't look up. 'It's not that I don't want to help, I'm just too busy.'

'Just for a little while,' I begged him. 'Then we'll come back.'

He laughed. 'If all you want to do is look, you go and have a look. And come back and report without delay!'

I was furious. 'Without delay? But by then he'll have sent off all his intelligence to the enemy!' He shrugged and ignored me.

Shuya really loved seeing me squirm (it was what she most enjoyed). She said, 'Orange, I've got an idea. Take the wooden-handled pistol, creep up behind him and wallop him on the back of the head. See if that doesn't make him talk.'

I refused to answer. I knew they didn't believe me. They were just humouring me, like I was a kid.

Tianlu was in his bedroom poring over the English dictionary. He overheard and came out and offered, 'I'll come with you if you like.'

Shuya didn't seem to like that, and began to backtrack. 'I don't think you should go. If he really is a spy, you might be in big trouble.'

Ah-hah! So she was jealous, I could tell from her voice. I ignored her and hung onto Tianlu's arm like we were best mates. Tianlu went red in the face from embarrassment.

When we were out in the walkway, he pulled his arm free. 'Don't do that, Orange, you're too old for that.'

'Who says? I'm only thirteen.'

'Yes, you're thirteen. You're a big girl.'

'But I want to hang onto you, you're my brother!'

I crooked my elbow through his arm and held him tight. I'd always been obstinate like that since I was little. If you told me I wasn't to do something, I'd go right ahead and do it.

Tianlu was so embarassed that it was like walking arm in arm with a stick of wood. I released him and hung onto the banisters as we went down, laughing so hard that I got a stitch.

Eventually, he relaxed and started to laugh too. 'You girls!'

I took him to the school and we hid behind a low wall opposite the school gate, pulling some branches across our faces. We'd arrived at the right time. It was early afternoon, and Mr Dong should be going out. We hadn't been waiting long when the old cook came trotting out of the gate. He was looking at the ground, swinging his little arms, clearly in a hurry. I was worried that his pigeon-toed feet might trip him up.

Once he'd gone past us, without a second's hesitation, I tugged at Tianlu's jacket. It was time to go. We clambered over the wall and followed him as silently as we could. Tianlu had long strides and walked fast, and within a couple of minutes he was ahead of me. I ran to catch up, and whispered, 'We've got to keep our distance, and keep out of sight!' I'd read a British detective novel once, and now I was putting it to good use.

Mr Dong kept looking around to see if anyone was following him. If he was upright and honest, why was he looking so guilty?

On and on we walked, past a few turnings and around some corners until we came to a narrow lane called Tiles Alley. It was a strange place. The house had tall grey brick walls – no windows – and black-painted doors which were all firmly shut. It was as silent as the grave, like no one had lived here for hundreds of years. We watched as Mr Dong stopped at one of the doors and knocked urgently. Someone let him in, then poked their head out, looked around, withdrew and slammed the door shut.

I stood rooted to the spot. 'Did you see that, Tianlu? Go and fetch someone!'

Tianlu didn't move. 'Hurry up!' I insisted.

He looked thoughtful. 'Can you smell something?'

'Smell?' I was puzzled.

'Sweetish, a bit weird.'

I sniffed. 'I think I can smell something.'

'It's opium. When I was a kid, I had an uncle who used opium, and the whole house smelled like that. These houses are all opium dens, I'm sure of it.'

I must have gawped at him. I just didn't know what to say.

'I heard Chengdu has a lot of underground opium dens. They must be around here. If the school finds out that Mr Dong smokes opium, they'll kick him out, that's obviously why he doesn't want anyone to see.'

Good heavens, not a spy but an opium addict. How embarrassing. What was I going to say to Kejun and Shuya when they asked?

Tianlu looked at my gloomy expression. He rubbed his hands together and thought for a moment. Then he whispered, 'Don't worry. You haven't done anything wrong. You're perfectly within your rights to have suspicions. If you hadn't followed him, you would never have known he was an addict. If everyone in China was like you, Orange, the country would have nothing to worry about! The spies would have no intelligence to report to the Japanese. They wouldn't be able to survive in Chengdu!'

Somehow, Tianlu's words of comfort were so heart-felt that I felt warm inside.

Chapter 20

Mum's Fur Waistcoat

At the beginning of the winter holidays, Kejun and Shuya both left home. Victory Li was taking my sister's reading group, about seven or eight people, by bus to Chongqing to join an Anti-Japanese War Youth event organized by Zengjiayan Communist Party South China branch. Kejun and two fellow journalism students got funding from a Chengdu newspaper to go to the Chinese Expeditionary Army Kunming Training Centre, and write a series of reports for the newspaper. The editor-in-chief told them that any news about the Expeditionary Force was always popular. Everyone would want to read their reports. They took the express mail bus to Kunming.

With both of them gone, the house suddenly

seemed empty. The first couple of days, Mum couldn't get her head around it and kept filling their bowls at mealtime anyway. 'You bring them up till they're adults, and as soon as they're fledged, they're flown,' she said with a sigh.

My father carried on eating and didn't comment.

Mum looked at Tianlu, then at me, then tapped Su and Kid on their foreheads. 'Now you two, I'm keeping you here. You're not leaving.'

Su was very sweet. 'Mum, I'm not leaving home, even when I'm a hundred years old,' she declared.

Mum laughed till she cried. 'Su, by the time you're a hundred, my bones will be rattling in my grave.'

My little brother, Kid, looked confused. 'Mum, why will your bones rattle?'

Tianlu rapped him smartly on the head with his chopsticks. Then he put some shredded potato into Kid's bowl. That kept him quiet.

Kid was six years old, and a bundle of mischief. Most war babies were scrawny and sallow because they'd grown up deprived of home comforts, good food and warm clothing. Not Kid. He had always been chubby and rosy-cheeked. He was known all through the neighbourhood. 'Such a little cherub!' people would exclaim whenever his name came up.

There were certain advantages in being loved by everyone. Whenever he went out, people would give him snacks – a handful of peanuts or a bit of pancake. But it had its downsides too. One day, Kid slipped out on his own and somehow got into the mulberry grove and started throwing bricks around. It was his bad luck that a family called the Mas lived on the edge of the grove and had an unbelievably ugly brown 'partridge hen' which was right in the middle of laying an egg among the trees when Kid was having fun throwing bricks around. She was a sitting target, took a hit, and died. Now Kid was in real trouble, because Mrs Ma had quite a reputation hereabouts. She was easily capable of kicking up a fuss about nothing. And now her best laying hen was dead. She wasn't going to let Kid off lightly.

Mrs Ma grabbed him by his ear and marched him home, carrying the dead hen, its head dangling, in her other hand. She burst into Pomegranate Gardens, thumped up the stairs, and flung the dead bird down in front of my mother.

'I've only got one thing to say,' she announced. 'You're going to pay me back!'

Kid might have been a bit naughty, but there was no real badness in him, and right now, he was so terrified that he peed steaming hot pee all the way down the leg of his padded trousers.

At first, Mum tried to fob Mrs Ma off. 'The schools are on holiday, and all the kids are out playing. What makes you think it was my son?'

Mrs Ma scoffed. 'Everyone knows your little boy. I recognized him a mile off!'

Mum couldn't deny that. But still, she poked the hen with her toe and muttered, 'How could a kid of five or six have the strength to kill your hen with a brick?'

Mrs Ma stepped forward, bent down and twisted the bird's head to one side. 'Be good enough to take a look at this. He hit my hen right on its skull! It's shattered! If you don't believe me, you have a go at banging someone on the head with a brick!'

And that was that. It was obvious from the few words they'd exchanged that this was a woman to be reckoned with. Mum would have to pay her back.

The trouble was that it was near the end of the month and there was hardly any money in the house. After some hard bargaining, the woman agreed to accept the fur-lined waistcoat my mother was wearing instead.

The waistcoat was made of patterned satin and lined with fox fur, old but warm and cosy. Mum had brought it with her when they left Nanjing in the winter of 1937 and wore it all the time. It was one of the few things of value that we had.

When she'd gone, Mum pointed an angry finger at Kid. 'And as for you, we'll cut that naughty hand of yours off!'

Kid was so terrified at the threat that he burst out crying.

I told Mum she shouldn't have given in so easily, and exchanged her lovely fur waistcoat for a manky dead hen. Mum sighed, 'Your father's a respectable man with a reputation to keep up. I didn't want the whole neighbourhood to get involved. If I hadn't given her what she wanted, she would have made sure everyone knew, and it would have looked really bad!'

There was nothing I could say to that. I aimed a kick at Kid. 'Cry! Go on, cry! But it won't bring the hen back to life!'

My mother was used to wearing that fur-lined waistcoat day in day out, and without it, she only had a padded jacket with worn-out stuffing, and a thin shirt.

The weather was freezing and she was not in the best of health. She caught a nasty cold, ran a temperature for two days, and then developed a chronic cough. We could hear her coughing and spluttering every night when she went to bed. It was horrible. Dad went to Shaanxi Street to the herbalists and bought a poultice for her chest, and some cough medicine made of steamed pear and sugar, but nothing did any good.

With Mum sick, I had to stay home. As Dad put it, I was almost the mistress of the house now. Every morning I got up early and went food shopping. By the time I got back, Tianlu had the stove going and was making the soupy rice for our breakfast. I picked over the greens, washed and drained them. After breakfast, I had to plait Su's hair and make sure Kid sat down at the table to learn his words and copy them out. Then Su and I divided up the housework, sweeping, making the beds, dusting, and tidying Dad's desk. Mum could sit on the walkway outside and wash our clothes, while I brought her water, emptied the dirty water away, and took the wet laundry down to the courtyard to hang it out in the sun.

Mum used to take a nap after lunch. She was so worried about Kid escaping and making trouble again, that she took him to bed with her and made him sleep too. The house fell silent. The only sound was the tick-tock of the old-fashioned clock on top of the chest and Kid's snuffling in the bed. Su sat at the table, copying the illustrations from her book *The Twelve Maidens of Jinling*. I shut myself in our room and read the poetry that Victory Li had lent Shuya.

Li's recommendations were all left-wing progressive writers. There was He Qifang's *Prophecy*, Bian Zhilin's *Ten Years of Poetry*, and Li Guangtian's poems, all collected together in *Han Garden Poems*. Sheona had given me a beautiful notebook with a green leather cover for my birthday. I didn't want to write just anything in it, so I copied out Bian Zhilin's lines, 'You stand on the bridge to see the view, while those who've climbed the tower to see the view, watch you. The bright moon ornaments your window, while you ornament others' dreams.' And, 'The night breeze is lonesome, I climb the mountain, touch the top of the white poplar and pluck the zither strings.' And He Qifang's 'The flowers that fall in the gully are the most fragrant, and the morning dew that no one remembers is the brightest.'

Tianlu used to go out after breakfast and stay out

until dinnertime. He came home with filthy clothes, his face and hair covered in dust, and the dirt so engrained under his fingernails that it wouldn't wash out. He was always ravenous. He gulped his bowl of brown rice straight down without even putting any vegetables with it, and if Su and Kid left anything in their bowls, he didn't bother asking, it all went down too.

I overheard Mum muttering to Dad, 'Do you know what Tianlu does every day? He won't tell me when I ask, and I'm getting worried.'

My father was relaxed. 'If he doesn't want to say, then don't ask him. He's growing up. He's entitled to keep a secret.'

But my mother wasn't happy. 'Orange, you're close to Tianlu, has he told you anything? What does he do all day?' she asked me.

'Mum, if Dad says don't ask, then don't ask. Stop worrying!' I told her. Mum slapped me on the head angrily, 'Useless girl!'

Little did she know that the very same question was gnawing away at me too. I didn't care who else he kept his secrets from, but why was he shutting me out? It was really upsetting me. I was the closest to him in the whole family, after all. Hadn't we been partners when we went after the spy? And now he had a secret and was keeping it from me!

One evening, when Mum, Su, and Kid were all in bed asleep, and Dad was hosting some foreign agronomists and had not come home, I was copying out the poem, 'You stand on the bridge to see the view' in my green leather notebook. It was a lovely poem and I really wanted to talk to someone about it, so I pushed open Tianlu's door and went in.

I got the shock of my life. In spite of the cold, Tianlu was bare-chested. He had pulled his jacket and vest all the way down to his waist, his head was tilted at an awkward angle, and he was reaching across with his left arm to his right shoulder, struggling to smear something on the shoulder muscle. He was grunting with pain.

He looked startled when I burst in, and hurriedly pulled his jacket back on and sat up straight. He didn't say a word, just waited for me to say what I'd come in for.

I didn't say anything either. I went over to the bed and pulled his jacket off his shoulder again. From the shoulder blade all the way down his back was one big mass of bruising and swelling. In some places, there was broken skin, which showed up like small, bright red peach blossoms. The ointment he was putting on had a strong smell, musk, or maybe borneol.

I gasped and almost cried out. Tianlu quickly put his finger to his lips, and glanced in the direction of the door. It was obvious he didn't want Mum to find out.

'Did you get in a fight?' I whispered.

He laughed. 'Course not! I found a building site. They're building a house, and they took me on as a labourer.'

'Is that what labouring does to you?' I almost forgot to whisper.

'It's carrying stones and bricks and timber, something I've never done before.'

'Are we really so short of money?' I honestly had no very clear idea of the family finances.

'Mum gave up her fur waistcoat and there's plenty more cold weather to come. She's not strong, she needs to keep warm. If I earn some money, I can get her waistcoat back.'

'But Mrs Ma won't give it up. She's a cheat and a bully.'

'I can pay her enough money for three hens. Or five, if three's not good enough.'

I didn't say any more. I dipped my finger in the ointment and rubbed it slowly over his back. I felt bad. Mum had such a terrible cough, and all because of losing her waistcoat. How come none of her own children cared, and only Tianlu had taken it to heart and was trying to help?

'Tianlu,' I said, 'tomorrow I'll come and help you on the building site.'

'Eh? Do you think just anyone can work on a building site? Your arms and legs are like sticks. What could you do?'

I had to admit he was right. I helped him back on with his jacket and sat down on the bed beside him. 'Seeing your shoulder and back makes me want to grow up quickly,' I said gloomily. 'I wish I could finish high school tomorrow and earn some money and help support the family.'

'Okay, so let's work it out. You'll finish high school by eighteen, right? You're a girl. What can you do?' Tianlu said.

I thought for a moment. 'I can be a primary school teacher.'

He smiled gently. 'Sure, you be a teacher, like your father, that's great.'

I was embarrassed. 'He's a university lecturer. I could only teach primary school.'

'That's great too! But you need to eat well and fatten yourself up a bit. And you need to study hard too. No school will hire you unless you get good marks.'

'I'm already getting very good marks. I came second in our end-of-term tests.'

He nodded. 'Second, that's a big improvement. But if you want to be a primary school teacher, you need to be able to play piano and chess, and do calligraphy and painting too. You've got the basics of playing the piano, keep practicing, and then you can teach the little ones.'

Tianlu was talking so much sense, I had to agree. He sounded a bit like my mum or dad but, oddly enough, I didn't mind him preaching to me. I felt good.

That winter, Tianlu worked three weeks on the building site until he'd saved enough money to redeem the fur waistcoat. And then we went to the mulberry grove to talk to Mrs Ma. She certainly was determined to be difficult. She knew we wanted the waistcoat back, and set an astronomical price. We argued every which way, and finally got it. Tianlu paid out enough money to buy five laying hens!

When he gave the waistcoat to Mum, she cried. 'Thank you, sweetheart, you're such a good boy, so thoughtful. She'll be a lucky woman, the girl you marry!'

Tianlu went red from ear to ear, scurried back to his room and shut the door, and didn't come out till dinnertime.

Kejun came home before the end of the holidays. His fact-finding trip had made him a much more serious person. He shut himself in his room and churned out article after article. He kept a diary too. He even said he wanted to write the story of the Chinese Expeditionary Army. He said he wanted the whole country to know how those brave men were giving their lives for China, and had fought for two years to keep the Japanese in Burma from breaking through the Chinese defence lines into Yunnan.

When he wasn't writing, he said little. He seemed to have a lot on his mind. He didn't tell us what, and we didn't dare ask. He was our big brother, and he had a big brother's dignity.

Shuya didn't come home. At first we thought it was because the road was blocked and her group had been delayed. We weren't too worried, because she wasn't travelling alone. Then, a week after school started, we got a letter from Chongqing. It was a bolt out of the blue. She wrote that she was going with Victory Li to Yan'an. There were over a hundred of them in the group, she said, all of them students about her age, and they were going to enroll in the Anti-Japanese War University. The trip to Yan'an would be dangerous, she wrote, because there were Japanese blockades along the road. But that didn't matter, the Communist Party South China branch had found them a guide and was making all the arrangements. It would all be fine. 'Dear Mum and Dad,' she finished, 'be happy for me and send me your blessings. We're working for freedom and a brighter future for humankind!'

My mother's hand trembled like a leaf as she held Shuya's letter. 'It was so difficult to get her out of Nanjing, and she's rushing into danger again! "Japanese blockades along the road." What is that girl thinking of? Why didn't she discuss it with us first?'

My dad was sunk in gloom and didn't utter a word for a whole day. Finally, at the dinner table, he pointed his chopsticks at each of us in turn and spoke, 'You children, you're growing up or already grown up. You'll choose your own road in life and we, your parents, we'll respect your decisions. But just remember one thing: no matter where you go or what you do, you must let us know first. You are the children of your parents first, and your country second.'

And he picked up his bowl. 'Eat up!'

Chapter 21
Joining Up

In 1944, seven years after the Anti-Japanese War started, China and its armies were in dire straits. The situation was critical. The Japanese had suffered a major defeat at the Battle of Imphal in India. Enraged and humiliated, they decided on a mad dash along the road from Yunnan into Burma, from where they could shore up their India campaign. Under the Japanese onslaught, the Chinese Nationalist army fell back all over southern China: Luoyang, then Hengyang, then Guilin, Liuzhou, and Nanning. The Japanese were staring defeat in the face but that only made them more frenzied. They made a forced march into Guizhou, and captured Dushan, an important town in the south of the province. At that point, they posed a direct threat to Chongqing, the wartime capital.

All of China was in shock.

The Huaxi Fields students could no longer sit quietly at their desks studying. Everyone was talking about joining up and fighting. The slogan was, 'We'll fight every inch of land with every inch of blood! One hundred thousand young people make one hundred thousand soldiers!'

Professor Xu from the Department of Physics and Professor Mei from Animal Husbandry came upstairs to talk to my dad about the situation. 'We have to discourage the students from being so fanatical. It's tantamount to signing your own death warrant,' said Professor Xu. 'One hundred thousand young people make one hundred thousand soldiers! And they make a hundred thousand corpses and a hundred thousand skeletons! We can't just let them go off to be cannon fodder, otherwise, why are we working so hard to run the university? Why are our students bothering to study at all? Winning the war isn't enough; without these young people, there's no future for China! No future for civilization!'

Professor Mei lit up a Camel cigarette and puffed away at it for a while. Then he said, 'As a teacher, of course I don't want to send my students off to the battlefield, but there's no alternative. China faces annihilation in this war. You can't make an omelette without breaking eggs! Our forebears knew that, and we must follow in their footsteps. We need to win the war before we can rebuild the country. You can't do it the other way around. If I were twenty again, you wouldn't keep me away from the fighting!'

My father had been listening in silence. The reason was that he didn't want to influence Kejun's decision. Looking back on it, it must have felt to him like he was waiting for the judge to deliver sentence: would it be death or a life sentence? If Kejun didn't sign up, my father might have been disappointed but he would accept it. If he signed up, Dad knew that in all likelihood, he would never see him again.

All the family was affected by the gloomy atmosphere. Even the rambunctious Kid sensed what was going on, and clung to Mum all day like a little lamb.

Kejun had a lot to do and had hardly been home for days. Mum wanted me to go to the university to find him, but my dad stopped her. Dad said my brother was helping out on the Youth Army Recruitment Committee. There were so much to do and it was mayhem. Kejun was busy filling in forms, drawing up lists, and doing publicity. It was best not to bother him.

Mum looked wrung out with anxiety. 'Will he… will he…?' she could hardly bring herself to finish the question, 'join up?'

'Prepare yourself,' Dad said.

Mum broke down and cried. She knew the war situation. She knew what her husband and her son were like. She cried because she needed to vent some of her grief.

Finally, Kejun managed a visit home. He told us that he was going to join the Chinese Expeditionary Army. He said cheerfully that he could be useful three ways: he could translate, he could be a war reporter, and if need be, he could take up arms and fight. He rolled up his sleeves and showed us his pumped-up muscles with a laugh. 'Look where exercise got me. Finally I'll get to use them!'

Kejun had always talked of the Expeditionary Army with such admiration. Now finally he was getting his chance to become one of them. His trip to Kunming doing interviews during the winter holidays had been a prelude, leading up to this, the main movement.

The day Kejun put on his army uniform, slung his rucksack over his shoulder, and left, every one of our neighbours in Pomegranate Gardens came out of their houses and lined up silently in the courtyard to see him off as he strode out through the gate. Only my parents were not there. They stood side by side upstairs, looking over the railings. My father squeezed my mother's hand very tight so that she wouldn't say anything or sob.

Kejun was first sent to India for training. On 7th July, on the seventh anniversary of the outbreak of the Anti-Japanese War, the Chinese Expeditionary Army linked up with the Allied Forces to launch a campaign against Myitkyina in Burma, which was in Japanese hands. In the first days of August, my brother was killed in Myitkyina.

It was all entirely predictable. From the day Kejun enlisted, my father and mother had been preparing themselves for the bad news. The months, the weeks and the days passed, and they waited. With every day that went by, we mentally crossed out another twenty-four hours. With every day that went by, victory was that much closer, and we allowed our hopes to grow.

But my elder brother would never come back. At

nineteen years old, he lay at rest in a foreign land.

That same August, Tianlu enrolled at the Chinese Air Force flight training school in Kunming. His ambition had always been to study in the Department of Chemical Engineering of University of Nanking and help rebuild China's industry. Why did he suddenly change his mind and apply to the military academy? He never said. Thinking back, it was probably after Mark died crossing the Hump and bequeathed him the model of the shark-mouth plane. The model hung over his bed, and must have become a part of his dreams, a part of his flesh and blood.

My father had received the news about Shuya going to Yan'an calmly. When Kejun signed up, Dad felt it was right and proper. But when Tianlu said he wanted to join the airforce, it was the last straw. It broke my dad's heart. His face filled with pain, his eyes looked suddenly old, his shoulders slumped. He wrung his hands, and wandered round and round the room. After a few minutes, he looked up and asked Tianlu, 'Is there anything to discuss?' And then, 'Could you reconsider?'

Tianlu stood in the doorway, not daring to meet my father's eyes, saying nothing at all.

Dad knew that Tianlu wasn't going to change his

mind. He knew what kind of a boy he was. He didn't say a word to discourage him. Instead, he told my mother to get together all the cash we had. Every day until Tianlu left, there were to be big chunks of meat for dinner. And Tianlu's favourite, egg drop fermented rice soup. Tianlu had to have a bowl every day, just for him. Tianlu dare not refuse it, though he found it hard to swallow, all on his own. But he knew that this was my father's way of expressing wordless love, so he couldn't refuse.

My mother was forty years old by then, and in just those few months, stiff white hairs had begun to appear on the top of her head, sticking up like needles. Every day when she bent down to do the laundry and cooking, the sight of that cockscomb of white hair on top of her head caused us pain.

Before school started again, Tianlu asked if I'd go for a walk with him. He walked silently with his hands in his pockets, and I followed, taking peeks at his serious expression, and wondering what all this was about. From the side, he looked completely different from Kejun, who had a straight nose, thin lips, and eyes that tilted upwards slightly. Cheerful and easy-going, he had always been attractive to girls.

Tianlu, on the other hand, had strong, rough-hewn features. It took a little while to see that, under it, he was thoughtful and deliberate by nature. No wonder my mother always treated him differently from the rest of us.

We found ourselves walking through the trees by the river. Tianlu stopped for a moment and glanced into the woods as if he was remembering something. It occurred to me that the first time I saw him was when I was up a mulberry tree here, clutching a handful of purple mulberries in my hand. Then we walked along the path through the cemetery, past the Catholic Church that had been bombed by the Japanese and then patched up. I remembered how, when I was nine, he had walked me to my piano practice one night. Some branches overhanging the cemetery caught in my hair, and I was scared and wanted to hold his hand, but he gave me a stick instead.

Still, he said nothing, and I kept silent too.

We carried on walking as far as my school, following the compound wall, and Tianlu suddenly asked, 'What class will you be in when you start school? Third year?'

I nodded.

He nodded too.

Then he said, 'After I've left, you'll be the oldest. It doesn't seem real, does it?' A smile flitted across his lips. 'No one wants to grow up, but you can't not grow up. Your mum and dad are getting old. It's all going to fall on your shoulders.'

'Don't say that!' I protested. 'You and Shuya will come back!'

He put his hands in his trouser pockets and looked up at the sky. 'Right, as soon as I can fly, I'll be flying over Huaxi Fields to see what you're doing. So watch it! I'll be able to see everything from the sky. If I find out that you're misbehaving, I'll throw a ball from the plane and hit you on the head.'

I grinned, and tried to laugh, but for some reason I couldn't get it out.

'So, when you come home next, what do you want to see us doing?'

He bowed his head and looked serious. 'Orange, when I get home, play the piano for me, the one you said, the flying bees one – '

'"Flight of the Bumblebee"!' I cried joyfully.

He finally laughed. 'That's right. "Flight of the Bumblebee". Such a pretty name, you can see the bees flying around in front of you. Next time I'm home, I want to hear you play it.'

'Okay,' I said, 'I'll practice it every day after you go, and wait for you to come home to listen to it. So you've absolutely got to come home!'

Chapter 22

Letters Wing Their Way

Dear Orange,

I got to Kunming about a week ago and everything's going well. The flying school courses are intensive and there's a huge amount of physical training. I sweat so much I get through two lots of fatigues every day. A Yenching University student who arrived at the same time as me actually collapsed, he got so exhausted. Yesterday, I washed his clothes for him. God, they were filthy! We soaked them in a big bowl but they stank. It wasn't his fault. It was just running ten thousand metres a day that did for him. Now the instructor's said that he can start with five thousand metres runs, and build up. Our PE instructor's pretty nice to us, very understanding.

All the teaching is in English, because the flight

instructors and theory instructors are American. This is a bit of a problem for me – my English isn't good enough. I just now agreed with the Yenching University student that I'll wash his clothes every day, and he'll help me with my English. Fair exchange, eh?

I forgot to say, he's my roommate, his name's Qian Husheng, and he's from Shanghai. He was studying physics, and was in the third year when he applied for the flying school. He knew Kejun. I think they played football together. I'm sure we're going to be good friends.

The lights are going out in a moment so I'll stop now. Please give my best to your mum and dad. I wrote to your dad the day after I arrived in Kunming, just to say I'd arrived safely. But I know both of them are very busy so from now on I'll write to you.

Tianlu

Dear Tianlu,

You can't imagine how happy I was to get your letter! I read it to Su and Kid, and they asked lots of questions, all kids' questions, so I won't bother you with them. Also, there must be a lot of things to do with your flying school that you can't talk about, I mean military secrets, right? But that's okay, I understand.

We started geometry this term, and it's horrendously difficult. You know I don't have much spatial awareness. And I find the dotted and solid lines in geometry even worse than musical notation, so complicated. Apparently, we'll soon be learning auxiliary lines too because you need them to solve the problem. It gives me a headache just thinking about them. Why didn't Mum make me as clever as Shuya when I was born? It's depressing.

Kid has moved into the room you used to share with Kejun. But your bed is still there, Mum is really hoping that you'll make it home over the New Year. It's only September, how funny that Mum's thinking of New Year already!

By the way, my dad has just started teaching a new course on insect pests, and is rearing wheat worms, rice worms and cotton worms in the laboratory. He's also got Pieridae butterfly caterpillars under a big gauze cover, they're hideous. I took Sheona to see them once and she ran outside and puked. She said all those fat bugs squirming around were disgusting. They made her itch all over, and she wouldn't be able to eat her dinner.

Yesterday, Professor Mei brought a nanny goat home and tethered her where he used to raise hens. He said that she was the last goat from the Department of Animal Husbandry, because they're not going to keep cows and goats anymore. They don't have the money, and lots of their students have joined the army, so there'll be fewer courses. I wish you could see Professor Mei milking the goat. It's so funny. The goat shuts her eyes like she's really enjoying it. The prof made each of us try the milk, but I didn't like it, it's too goaty. The prof says that goat milk is more nutritious than cow's milk. He wants us children to look after her. Whenever we have time, we have to go and cut grass for her. And all the families will take turns to get the milk. Mum was very happy about that, she thinks my dad could really do with something nutritious.

I've really blabbed on in this letter, I don't even know if you'll have time to read it all.

From now on, I'm going to write to you every day, every single day.

Orange

Dear Orange,

Yesterday our instructor put us in a trainer plane.

It was so exciting. It feels very strange sitting in the cockpit, like sitting in a steel box. I could smell something very odd, maybe the smell of munitions, or the smell of bodies after they've been hit by bullets and vapourized.

Sorry, I shouldn't say things like that. I don't want to alarm you. Sometimes I let my imagination run away with me. Orange, you're the sweetest girl in the world. Promise me you'll live like a brilliant ray of sunshine, and don't let all the terror around us get to you.

Let me talk about more fun stuff. Sitting in a plane, even if it's still on the ground, I feel very high up. It's a fantastic feeling. I can see for miles. The world feels huge and I feel like my life has opened up too. I can see field after field of sogon grass on either side of the runway. They're carved up into irregular shapes by streams and ponds, yellow and green, old growth and new growth, undulating away into the distance and merging with the mountains. You know what it reminds me of? You said you were learning geometry, and I imagine those patches of grass are geometric shapes in your exercise book. I imagine you sitting in your classroom drawing them out, and me piloting the plane drawing lines in the grass, doing the same thing in a different space and time. Wouldn't that be wonderful?

I'm fine, just fine, everything's great. Don't worry about me, and tell Mum and Uncle not to worry too.

Tianlu

Dear Tianlu,

I have to report something that will make you angry: Kid broke your airplane model. He said he just wanted to hold it and look at it. I took it down from your mosquito net and gave it to him, but he thought it was the same as a paper plane and you could make it fly! He stood on our walkway and threw it down, and unfortunately it landed on the Meis' pot that they use for boiling herbal medicine. The plane fell to bits and the pot shattered too, into eight pieces. Mum had to go out and buy them a new one.

I don't know if the airplane can be repaired. Anyway, the bits are all in your drawer. Let's see when you come back. If it can't be mended, you'll be able to get a new model, right? Because soon you'll be a pilot.

Mum gave Kid a walloping and he's promised never to touch your things again. But children say things and then forget them. I promise I'll keep a close eye on him in future.

Winter will be here soon and Mum's worried about getting a chest infection again so she's already wearing the waistcoat. She says she's got to justify all those days on the building site you did to earn the money to buy it back.

When will you be able to fly a plane? I had a bet with Su about which of us will spot you in the sky first. I am sure I'll be first, because every time I see a plane flying overhead, I always have to go out and look, even during class time. The teachers know you're training as a pilot, and they always tell me, 'Go on, out you go, take a look and you'll feel better.'

I'll stop now. The lights will be turned off soon. We often have powercuts at our school. The head says the city doesn't have enough electricity and war work gets priority. I can't wait for you to be able to fly up and hit some Japanese planes.

Orange

Dear Orange,

Thank you for your encouragement. When I think of all of you in Huaxi Fields looking out for me, it makes me study harder. In our tests last week, I came third overall. I got one question wrong in the pilot theory test and in the flight practice test I didn't have good control of the joystick. The instructor says sometimes I'm too impatient, and overdo it. I'll try and do better next time.

We got one day off this week, and Husheng and I went to look around Kunming. We each had a bowl of over-the-bridge noodles. They're rice noodles and they're really peculiar, they don't need cooking. They bring you a bowl of boiling hot chicken broth and put the meat and vegetables and noodles in it and it's ready to eat! They're a Kunming speciality and there's a story about them, which I'll tell you when I get home and we have more time. So I'm going to leave you in suspense for now!

The local people are really great. The noodle shop owner refused to charge us a cent once she found out we were at the Training School. She said, 'You're going to fly up and pop off the Japanese. You pop one more for me!' That made the two of us feel very humbled. People are so kind to us and we still don't know when we'll be able to fly, it's embarrassing. So we originally planned to go to Dianchi Lake after our lunch, to see if we could spot the black-headed gulls they talk about, but we went straight back to the school. I mustn't forget my mission, to study, study and study even harder.

And mind you study hard too, Orange. We're fighting the battle now, and you'll be building the country afterwards. China needs to get stronger.

Tianlu

Dear Tianlu,

I have good news to report! I came first in the end-of-winter-term exams! The head personally gave me my commendation, and said to me, 'Orange, you've finally got the hang of it.' What she doesn't know is, I got the first place because of you. You're studying so hard, I'm determined not to fall behind.

Last time you wrote, you asked if there was any news from Shuya. There isn't. My mother made her a dark blue, fitted, padded jacket with a stand-up collar, fastened with a beautiful cloud-knot button she'd made with some dark red corduroy that Mrs Xing gave her. Shuya will look beautiful in it. But Mum didn't have an address to send the jacket to. She sometimes holds it in her arms and cries over it when she thinks no one's looking. Su told me. Dad tried to comfort her, he told her children grow up and have their own lives to lead and she shouldn't worry. Mum said, even so, she should have written to let us know she's all right. Dad thought a bit, then said there was only one explanation: there's a big Japanese-occupied area between Yan'an in the northwest, and Chengdu in the southwest, so the postal services can't get through.

Tianlu, do you think Shuya has written and her letter never arrived, or has she not written at all? We're all very worried.

It's such a relief that we get letters from you. Mum has all your letters numbered in order, and she makes Su read them to her one by one. Su says she can recite them all off by heart, but she still wants to hear them.

And before I forget, Mum wants me to ask you, do you need anything for when you go to India? Will you need summer clothes, or winter padded jacket and trousers? And she's worried you won't like the food. Would you like her to make you some rice noodles to take with you?

Looking forward to hearing from you.

Orange

Dear Orange,

I'm writing this letter from an Indian army camp. Three days ago, we flew here from Kunming in a Flying Tigers transport plane. We're doing three months' intensive training, and if we pass our exams, we can join the CACW, the Chinese-American Composite Wing, in China and go into battle. Our American instructor said that he had never sent trainee pilots up in such a short time before, but they're making an exception of us, because we're needed.

When we flew over the Hump, the snow-capped mountains seemed to go on forever, they're spectacular! I don't know how to describe it to you, even though I really want to. I can't find the words to do it justice. I'm so boring, if only I was as good at writing as Kejun. But as we were making the flight, I thought of Mark, who died here, on what they call the 'Roof of the World'. His body will always lie in these mysterious mountains, and that's right and proper, isn't it?

I hope if I ever die for my country I'll be as lucky as Mark.

Hah! That slipped out, didn't it? Wash your mouth out, Tianlu!

Indian food is very weird. They pound all the ingredients to a pulp, and then mix them with spices and call it curry. Everything's yellow and doesn't look appetizing at all. But we generally don't eat the local food, we eat steak. Americans are very advanced except in what they eat. We get really good steak but it isn't properly cooked. When you cut into it with your knife, blood leaks from the meat. The first time I ate steak, I retched. I just couldn't get it down. Husheng was okay. He'd eaten American steaks in Shanghai before. Our senior officer forced me to eat it all up anyway. He said I needed it because the training was very intensive. Guess what I did? I gave it a little chew, then I shut my eyes and swallowed, and then gulped down lots of water so I wouldn't bring it all up again. Actually, eating depends on willpower. I wanted to eat it, so I ate it.

Please don't tell Mum that. She'll feel sorry for me. Just think, if you could buy a piece of steak as big as your fist in Chengdu, Mum would be ecstatic. She'd make it last for lots of meals.

I'll stop here. This is our afternoon break, and we'll be back in class soon.

Oh, one more thing, tell Mum it's very hot in

India, we don't need padded jackets, so she doesn't need to worry about what I'm wearing.

Tianlu

Dear Tianlu,

I told Kid you were eating curry in India. He's so greedy, he kept on at me to tell him what it looked like and how it tasted. I couldn't tell him, so I said to ask my dad. Poor Kid, he's never known anything but this war, he's never had treats to eat, or decent toys to play with. By the way, he's cut loads of grass for Professor Mei's nanny goat. He even went out yesterday in the rain and almost slipped into the river. When he got home, he got another spanking from Mum. Every time it's our turn for the milk, Kid's always there waiting with his bowl held out. Professor Mei says the milk is good for you even when it's fresh, but Mum worries, and insists on boiling it first. Dad gets most of it and the rest goes to Kid. My father has liver trouble nowadays, and Uncle Fan told him to try and eat better. We're lucky that Prof Mei brought back the nanny goat.

Dad wants me to tell you that you should get to like steaks! Because steak builds you up and when you come back to China, you'll need to be strong as well as courageous.

Su folded ten paper airplanes yesterday and hung one on every door frame, every bed, and every bookshelf in our house. She said that if there are planes everywhere in the house, it's like seeing you all the time. She made the biggest and most beautiful one for Kid, and drew a little man wearing a helmet in the cockpit. She told him the pilot was you and the plane was your plane. He took it to bed and went to sleep with it, and when he woke up, it was squashed flat. He burst into tears and Su had to fold another one for him.

We all miss you very much. All of us, every minute of the day.

Orange

Dear Orange,

I managed to get hold of a model plane for Kid. It's different from Mark's, slightly larger. I think Kid'll like it. I wanted to mail it to China, but our commanding officer said that the Hump's only for transporting vital materials, and letters, nothing else. That's understandable. I've put the model in my trunk, and I'll bring it with me when I come back to China. You can tell Kid about it.

We're doing parachute training these days. My first jump, I got cramp and I couldn't get myself out of the door. The instructor had to give me a push. It's not that I was afraid, it was because my body wouldn't obey my instructions. It was embarrassing but the instructor said it often happens with your first time.

Husheng was even more embarrassed. He pissed himself. I was the only one he told, so if you ever meet him one day, whatever you do, don't mention it.

I was much more relaxed jumping today. I kept my eyes open, and after the parachute opened, I was suddenly buoyed up and I felt like a cloud. I could see everything on the earth beneath my feet, the colours, the fields, the mountains and rivers. The earth is so beautiful. If only there was no war, life would be beautiful too.

Don't laugh at me, I'm no good at expressing my feelings.

The instructor says that as pilots, we don't get the chance to parachute anyway. There's a mechanism in our seats, that if the plane's hit, it pops up and automatically ejects us. It's safe, so don't worry about me. But you all look after Uncle, get him to take more rest and stop traveling to the villages to promote his improved crop strains. He should train up younger people to do those things.

Tianlu

Dear Tianlu,

When you fly, does it feel something like being a bird? I'd love to know. I want to see you flying too.

This week I was able to play 'Flight of the Bumblebee' straight through without any mistakes for the first time. When Mrs Fan heard me play, she said it wasn't bad. She said I'd caught the playful feeling, and if only I could up the speed, it would be perfect. She actually used the English word 'perfect'! And you know how demanding she is with her piano students.

It's all because of you. One day, when you come home, I'm looking forward to being able to say proudly, 'My dear brother, I'll play "Flight of the Bumblebee" for you anytime. Just say the word!'

Don't worry about Dad. We'll look after him. A few days ago, he got a letter from the US Department of Agriculture inviting him to go there to work on research into a disease-resistant wheat variety. But Dad said he's going to wait for victory so that he can go with his head held high and be proud of his country.

Orange

Dear Orange,

I've finished my training in India and have officially become a pilot of the CACW. Originally the plan was for our cohort to go to the United States for a few months after receiving basic training in India. But that's out of the question now. The war is in its eighth year, and so many men have been lost that we're urgently needed. Besides, we've already written our wills. We can't wait to go into battle and serve our country, and give our lives if necessary! So when you read this letter, I might be in the air fighting an enemy plane. I want to see it vapourized right in front of my eyes! I might also be hit by an enemy bullet and die. But in the words on the stele at the entrance to our training school, 'If we die, we take the enemy down with us.'

Orange, my little sister, let me say something as your big brother: if I really do give my life for my country, then it's nothing more than my duty. Please, please promise me you'll be happy forever. And live for me too. You're only fourteen, you're going to grow up, you'll live to see the day when the war is won, when the Japanese surrender, when the whole country rejoices. When that day comes, when you all parade down the streets holding torches aloft, and waving red flags, think of my spirit sitting on your torch, imagine its flame is my laughter, know that I'll be with you.

I hope this letter is not goodbye, but if it is, I have no regrets. Because ever since I came to your home at fourteen, I've had so many happy times with Uncle, Mum, Kejun, Shuya, Su and Kid and you, especially you, Orange.

Tianlu

Chapter 23

Happy Times

When I next saw Tianlu, I had the last letter he wrote to me in my jacket pocket. That was the one where he said his last goodbye. I was so cross with him. 'Why did you talk nonsense like that? It was rubbish! No one wanted to say goodbye to you. None of us were having that, not my dad, nor my mum, and certainly not Su or Kid or me! We would have got you home one way or another, we'd have trussed you up and dragged you home with a rope, whether it took one year or ten years!'

He laughed, and aimed a swipe at my head with his big hand but I dodged. He was treating me like a kid but I was sitting with him as a member of the Chengdu Battlefield Entertainment Corps. We sat side by side on the sports field of the Kunming Air Force Camp, and he was the one I had come to 'entertain'.

I never imagined I would see Tianlu again so soon.

The Entertainment Corps was there to raise the troops' morale, and Sheona was supposed to be in it. She played the piano really well, and was due to play at their gala. But things don't always go according to plan. The day before the gala, she was riding her bike along a gravel path at her school and skidded and went head over heels. Her arms and knees were badly grazed, and her elbows were pouring with blood. Her father bandaged her up so tight that she looked like a doll.

I went to see her, and when her mother wasn't around, she whispered in my ear, 'The Entertainment Corps came to see me about playing for the gala, but my father's worried in case I get an infection, so I'm grounded. I told them, "Ask Orange, she's been playing the piano for six years. She can play for you."'

I was so startled that my head shot up but she pulled it down again and whispered, 'Don't let on you know. They don't have time to find anyone better to replace me, so they'll come to you.'

I didn't say anything. I couldn't because she had my head pressed down. I just waved my hands.

She looked hard at me. 'Orange, don't tell me you don't want to see Tianlu?'

I suddenly understood – my dear friend Sheona had fallen off deliberately. She'd hurt herself so that I could go to the gala and see Tianlu again.

I'll always remember Sheona. I haven't seen her in seventy years but I imagine her living in some town or village in America, playing the piano, growing flowers, looking after her grandchildren, enjoying her family. Or perhaps she's departed this life and is long dead and buried. But I'll never forget her, with her blond plaits and her girlish shrieks whenever I climbed trees or jumped in the river.

We had a three-day stay at the camp to entertain the troops. For the whole three days, I was Tianlu's guest and he ran around thinking up treats for me. He got hold of two tins of corned beef, then bartered them in the market in Kunming for a bag of green and yellow mangoes as big as your fist. Silly boy, didn't he know that girls like meat? I hadn't had a whiff of meat for six months in Chengdu.

But I liked mangoes too. I had never tasted fruit as sweet and fragrant. I peeled off the skin, and the pale yellow juice ran down my fingers over my hand. I put my fingers in my mouth and sucked them and the sweetness took my breath away. 'Shen Tianlu!' I cried, 'What a wonderful place Kunming is!'

He watched me and didn't say a word. He smiled, just smiled. When I think back, his eyes must have been brimming with love and tenderness, but I was a clueless girl back then, and much too busy peeling and devouring the mangoes and sucking up the juice to notice.

My mouth and fingers were coated in sticky juice by the time I'd finished. I was in a horrible mess. But as if by magic, he produced a very old but freshly laundered handkerchief and wiped the tip of my nose and was going to wipe my lips. Then he hesitated a moment, and gave me the handkerchief so I could clean my own face.

'No, you do it for me,' I said, pursing my lips.

He looked flustered and went red. Clutching the hanky, he looked from it to me and back again. I couldn't help bursting out laughing. I laughed so hard that I nearly spat mango juice all over his chest.

'Orange!' he remonstrated.

I held my hands up so he could see that I really couldn't wipe my own face, my fingers were all stuck together.

He wavered, and then wavered some more, and finally lifted the hanky and hurriedly dabbed at my mouth. I found that so funny, I was convulsed with laughter again. He was obviously worried his mates would hear me, and clamped his hand over my mouth. 'Orange! Orange!' he implored. 'Do behave yourself! You're fifteen now, be a bit more grown up!'

It was true I was growing up, but he was my big brother Tianlu, after all. Why shouldn't I mess around with him?

He introduced me to his friend Husheng. Husheng was wearing a flying suit and saluted me solemnly, called me 'Miss Wang', and then reached out to shake hands with me. Tianlu explained to me that Husheng was from Shanghai and in their dialect, Huang (my surname) and Wang, sounded the same. Husheng was so embarrassed that he went red and wouldn't speak Shanghainese anymore. He kept apologizing in English instead. He was very short – side by side with Tianlu, he looked quite pocket-sized. He had a round face, double eyelids, long eyelashes, and very dark pupils, but his skin was pale, even the fierce sun of the Yunnan plateau had not succeeded in tanning it. He was shy but sweet. He had a rather delicate appearance, not like a soldier at all.

I really wanted to sit in Tianlu's plane. Most of all, I wanted him to take me up in it so we could fly over Pomegranate Gardens, and everyone – Mum, Su, Sheona, Professor Mei and Uncle Xu – could see what a hero Tianlu was.

I was so ignorant that I actually asked him. Tianlu was taken aback. He obviously didn't know what to say and twisted his hands together and cracked his knuckles. However, finally, he went to his officer and asked if I could sit in the trainer plane for five minutes, maximum ten. He reported back to me that the officer had glanced at him, and said slowly, 'You really think that's appropriate?'

'It's the first time I've made a special request and I was embarrassed.' He laughed. 'But even though he was so scornful, I really wanted to let you sit in it. After all, you're my little sister.'

I was very disappointed not to be able to sit in a Flying Tiger plane, but knowing that Tianlu was ready to stick his neck out for me and ask his officer gave me a warm feeling inside. During the three days in that airforce camp, I got that feeling of warmth all the time.

I was foolish enough to believe that happiness was a normal daily occurrence and would last forever, like the packet of chewing gum that Tianlu gave me. So long as I never stopped chewing on it, there'd always be a sweet taste in my mouth.

'Orange, what will you play at the gala?' Tianlu asked, at least half a dozen times. 'There are lots of Americans in the camp, and they're not all tone-deaf like me.' He was obviously anxious, especially when I didn't answer.

But I shrugged my shoulders like the Americans in the camp did. 'It doesn't matter what I play, the main thing is for people to have a good time.'

He was about to say something more, but stopped himself and looked at me with real unease.

'You look like you haven't slept the last couple of nights,' I teased him. 'Are you worried I'll go up on that stage and make a mess of it and let you down?'

'Oh dear, can't I say anything right?' he muttered.

The more anxious he got, the funnier I found it. I'd always enjoyed pulling his leg, ever since I was a kid, and that hadn't changed. I pretended to ignore him and went and talked to Husheng. 'Do another picture of me,' I asked him. Husheng's sketches of me were much better-looking than I was in real life. I came out looking like a girl in a magazine. He was convinced he drew badly, but I liked the way his pencil made me into a beautiful young woman.

'Miss Wang,' he said awkwardly, 'I'm really sorry. I only sketch in my spare time.'

I picked up the sketch and flattered him shamelessly. 'But Husheng, you're so much better than the art teacher in our school! He always makes people really ugly. You draw really well, better than anyone I know.'

That cheered him up. He went bright red and giggled, and a faint dimple appeared at the corner of his mouth.

There was a basketball match between the Entertainment Corps and the pilots. The first half of the game, we lost hopelessly, but in the second half, they gave away a few points, and when it came to shooting into the net, they deliberately held onto the ball, so the final score wasn't too bad.

While the boys from the Entertainment Corps played basketball, we girls weren't idle. We went around all the dormitories and collected a huge bundle of sheets. Then we put them in the sinks and, laughing and joking, thumped them and trod them under our bare feet. The place was flooded with water by the time we'd finished, and we'd used up every scrap of soap in the camp. We laid the bed covers out to dry in the sunshine – and then had no idea what to do. We'd unstitched the bed covers, but none of us knew how to stitch them back up again. The pilots had to help us out and do it themselves. They didn't complain, in fact they made a point of saying how nice and clean the bedding smelled.

'You're all angels,' said Tianlu, looking at his nice clean sheets. We girls sat on the freshly made-up bed and cracked up laughing.

'It's true,' he protested. 'You've galvanized us. Before you came, I hadn't washed my bedding in three months. Some of the men left it even longer, like six months, and the sheets were stiff with dirt, you could stand them upright.'

I knew this wasn't true. The pilots' beds were much cleaner than the students' beds at our school, no doubt because their commanding officer kept them in line. Tianlu was just badmouthing his mates as a compliment to us.

He'd only been gone a few months. Where had he

learnt to sweet-talk the girls?

It was true I was fifteen, but I was still a kid in Tianlu's eyes. He was so kind and took such good care of me. In fact, it was like I was a piece of precious porcelain and he was afraid I might break. I sensed he didn't know the right place to keep me. In his pocket? In his eyes? In his heart?

How I loved being spoiled. My father was an agronomist. He loved the soil and seeds more than us. My mother had given birth to five children, and slaved away day and night in the house. She never had a minute to spare. That generation had it tough. They had no time to share the beauty of life with us. But Tianlu understood. He was so sensitive, and endlessly patient as he waited for me to grow up.

Six years before, when God gave Tianlu to our family, I was a kid who knew nothing and cared even less. But he gave us the best of boys to be my guide. Where once I could hardly see what was in front of my nose, now I looked up and could see a ray of light in the clouds. I felt blessed.

The gala was on the third and last night of our stay. My piano solo came about in the middle of the programme, number five. I'll never forget it. The piano was borrowed from the local school in Kunming. It was an old one and the paint was cracked, but it played fine. I wore a white tulle skirt that Sheona lent me. As I walked onto the rudimentary stage in the camp assembly room, I was enormously excited. Of course there were no spotlights, that would have been asking too much. But they'd hung light bulbs at each corner of the stage and they were bright enough to show me the fine sheen of sweat on the tip of my nose when I lowered my eyes. In the ten seconds it took me to walk to the front of the stage, there was a storm of applause that felt like heavy rain beating on my body. I felt my heart hammering but I couldn't hear it, there was too much noise. In a daze, I sat down at the piano.

Did I think of Tianlu as I sat down? Actually, no. At that moment, there was only me and the black and white keys and the sheet music. Everything else was indistinct. I felt like I was floating on some kind of a cloud.

I played 'Flight of the Bumblebee'. In the months since Tianlu left home to join the army, I'd worked my socks off to practice this piece. I'd persevered every single day, I hadn't slacked off for a minute. That was why Sheona had thrown herself off her bike, to give me the chance to shine.

The lights were bright. It was March in Kunming, and mild. The cramped auditorium smelled strongly of hurriedly-applied whitewash and sweaty young soldiers, and as my fingers warmed the old piano keys, there was the smell of celluloid too. I could even smell the faint fragrance on the rapidly-beating wings of my bumblebee. How utterly beautiful this was! I was so intoxicated by the music, by the unearthly silence in the auditorium, and by my own happiness, that I forgot to look at the audience to see the expression on Tianlu's face.

My fingers whizzed over the keys. My heart pounded in my chest. My eyes saw nothing. The eighty-eight piano keys were a river of black and white. I used all ten fingers to gather the flowers that splashed out of the river water. I didn't need my eyes. I used my sense of touch, my ears, and all my nerve endings, and as the last note flew into the air, I closed my eyes altogether. I felt that another second of that and I would faint.

The applause was tumultuous. I stood up, smiling stupidly, with no clue what to do. The stage manager pretended to go on stage to move the piano, and gave me a little push. I remembered that I was supposed to make a ladylike curtsey.

I couldn't see Tianlu. My eyes swept over the audience but I couldn't see him anywhere. Where could he be?

Flustered, I ran off the stage and out of the side door. Then, in the gathering dusk, I saw him. The lights in the auditorium spilled through the door, and framed his tall lean figure in its military uniform. He looked as still and solid as a tree. He had been standing with his back to the door, but he must have had eyes in the back of his head because at the sound of my running footsteps, he turned towards me. In that instant, I thought I saw tears in his eyes.

Was he crying? Could he cry? No, surely not. I must be wrong. I'd never been particularly observant.

How solemn he looked in the half-dark! I didn't dare ask him anything. We stood face-to-face, quite silent, letting the night breeze carry our breath to each other's ears.

Just as I was beginning to think I couldn't take any more of this solemnity, he sighed, reached out his arms, and with the utmost care, drew me to his chest.

'Orange,' he whispered tenderly. 'Now I remember

the name of that piece, 'Flight of the Bumblebee', right?'

'I played it for you, Tianlu,' I said.

'I know, I know.'

'Did I play well?'

'No one could have played it better.'

'Then pinky-swear, when this war is over and you come home, you'll listen to me play the piano every day.'

'I will. Every day.'

I pressed my ear against his chest and listened to his heart beating, fast, and loud. So loud that they might have been bullets fired from the barrel of a gun.

I felt completely at peace. Even if they were bullets, they were being fired at the enemy. With him, I was safe. We could all be safe.

Epilogue

Tianlu was killed two months later, in May of 1945.

Everything had been going well: the US army bombed Tokyo, the Soviet Red Army occupied Berlin, and fifty-one countries gathered in San Francisco for the United Nations Conference. The world was being transformed. In China too, the situation was encouraging: the Japanese were driven out of western Hunan, Fuzhou was recaptured, and Nanning was encircled by the Nationalist Army. The five divisions that had been stationed in India and the thirty divisions of the Expeditionary Army had been reequipped and were ready to go into battle.

That month, our pomegranate tree was covered in flaming red blossom. It looked like the whole tree was on fire, shouting, bursting with life.

Mum stood on the walkway and looked at the tree. She murmured happily to herself, 'What a good omen!' She was remembering that this time last year, there had been only a few scrappy flowers on the tree, and Shuya had left for Yan'an and there was still no news of her, and Kejun had died and we hadn't been able to bring his body home.

Su was on the walkway too, skipping energetically and pouring with sweat. When she heard Mum, she said scornfully, 'That's superstitious.'

My mother didn't get annoyed. 'You're just a child. What would you know? The lives of plants and trees and human beings have always been interlinked. When living things do well, then families do well too. I had a dream about Tianlu. He was calling to me, "Mum! Leave two pomegranates for me!"

'Su leaned against the wall and laughed. 'Tianlu's a Flying Tiger now, d'you really think he's missing your pomegranates?'

'Why not? You can travel all over the world but home things are the best. I'm sure he'll be home in September, latest October, when the pomegranates are ripe.'

We were only just in May, but everything in

Huaxi Fields was so lush and green that it took Kid no time at all to pick the daily basket of fresh green grass for the goat. Sheona, who loved pretty things, had started wearing a checked summer dress with a collar and shirt-waist. But in the northern part of Hubei, the battles between the Chinese and the Japanese were still going on. First, the Japanese army launched attacks from Henan and Hubei, trying to wrest control over the Nanyang and Laohekou military bases. The Chinese army could not hold the lines and retreated steadily, suffering heavy casualties. But after the Japanese army captured Nanyang and Laohekou, the Chinese army regrouped, and launched a counter-offensive, regaining lost ground bit by bit. Battle after bitter battle was fought, and neither side had time to draw breath. Tianlu's unit was dispatched to lend air support in northern Hubei and deal the Japanese army a mortal blow.

Husheng died first. He was hit by anti-aircraft fire during a bombing mission, and his plane caught fire. After ejecting, he unfortunately landed behind Japanese lines. Surrounded by Japanese soldiers, he took out his pistol, calmly shot as many as he could, and saved the last bullet for himself.

Then it was Tianlu's turn. He went up that day in a P47 fighter jet and engaged with Japanese fighters soon after takeoff. Fifteen or so minutes later, Tianlu had shot his last bullet, and his fuselage had been holed all over. He knew that he had no hope of getting home, so he picked a Mitsubishi A6M Zero, the newest fighter the Japanese had, pulled his plane into a steep ascent, then dived into it. He took the enemy plane down with him as he died.

Tianlu's will and personal possessions only arrived back in Pomegranate Gardens in August, by which time the Japanese had already surrendered.

My mother was completely unprepared. We'd won the war over the Japanese, after all. Surely Tianlu would soon be home. When the neatly-turned-out air force captain with the solemn expression stood in front of her holding Tianlu's bag and papers, she kept looking behind him, hoping that Tianlu was teasing her.

Suddenly, Su and Kid realized what had happened. They clung to her and begged her, 'Mum, don't cry! Mum, don't cry!'

'But I must cry,' said Mum. 'If I don't cry it out, I'll die.'

Mum didn't stop crying for a month. After that,

her vision was always blurred, and she had a wavering dark shadow in front of her eyes. She insisted the shadow was Tianlu, haunting her because he couldn't bear to leave her.

Before winter arrived, the rest of us took a steamer down river back to Nanjing. Kid had not been born the year we left, and he was eight years old when we got back.

Professor Mei and Uncle Xu and their families travelled on the same boat with us. Sheona's family had already gone back to the US via Vietnam, taking Mark's big suitcase with them. Uncle Tao's bones stayed behind in Chengdu, in Huaxi Fields.

We never did get a letter from Shuya, and we had no idea how to trace her. Then in about 1950, we had an unexpected visitor, a small man, dressed in a gray tunic, with a side parting and small features – eyes, nose, and mouth all crowded together. At a guess, he was thirty, or perhaps forty; it was hard to tell. He introduced himself as Victory Li, a friend of my sister who had been with her during the war. He told us Shuya had died in the last month of the war. The Eighth Route Army had launched a major counter-offensive against the Japanese in North China. By that time, my sister had left Yan'an Anti-Japanese University and was working in a military hospital in the Shanxi-Suiyuan Anti-Japanese Base Area. During one of the battles, she'd gone with a stretcher team on a mission to rescue a casualty, and was hit in the head by a Japanese shell. She died instantly.

Mum didn't cry this time. I think it was because she had already accepted that Shuya was dead. From 1944 to 1950, for six long years, we hadn't received a single letter from or about her. My mother had suffered so much that she could scarcely suffer anymore.

My father's chronic liver disease got worse. One day in the 1950s when he was teaching his students, he collapsed, vomiting blood. It wasn't easy to get an ambulance back then, and all his students could do was to borrow a trolley from the school cafeteria and rush him to the hospital on foot. It took them a while and he died before he reached the operating table.

My mother lived to be over seventy. Sadly, in the last ten years of her life, she was completely blind, and could not see her grandchildren. She had cried herself blind with the deaths of her children during the war, and her eyesight never recovered.

In 1984 or thereabouts, I was in my fifties and

about to retire when I finally saved enough money to buy a Pearl River piano. My playing was so rusty that I had to start almost from scratch with the Beyer and Thompson lessons for kiddies, but a year later, I could stumble my way through 'Flight of the Bumblebee' again. Now, another thirty years have passed, and 'Flight of the Bumblebee' is my signature piece. I have played it at the faculty and staff parties, I have played it for the Association of Retired Workers, and for the Senior Citizens Choir. Every time I play it, Tianlu's words come back to me, 'What a beautiful name for a piece. I can see the way the bumblebee flies. Next time I'm home, you must play it for me.'

Every May, when the pomegranate blossom is out, the bees buzz around my house, but the man who wanted to hear me play 'Flight of the Bumblebee' is gone and will never come back.

This is the story of Tianlu and me. You may wonder, after eighty years, how I remember every single thing that happened so clearly. Well, it's like this: I've never grown old because when Tianlu died, he became part of me, of my body. He'll always be twenty, splendid, and passionate, and he lives in me.

Afterword, by Huang Beijia
Splendid Land, Endless Days

It must have been five years ago that Mr Wang Zhenyu of Phoenix Publishing&Media Group (PPMG) asked me to be a judge for their Top Ten Books of the Year. I found myself walking into a room full of books and was instantly dazzled. The best works published by the group's various imprints were spread out in seven or eight bookcases. The sun shone on all sorts of book covers, from the dignified to the humorous. It was a glorious sight.

With so many books randomly arranged, it was serendipity that my eyes alighted on *Wind over Huaxi Fields*. After the judging was over, I asked if I could take this impressive volume of several hundred pages home with me. I delved into it and read to the end in two days. Then I read it all over again. I realized I was smitten by the story of the National Southwest Associated Universities that relocated to Huaxi Fields, Chengdu, during the Anti-Japanese War.

I imagined those eminent professors who refused to live under foreign rule, making the long trip westward with their wives and young children, along with their beloved books, scientific instruments, the seeds and animals they were using for experiments, and huge numbers of students. They fled from the enemy-occupied east to the southwest on buses and in cars, by boat, and on foot. When they arrived in the city of Chengdu, they set up camp in the Huaxi Fields area and made it the university district. There, both culture and teaching and the national spirit continued to flourish in an unbroken tradition. I imagined how those enthusiastic young students pored over their books as war raged around them, read and studied and discussed, and learned to think for themselves, and finally faced the bullets of the Japanese invaders with their bodies. And what about the children who followed their parents all the way to the west? They grew up far from home, absorbing the fervour and the serious-mindedness of their elders alongside their daily studies. What kind of adults would they – should they – turn into?

I spent the next five years writing a novel, in between working on quite a number of novellas and short stories as well, but I couldn't get this fascinating story out of my mind. Last spring, I went to Sichuan to do readings in schools, and finally had the opportunity to visit Huaxi Fields in Chengdu, and to get a feel of a place that eighty years ago was both tranquil and tumultuous.

The five eastern universities that moved to Chengdu during the Anti-Japanese War, Yenching University (Beijing), University of Nanking and Ginling College (Nanjing), Cheeloo University (Jinan), and West China Union University (Chengdu), all moved back east with the victory against Japan in 1945. Today, only the West China School of Medicine remains, and is located in Sichuan University. Strolling through its quietly elegant campus, one is transported back to the days of the Republic of China, the nameplates on each of the old school buildings a concise testimony to that short-lived period eighty years ago. Climbing up the wide, creaking wooden staircases, one's ears seem to hear clattering footsteps and youthful laughter, and snatches of erudite conversation in English. I found myself ducking aside to let those phantoms hurry past.

I also saw the students of today, sitting on the campus benches, reading and reciting in twos and threes. They were eighteen or twenty years old, bright-eyed and smiling, so young and beautiful! Were there any descendants of the teachers and students of the five universities among them? Were they aware of what had happened in this very place? Did the passions of past generations still course through their veins?

I returned to Nanjing from Chengdu, and set about writing *Flight of the Bumblebee*. The story is told by an old woman, but its rhythm is bright and free. It is the old woman's emotional look back at her childhood from her twilight years, as she relives old scenes, and says goodbye to her life. I have written it for today's children, with Orange as my chief character, so I have made every effort to write a story which is entertaining and full of everyday events. But as I came to the end, I could not help being overcome with sadness. My eyes blurred with tears and I could hardly type the words. I mourned these young lives and young souls, meteors shooting across the sky, so dazzling yet so brief. Their vivid, smiling faces still have the power to move us after all these years.

Now that I have finished this book, I want to express my gratitude to Mr Dai Jun, the author of *Wind over Huaxi Fields*. I never knew him, but his words inspired *Flight of the Bumblebee,* and grounded it in fact. Thanks also to Mr Wang Zhenyu of the Phoenix Publishing&Media Group. If he had not invited me to be a judge of their books, I would never have come across this fascinating subject. I thank Yong Bo, the president of Phoenix Juvenix and Children's Publishing Ltd. who, when he found out that I wanted to go to Huaxi Fields to see it for myself, immediately sent someone from Nanjing to accompany me. With this book, as with every book, the process of its creation involves it passing through countless hands, and it has taken its time, and acquired a life of its own, and a human warmth.

Huang Beijia is one of China's most important children's writers. Born in 1955. Writer, known in the 1980s for her stories about intellectuals, their emotional lives and Chinese masculinity. More recently better known for her children's books. Nominated for the Hans Christian Andersen Award 2020.

Nicky Harman lives in the UK and is a full-time translator of Chinese literary works. She has won several awards, including the 2020 Special Book Award, China, the 2015 Mao Tai Cup People's Literature Chinese-English translation prize, and the 2013 China International Translation Contest, Chinese-to-English section. When not translating, she promotes contemporary Chinese fiction through teaching, blogs, talks and her work on Paper-Republic.org.

Ingram Content Group UK Ltd.
Milton Keynes UK
UKHW011831190323
418793UK00004B/646